The Blue Castle

L. M. MONTGOMERY

The Blue Castle

HESPERUS

Published by Hesperus Press Limited
28 Mortimer Street, London W1W 7RD
www.hesperuspress.com

The Blue Castle first published 1926
First published by Hesperus Press Limited, 2013

Designed and typeset by Madeline Meckiffe
Printed in Great Britain by CPI Group (UK) Ltd

isbn: 978-1-84391-394-8

ONE

If it had not rained on a certain May morning Valancy Stirling's whole life would have been entirely different. She would have gone, with the rest of her clan, to Aunt Wellington's engagement picnic and Dr Trent would have gone to Montreal. But it did rain and you shall hear what happened to her because of it.

Valancy wakened early, in the lifeless, hopeless hour just preceding dawn. She had not slept very well. One does not sleep well, sometimes, when one is twenty-nine on the morrow, and unmarried, in a community and connection where the unmarried are simply those who have failed to get a man.

Deerwood and the Stirlings had long since relegated Valancy to hopeless old maidenhood. But Valancy herself had never quite relinquished a certain pitiful, shamed, little hope that Romance would come her way yet – never, until this wet, horrible morning, when she wakened to the fact that she was twenty-nine and unsought by any man.

Ay, there lay the sting. Valancy did not mind so much being an old maid. After all, she thought, being an old maid couldn't possibly be as dreadful as being married to an Uncle Wellington or an Uncle Benjamin, or even an Uncle Herbert. What hurt her was that she had never had a chance to be anything but an old maid. No man had ever desired her.

The tears came into her eyes as she lay there alone in the faintly greying darkness. She dared not let herself cry as hard as she wanted to, for two reasons. She was afraid that crying might bring on another attack of that pain around the heart. She had had a spell of it after she had got into bed – rather worse than any she had had yet. And she was afraid her mother would notice her red eyes at breakfast and keep at her with minute, persistent, mosquito-like questions regarding the cause thereof.

'Suppose,' thought Valancy with a ghastly grin, 'I answered with the plain truth, "I am crying because I cannot get married." How horrified Mother would be – though she is ashamed every day of her life of her old maid daughter.'

But of course appearances should be kept up. 'It is not,' Valancy could hear her mother's prim, dictatorial voice asserting, 'it is not maidenly to think about men.'

The thought of her mother's expression made Valancy laugh – for she had a sense of humour nobody in her clan suspected. For that matter, there were a good many things about Valancy that nobody suspected. But her laughter was very superficial and presently she lay there, a huddled, futile little figure, listening to the rain pouring down outside and watching, with a sick distaste, the chill, merciless light creeping into her ugly, sordid room.

She knew the ugliness of that room by heart – knew it and hated it. The yellow painted floor, with one hideous, 'hooked' rug by the bed, with a grotesque, 'hooked' dog on it, always grinning at her when she awoke; the faded, dark red paper; the ceiling discoloured by old leaks and crossed by cracks; the narrow, pinched little washstand; the brown-paper lambrequin with purple roses on it; the spotted old looking glass with the crack across it, propped up on the inadequate dressing-table; the jar of ancient potpourri made by her mother on her mythical honeymoon; the shell-covered box, with one burst corner, which Cousin Stickles had made in her equally mythical girlhood; the beaded pincushion with half its bead fringe gone; the one stiff, yellow chair; the faded old motto, 'Gone but not forgotten', worked in coloured yarns about great-grandmother Stirling's grim old face; the old photographs of ancient relatives long banished from the rooms below. There were only two pictures that were not of relatives. One, an old chromo of a puppy sitting on a rainy doorstep. That picture always made Valancy unhappy. That forlorn little dog crouched on the doorstep in the driving rain! Why didn't someone open the door and let him in? The other picture was a faded, passe-partouted engraving of Queen Louise coming down a stairway, which Aunt Wellington had lavishly given her on her tenth birthday. For nineteen years she had looked at it and hated it, beautiful, smug, self-satisfied Queen Louise. But she never dared destroy it or remove it. Mother and Cousin Stickles would have been aghast, or, as Valancy irreverently expressed it in her thoughts, would have had a fit.

Every room in the house was ugly, of course. But downstairs appearances were kept up somewhat. There was no money for rooms nobody ever saw. Valancy sometimes felt that she could have done something for her room herself, even without money, if she were permitted. But her mother had negatived every timid suggestion and Valancy did not persist. Valancy never persisted. She was afraid to. Her mother could not brook opposition. Mrs Stirling would sulk for days if offended, with the airs of an insulted duchess.

The only thing Valancy liked about her room was that she could be alone there at night to cry if she wanted to.

But, after all, what did it matter if a room, which you used for nothing except sleeping and dressing in, were ugly? Valancy was never permitted to stay alone in her room for any other purpose. People who wanted to be alone, so Mrs Frederick Stirling and Cousin Stickles believed, could only want to be alone for some sinister purpose. But her room in the Blue Castle was everything a room should be.

Valancy, so cowed and subdued and overridden and snubbed in real life, was wont to let herself go rather splendidly in her daydreams. Nobody in the Stirling clan, or its ramifications, suspected this, least of all her mother and Cousin Stickles. They never knew that Valancy had two homes – the ugly red brick box of a home, on Elm Street, and the Blue Castle in Spain. Valancy had lived spiritually in the Blue Castle ever since she could remember. She had been a very tiny child when she found herself possessed of it. Always, when she shut her eyes, she could see it plainly, with its turrets and banners on the pine-clad mountain height, wrapped in its faint, blue loveliness, against the sunset skies of a fair and unknown land. Everything wonderful and beautiful was in that castle. Jewels that queens might have worn; robes of moonlight and fire; couches of roses and gold; long flights of shallow marble steps, with great, white urns, and with slender, mist-clad maidens going up and down them; courts, marble-pillared, where shimmering fountains fell and nightingales sang among the myrtles; halls of mirrors that reflected only handsome knights and lovely women – herself the loveliest of all, for whose glance men died. All that supported her through the boredom of her days was the hope of going on a dream spree at night. Most, if not all, of the Stirlings would have died of horror if they had known half the things Valancy did in her Blue Castle.

For one thing she had quite a few lovers in it. Oh, only one at a time. One who wooed her with all the romantic ardour of the age of chivalry and won her after long devotion and many deeds of derring-do, and was wedded to her with pomp and circumstance in the great, banner-hung chapel of the Blue Castle.

At twelve, this lover was a fair lad with golden curls and heavenly blue eyes. At fifteen, he was tall and dark and pale, but still necessarily handsome. At twenty, he was ascetic, dreamy, spiritual. At twenty-five, he had a clean-cut jaw, slightly grim, and a face strong and rugged rather than handsome. Valancy never grew older than twenty-five in her Blue Castle, but recently – very recently – her hero had had reddish, tawny hair, a twisted smile and a mysterious past.

I don't say Valancy deliberately murdered these lovers as she outgrew them. One simply faded away as another came. Things are very convenient in this respect in Blue Castles.

But, on this morning of her day of fate, Valancy could not find the key of her Blue Castle. Reality pressed on her too hardly, barking at her heels like a maddening little dog. She was twenty-nine, lonely, undesired, ill-favoured – the only homely girl in a handsome clan, with no past and no future. As far as she could look back, life was drab and colourless, with not one single crimson or purple spot anywhere. As far as she could look forward it seemed certain to be just the same until she was nothing but a solitary, little withered leaf clinging to a wintry bough. The moment when a woman realises that she has nothing to live for – neither love, duty, purpose nor hope – holds for her the bitterness of death.

'And I just have to go on living because I can't stop. I may have to live eighty years,' thought Valancy, in a kind of panic. 'We're all horribly long-lived. It sickens me to think of it.'

She was glad it was raining – or rather, she was drearily satisfied that it was raining. There would be no picnic that day. This annual picnic, whereby Aunt and Uncle Wellington – one always thought of them in that succession – inevitably celebrated their engagement at a picnic thirty years before, had been, of late years, a veritable nightmare to Valancy. By an impish coincidence it was the same day as her birthday and, after she had passed twenty-five, nobody let her forget it.

Much as she hated going to the picnic, it would never have occurred to her to rebel against it. There seemed to be nothing of the revolutionary in her nature. And she knew exactly what everyone would say to her at the picnic. Uncle Wellington, whom she disliked and despised even though he had fulfilled the highest Stirling aspiration, 'marrying money', would say to her in a pig's whisper, 'Not thinking of getting married yet, my dear?' and then go off into the bellow of laughter with which he invariably concluded his dull remarks. Aunt Wellington, of whom Valancy stood in abject awe, would tell her about Olive's new chiffon dress and Cecil's last devoted letter. Valancy would have to look as pleased and interested as if the dress and letter had been hers or else Aunt Wellington would be offended. And Valancy had long ago decided that she would rather offend God than Aunt Wellington, because God might forgive her but Aunt Wellington never would.

Aunt Alberta, enormously fat, with an amiable habit of always referring to her husband as 'he', as if he were the only male creature in the world, who could never forget that she had been a great beauty in her youth, would condole with Valancy on her sallow skin – 'I don't know why all the girls of today are so sunburned. When I was a girl my skin was roses and cream. I was counted the prettiest girl in Canada, my dear.'

Perhaps Uncle Herbert wouldn't say anything – or perhaps he would remark jocularly, 'How fat you're getting, Doss!' And then everybody would laugh over the excessively humorous idea of poor, scrawny little Doss getting fat.

Handsome, solemn Uncle James, whom Valancy disliked but respected because he was reputed to be very clever and was therefore the clan oracle – brains being none too plentiful in the Stirling connection – would probably remark with the owl-like sarcasm that had won him his reputation, 'I suppose you're busy with your hope-chest these days?'

And Uncle Benjamin would ask some of his abominable conundrums, between wheezy chuckles, and answer them himself.

'What is the difference between Doss and a mouse? The mouse wishes to harm the cheese and Doss wishes to charm the he's.'

Valancy had heard him ask that riddle fifty times and every time she wanted to throw something at him. But she never did. In the first place, the Stirlings simply did not throw things; in the second place, Uncle Benjamin was a wealthy and childless old widower and Valancy had been brought up in the fear and admonition of his money. If she offended him he would cut her out of his will – supposing she were in it. Valancy did not want to be cut out of Uncle Benjamin's will. She had been poor all her life and knew the galling bitterness of it. So she endured his riddles and even smiled tortured little smiles over him.

Aunt Isabel, downright and disagreeable as an east wind, would criticise her in some way – Valancy could not predict just how, for Aunt Isabel never repeated a criticism – she found something new with which to jab you every time. Aunt Isabel prided herself on saying what she thought, but didn't like it so well when other people said what they thought to her. Valancy never said what she thought.

Cousin Georgiana – named after her great-great-grandmother, who had been named after George the Fourth – would recount dolorously the names of all relatives and friends who had died since the last picnic and wonder 'which of us will be the first to go next'.

Oppressively competent, Aunt Mildred would talk endlessly of her husband and her odious prodigies of babies to Valancy, because Valancy would be the only one she could find to put up with it. For the same reason, Cousin Gladys – really First Cousin Gladys once removed, according to the strict way in which the Stirlings tabulated relationship – a tall, thin lady who admitted she had a sensitive disposition, would describe minutely the tortures of her neuritis. And Olive, the wonder girl of the whole Stirling clan, who had everything Valancy had not – beauty, popularity, love – would show off her beauty and presume on her popularity and flaunt her diamond insignia of love in Valancy's dazzled, envious eyes.

There would be none of all this today. And there would be no packing up of teaspoons. The packing up was always left for Valancy and Cousin Stickles. And once, six years ago, a silver teaspoon from Aunt Wellington's wedding set had been lost. Valancy never heard the last of that silver teaspoon. Its ghost appeared Banquo-like at every subsequent family feast.

Oh, yes, Valancy knew exactly what the picnic would be like and she blessed the rain that had saved her from it. There would be no picnic this year. If Aunt Wellington could not celebrate on the sacred day itself she would have no celebration at all. Thank whatever gods there were for that.

Since there would be no picnic, Valancy made up her mind that, if the rain held up in the afternoon, she would go up to the library and get another of John Foster's books. Valancy was never allowed to read novels, but John Foster's books were not novels. They were 'nature books' – so the librarian told Mrs Frederick Stirling – 'all about the woods and birds and bugs and things like that, you know'. So Valancy was allowed to read them – under protest, for it was only too evident that she enjoyed them too much. It was permissible, even laudable, to read to improve your mind and your religion, but a book that was enjoyable was dangerous. Valancy did not know whether her mind was being improved or not; but she felt vaguely that if she had come across John Foster's books years ago life might have been a different thing for her. They seemed to her to yield glimpses of a world into which she might once have entered, though the door was forever barred to her now. It was only within the last year that John Foster's books had been in the Deerwood library, though the librarian told Valancy that he had been a well-known writer for several years.

'Where does he live?' Valancy had asked.

'Nobody knows. From his books he must be a Canadian, but no more information can be had. His publishers won't say a word. Quite likely John Foster is a nom de plume. His books are so popular we can't keep them in at all, though I really can't see what people find in them to rave over.'

'I think they're wonderful,' said Valancy, timidly.

'Oh – well –' Miss Clarkson smiled in a patronising fashion that relegated Valancy's opinions to limbo, 'I can't say I care much for bugs myself. But certainly Foster seems to know all there is to know about them.'

Valancy didn't know whether she cared much for bugs either. It was not John Foster's uncanny knowledge of wild creatures and insect life that enthralled her. She could hardly say what it was – some tantalising lure of a mystery never revealed – some hint of a great secret just a little further on – some faint, elusive echo of lovely, forgotten things – John Foster's magic was indefinable.

Yes, she would get a new Foster book. It was a month since she had Thistle Harvest, so surely Mother could not object. Valancy had read it four times – she knew whole passages off by heart.

And – she almost thought she would go and see Dr Trent about that queer pain around the heart. It had come rather often lately, and the palpitations were becoming annoying, not to speak of an occasional dizzy moment and a queer shortness of breath. But could she go to him without telling anyone? It was a most daring thought. None of the Stirlings ever consulted a doctor without holding a family council and getting Uncle James' approval. Then, they went to Dr Ambrose Marsh of Port Lawrence, who had married Second Cousin Adelaide Stirling.

But Valancy disliked Dr Ambrose Marsh. And, besides, she could not get to Port Lawrence, fifteen miles away, without being taken there. She did not want anyone to know about her heart.

There would be such a fuss made and every member of the family would come down and talk it over and advise her and caution her and warn her and tell her horrible tales of great-aunts and cousins forty times removed who had been 'just like that and dropped dead without a moment's warning, my dear'.

Aunt Isabel would remember that she had always said Doss looked like a girl who would have heart trouble – 'so pinched and peaked always'; and Uncle Wellington would take it as a personal insult, when 'no Stirling ever had heart disease before'; and Georgiana would forebode in perfectly audible asides that 'poor, dear little Doss isn't long for this world, I'm afraid'; and Cousin Gladys would say, 'Why, my heart has been like that for years', in a tone that implied no one else had any business even to have a heart; and Olive – Olive would merely look beautiful and superior and disgustingly healthy, as if to say, 'Why all this fuss over a faded superfluity like Doss when you have me?'

Valancy felt that she couldn't tell anybody unless she had to. She felt quite sure there was nothing at all seriously wrong with her heart and no need of all the pother that would ensue if she mentioned it. She would just slip up quietly and see Dr Trent that very day. As for his bill, she had the two hundred dollars that her father had put in the bank for her the day she was born, but she would secretly take out enough to pay Dr Trent. She was never allowed to use even the interest of this.

Dr Trent was a gruff, outspoken, absent-minded old fellow, but he was a recognised authority on heart-disease, even if he were only a general practitioner in out-of-the-world Deerwood. Dr Trent was over seventy and there had been rumours that he meant to retire soon. None of the Stirling clan had ever gone to him since he had told Cousin Gladys, ten years before, that her neuritis was all imaginary and that she enjoyed it. You couldn't patronise a doctor who insulted your first-cousin-once-removed like that – not to mention that he was a Presbyterian when all the Stirlings went to the Anglican church. But Valancy, between the devil of disloyalty to clan and the deep sea of fuss and clatter and advice, thought she would take a chance with the devil.

TWO

When cousin Stickles knocked at her door, Valancy knew it was half-past seven and she must get up. As long as she could remember, Cousin Stickles had knocked at her door at half-past seven. Cousin Stickles and Mrs Frederick Stirling had been up since seven, but Valancy was allowed to lie abed half an hour longer because of a family tradition that she was delicate. Valancy got up, though she hated getting up more this morning than ever she had before. What was there to get up for? Another dreary day like all the days that had preceded it, full of meaningless little tasks, joyless and unimportant, that benefited nobody. But if she did not get up at once she would not be ready for breakfast at eight o'clock. Hard and fast times for meals were the rule in Mrs Stirling's household. Breakfast at eight, dinner at one, supper at six, year in and year out. No excuses for being late were ever tolerated. So up Valancy got, shivering.

The room was bitterly cold with the raw, penetrating chill of a wet May morning. The house would be cold all day. It was one of Mrs Frederick's rules that no fires were necessary after the 24th of May. Meals were cooked on the little oil-stove in the back porch. And though May might be icy and October frostbitten, no fires were lighted until the 21st of October by the calendar. On the 21st of October Mrs Frederick began cooking over the kitchen range and lighted a fire in the sitting room stove in the evenings. It was whispered about in the connection that the late Frederick Stirling had caught the cold which resulted in his death during Valancy's first year of life because Mrs Frederick would not have a fire on the 20th of October. She lighted it the next day – but that was a day too late for Frederick Stirling.

Valancy took off and hung up in the closet her nightdress of course, unbleached cotton, with high neck and long, tight sleeves. She put on undergarments of a similar nature, a dress of brown gingham, thick, black stockings and rubber-heeled boots. Of late years she had fallen into the habit of doing her hair with the shade of the window by the looking-glass pulled down. The lines on her face did not show so plainly then. But this morning she jerked the shade to the very top and looked at herself in the leprous mirror with a passionate determination to see herself as the world saw her.

The result was rather dreadful. Even a beauty would have found that harsh, unsoftened side-light trying. Valancy saw straight black hair, short and thin, always lustreless despite the fact that she gave it one hundred strokes of the brush, neither more nor less, every night of her life and faithfully rubbed Redfern's Hair Vigor into the roots, more lustreless than ever in its morning roughness; fine, straight, black brows; a nose she had always felt was much too small even for her small, three-cornered, white face; a small, pale mouth that always fell open a trifle over little, pointed white teeth; a figure thin and flat-breasted, rather below the average height. She had somehow escaped the family high cheekbones, and her dark-brown eyes, too soft and shadowy to be black, had a slant that was almost Oriental. Apart from her eyes she was neither pretty nor ugly – just insignificant-looking, she concluded bitterly. How plain the lines around her eyes and mouth were in that merciless light! And never had her narrow, white face looked so narrow and so white.

She did her hair in a pompadour. Pompadours had long gone out of fashion, but they had been in when Valancy first put her hair up and Aunt Wellington had decided that she must always wear her hair so.

'It is the only way that becomes you. Your face is so small that you must add height to it by a pompadour effect,' said Aunt Wellington, who always enunciated commonplaces as if uttering profound and important truths.

Valancy had hankered to do her hair pulled low on her forehead, with puffs above the ears, as Olive was wearing hers. But Aunt Wellington's dictum had such an effect on her that she never dared change her style of hairdressing again. But then, there were so many things Valancy never dared do.

All her life she had been afraid of something, she thought bitterly. From the very dawn of recollection, when she had been so horribly afraid of the big black bear that lived, so Cousin Stickles told her, in the closet under the stairs.

'And I always will be – I know it – I can't help it. I don't know what it would be like not to be afraid of something.'

Afraid of her mother's sulky fits – afraid of offending Uncle Benjamin – afraid of becoming a target for Aunt Wellington's contempt – afraid of Aunt Isabel's biting comments – afraid of Uncle James' disapproval – afraid of offending the whole clan's opinions and prejudices – afraid of not keeping up appearances – afraid to say what she really thought of anything – afraid of poverty in her old age. Fear – fear – fear – she could never escape from it. It bound her and enmeshed her like a spider's web of steel. Only in her Blue Castle could she find temporary release. And this morning Valancy could not believe she had a Blue Castle. She would never be able to find it again. Twenty-nine, unmarried, undesired – what had she to do with the fairy-like chatelaine of the Blue Castle? She would cut such childish nonsense out of her life forever and face reality unflinchingly.

She turned from her unfriendly mirror and looked out. The ugliness of the view always struck her like a blow; the ragged fence, the tumble-down old carriage-shop in the next lot, plastered with crude, violently coloured advertisements; the grimy railway station beyond, with the awful derelicts that were always hanging around it even at this early hour. In the pouring rain everything looked worse than usual, especially the beastly advertisement, 'Keep that schoolgirl complexion.' Valancy had kept her schoolgirl complexion. That was just the trouble. There was not a gleam of beauty anywhere – 'exactly like my life', thought Valancy drearily. Her brief bitterness had passed. She accepted facts as resignedly as she had always accepted them. She was one of the people whom life always passes by. There was no altering that fact.

In this mood Valancy went down to breakfast.

THREE

Breakfast was always the same. Oatmeal porridge, which Valancy loathed, toast and tea, and one teaspoonful of marmalade. Mrs Frederick thought two teaspoonfuls extravagant – but that did not matter to Valancy, who hated marmalade, too. The chilly, gloomy little dining-room was chillier and gloomier than usual; the rain streamed down outside the window; departed Stirlings, in atrocious, gilt frames, wider than the pictures, glowered down from the walls. And yet Cousin Stickles wished Valancy many happy returns of the day!

'Sit up straight, Doss,' was all her mother said.

Valancy sat up straight. She talked to her mother and Cousin Stickles of the things they always talked of. She never wondered what would happen if she tried to talk of something else. She knew. Therefore she never did it.

Mrs Frederick was offended with Providence for sending a rainy day when she wanted to go to a picnic, so she ate her breakfast in a sulky silence for which Valancy was rather grateful. But Christine Stickles whined endlessly on as usual, complaining about everything – the weather, the leak in the pantry, the price of oatmeal and butter – Valancy felt at once she had buttered her toast too lavishly – the epidemic of mumps in Deerwood.

'Doss will be sure to ketch them,' she foreboded.

'Doss must not go where she is likely to catch mumps,' said Mrs Frederick shortly.

Valancy had never had mumps – or whooping cough – or chicken-pox – or measles – or anything she should have had – nothing but horrible colds every winter. Doss' winter colds were a sort of tradition in the family. Nothing, it seemed, could prevent her from catching them. Mrs Frederick and Cousin Stickles did their heroic best. One winter they kept Valancy housed up from

November to May, in the warm sitting room. She was not even allowed to go to church. And Valancy took cold after cold and ended up with bronchitis in June.

'None of my family were ever like that,' said Mrs Frederick, implying that it must be a Stirling tendency.

'The Stirlings seldom take cold,' said Cousin Stickles resentfully. She had been a Stirling.

'I think,' said Mrs Frederick, 'that if a person makes up her mind not to have colds she will not have colds.'

So that was the trouble. It was all Valancy's own fault.

But on this particular morning Valancy's unbearable grievance was that she was called Doss. She had endured it for twenty-nine years, and all at once she felt she could not endure it any longer. Her full name was Valancy Jane. Valancy Jane was rather terrible, but she liked Valancy, with its odd, out-land tang. It was always a wonder to Valancy that the Stirlings had allowed her to be so christened. She had been told that her maternal grandfather, old Amos Wansbarra, had chosen the name for her. Her father had tacked on the Jane by way of civilising it, and the whole connection got out of the difficulty by nicknaming her Doss. She never got Valancy from anyone but outsiders.

'Mother,' she said timidly, 'would you mind calling me Valancy after this? Doss seems so – so – I don't like it.'

Mrs Frederick looked at her daughter in astonishment. She wore glasses with enormously strong lenses that gave her eyes a peculiarly disagreeable appearance.

'What is the matter with Doss?'

'It – seems so childish,' faltered Valancy.

'Oh!' Mrs Frederick had been a Wansbarra and the Wansbarra smile was not an asset. 'I see. Well, it should suit you then. You are childish enough in all conscience, my dear child.'

'I am twenty-nine,' said the dear child desperately.

'I wouldn't proclaim it from the house-tops if I were you, dear,' said Mrs Frederick. 'Twenty-nine! I had been married nine years when I was twenty-nine.'

'I was married at seventeen,' said Cousin Stickles proudly.

Valancy looked at them furtively. Mrs Frederick, except for those terrible glasses and the hooked nose that made her look, more like a parrot than a parrot itself could look, was not ill-looking. At twenty she might have been quite pretty. But Cousin Stickles! And yet Christine Stickles had once been desirable in some man's eyes. Valancy felt that Cousin Stickles, with her broad, flat, wrinkled face, a mole right on the end of her dumpy nose, bristling hairs on her chin, wrinkled yellow neck, pale, protruding eyes, and thin, puckered mouth, had yet this advantage over her – this right to look down on her. And even yet Cousin Stickles was necessary to Mrs Frederick. Valancy wondered pitifully what it would be like to be wanted by some one – needed by someone. No one in the whole world needed her, or would miss anything from life if she dropped suddenly out of it. She was a disappointment to her mother. No one loved her. She had never so much as had a girl friend.

'I haven't even a gift for friendship,' she had once admitted to herself pitifully.

'Doss, you haven't eaten your crusts,' said Mrs Frederick rebukingly.

It rained all the forenoon without cessation. Valancy pieced a quilt. Valancy hated piecing quilts. And there was no need of it. The house was full of quilts. There were three big chests, packed with quilts, in the attic. Mrs Frederick had begun storing away quilts when Valancy was seventeen and she kept on storing them, though it did not seem likely that Valancy would ever need them. But Valancy must be at work and fancy work materials were too expensive. Idleness was a cardinal sin in the Stirling household. When Valancy had been a child she had been made to write down every night, in a small, hated, black notebook, all the minutes she had spent in idleness that day. On Sundays her mother made her tot them up and pray over them.

On this particular forenoon of this day of destiny Valancy spent only ten minutes in idleness. At least, Mrs Frederick and Cousin Stickles would have called it idleness. She went to her room to get a better thimble and she opened *Thistle Harvest* guiltily at random.

'The woods are so human,' wrote John Foster, 'that to know them one must live with them. An occasional saunter through them, keeping to the well-trodden paths, will never admit us to their intimacy. If we wish to be friends we must seek them out and win them by frequent, reverent visits at all hours; by morning, by noon, and by night; and at all seasons, in spring, in summer, in autumn, in winter. Otherwise we can never really know them and any pretence we may make to the contrary will never impose on them. They have their own effective way of keeping aliens at a distance and shutting their hearts to mere casual sightseers. It is of no use to seek the woods from any motive except sheer love of them; they will find us out at once and hide all their sweet, old-world secrets from us. But if they know we come to them because we love them they will be very kind to us and give us such treasures of beauty and delight as are not bought or sold in any market-place. For the woods, when they give at all, give unstintedly and hold nothing back from their true worshippers. We must go to them lovingly, humbly, patiently, watchfully, and we shall learn what poignant loveliness lurks in the wild places and silent intervales, lying under starshine and sunset, what cadences of unearthly music are harped on aged pine boughs or crooned in copses of fir, what delicate savours exhale from mosses and ferns in sunny corners or on damp brooklands, what dreams and myths and legends of an older time haunt them. Then the immortal heart of the woods will beat against ours and its subtle life will steal into our veins and make us its own forever, so that no matter where we go or how widely we wander we shall yet be drawn back to the forest to find our most enduring kinship.'

'Doss,' called her mother from the hall below, 'what are you doing all by yourself in that room?'

Valancy dropped *Thistle Harvest* like a hot coal and fled downstairs to her patches; but she felt the strange exhilaration of spirit that always came momentarily to her when she dipped into one of John Foster's books. Valancy did not know much about woods – except the haunted groves of oak and pine around her Blue Castle. But she had always secretly hankered after them and a Foster book about woods was the next best thing to the woods themselves.

At noon it stopped raining, but the sun did not come out until three. Then Valancy timidly said she thought she would go uptown.

'What do you want to go uptown for?' demanded her mother.

'I want to get a book from the library.'

'You got a book from the library only last week.'

'No, it was four weeks.'

'Four weeks. Nonsense!'

'Really it was, Mother.'

'You are mistaken. It cannot possibly have been more than two weeks. I dislike contradiction. And I do not see what you want to get a book for, anyhow. You waste too much time reading.'

'Of what value is my time?' asked Valancy bitterly.

'Doss! Don't speak in that tone to me.'

'We need some tea,' said Cousin Stickles. 'She might go and get that if she wants a walk – though this damp weather is bad for colds.'

They argued the matter for ten minutes longer and finally Mrs Frederick agreed rather grudgingly that Valancy might go.

FOUR
❧

'Got your rubbers on?' called Cousin Stickles, as Valancy left the house.

Christine Stickles had never once forgotten to ask that question when Valancy went out on a damp day.

'Yes.'

'Have you got your flannel petticoat on?' asked Mrs Frederick.

'No.'

'Doss, I really do not understand you. Do you want to catch your death of cold again?' Her voice implied that Valancy had died of a cold several times already. 'Go upstairs this minute and put it on!'

'Mother, I don't need a flannel petticoat. My sateen one is warm enough.'

'Doss, remember you had bronchitis two years ago. Go and do as you are told!'

Valancy went, though nobody will ever know just how near she came to hurling the rubber-plant into the street before she went. She hated that grey flannel petticoat more than any other garment she owned. Olive never had to wear flannel petticoats. Olive wore ruffled silk and sheer lawn and filmy laced flounces. But Olive's father had 'married money' and Olive never had bronchitis. So there you were.

'Are you sure you didn't leave the soap in the water?' demanded Mrs Frederick. But Valancy was gone. She turned at the corner and looked back down the ugly, prim, respectable street where she lived. The Stirling house was the ugliest on it – more like a red brick box than anything else. Too high for its breadth, and made still higher by a bulbous glass cupola on top. About it was the desolate, barren peace of an old house whose life is lived.

There was a very pretty house, with leaded casements and dubbed gables, just around the corner – a new house, one of those houses you love the minute you see them. Clayton Markley had built it for his bride. He was to be married to Jennie Lloyd in June. The little house, it was said, was furnished from attic to cellar, in complete readiness for its mistress.

'I don't envy Jennie the man,' thought Valancy sincerely – Clayton Markley was not one of her many ideals – 'but I do envy her the house. It's such a nice young house. Oh, if I could only have a house of my own – ever so poor, so tiny – but my own! But then,' she added bitterly, 'there is no use in yowling for the moon when you can't even get a tallow candle.'

In dreamland nothing would do Valancy but a castle of pale sapphire. In real life she would have been fully satisfied with a little house of her own. She envied Jennie Lloyd more fiercely than ever today. Jennie was not so much better looking than she was, and not so very much younger. Yet she was to have this delightful house. And the nicest little Wedgwood teacups – Valancy had seen them; an open fireplace, and monogrammed linen; hemstitched tablecloths, and china-closets. Why did everything come to some girls and nothing to others? It wasn't fair.

Valancy was once more seething with rebellion as she walked along, a prim, dowdy little figure in her shabby raincoat and three-year-old hat, splashed occasionally by the mud of a passing motor with its insulting shrieks. Motors were still rather a novelty in Deerwood, though they were common in Port Lawrence, and most of the summer residents up at Muskoka had them. In Deerwood only some of the smart set had them; for even Deerwood was divided into sets. There was the smart set – the intellectual set – the old-family set – of which the Stirlings were members – the common run, and a few pariahs. Not one of the Stirling clan had as yet condescended to a motor, though Olive was teasing her father to have one. Valancy had never even been in a motorcar. But she did not hanker after this. In truth, she felt rather afraid of motorcars, especially at night. They seemed to be too much like big purring beasts that might turn and crush you – or make some terrible savage leap somewhere. On the steep mountain trails around her Blue Castle only gaily caparisoned steeds might proudly pace; in real life Valancy would have been quite contented to drive in a buggy behind a nice horse. She got a buggy drive only when some uncle or cousin remembered to fling her 'a chance', like a bone to a dog.

FIVE

Of course she must buy the tea in Uncle Benjamin's grocery store. To buy it anywhere else was unthinkable. Yet Valancy hated to go to Uncle Benjamin's store on her twenty-ninth birthday. There was no hope that he would not remember it.

'Why,' demanded Uncle Benjamin, leeringly, as he tied up her tea, 'are young ladies like bad grammarians?'

Valancy, with Uncle Benjamin's will in the background of her mind, said meekly, 'I don't know. Why?'

'Because,' chuckled Uncle Benjamin, 'they can't decline matrimony.'

The two clerks, Joe Hammond and Claude Bertram, chuckled also, and Valancy disliked them a little more than ever. On the first day Claude Bertram had seen her in the store she had heard him whisper to Joe, 'Who is that?' And Joe had said, 'Valancy Stirling – one of the Deerwood old maids.' 'Curable or incurable?' Claude had asked with a snicker, evidently thinking the question very clever. Valancy smarted anew with the sting of that old recollection.

'Twenty-nine,' Uncle Benjamin was saying. 'Dear me, Doss, you're dangerously near the second corner and not even thinking of getting married yet. Twenty-nine. It seems impossible.'

Then Uncle Benjamin said an original thing. Uncle Benjamin said, 'How time does fly!'

'I think it crawls,' said Valancy passionately. Passion was so alien to Uncle Benjamin's conception of Valancy that he didn't know what to make of her. To cover his confusion, he asked another conundrum as he tied up her beans – Cousin Stickles had remembered at the last moment that they must have beans. Beans were cheap and filling.

'What two ages are apt to prove illusory?' asked Uncle Benjamin; and, not waiting for Valancy to 'give it up', he added, 'Mir-age and marri-age.'

'M-i-r-a-g-e is pronounced mirazh,' said Valancy shortly, picking up her tea and her beans. For the moment she did not care whether Uncle Benjamin cut her out of his will or not. She walked out of the store while Uncle Benjamin stared after her with his mouth open. Then he shook his head.

'Poor Doss is taking it hard,' he said.

Valancy was sorry by the time she reached the next crossing. Why had she lost her patience like that? Uncle Benjamin would be annoyed and would likely tell her mother that Doss had been impertinent – 'to me!' – and her mother would lecture her for a week.

'I've held my tongue for twenty years,' thought Valancy. 'Why couldn't I have held it once more?'

Yes, it was just twenty, Valancy reflected, since she had first been twitted with her loverless condition. She remembered the bitter moment perfectly. She was just nine years old and she was standing alone on the school playground while the other little girls of her class were playing a game in which you must be chosen by a boy as his partner before you could play. Nobody had chosen Valancy – little, pale, black-haired Valancy, with her prim, long-sleeved apron and odd, slanted eyes.

'Oh,' said a pretty little girl to her, 'I'm so sorry for you. You haven't got a beau.'

Valancy had said defiantly, as she continued to say for twenty years, 'I don't want a beau.' But this afternoon Valancy once and for all stopped saying that.

'I'm going to be honest with myself anyhow,' she thought savagely. 'Uncle Benjamin's riddles hurt me because they are true. I do want to be married. I want a house of my own – I want a husband of my own – I want sweet, little fat babies of my own –' Valancy stopped suddenly aghast at her own recklessness. She felt sure that Rev. Dr Stalling, who passed her at this moment, read her thoughts and disapproved of them thoroughly. Valancy was afraid of Dr Stalling – had been afraid of him ever since the Sunday, twenty-three years before, when he had first come to St Albans'. Valancy had been too late for Sunday School that day and she had gone into the church timidly and sat in their pew. No one else was in the church – nobody except the new rector, Dr Stalling. Dr Stalling stood up in front of the choir door, beckoned to her, and said sternly, 'Little boy, come up here.'

Valancy had stared around her. There was no little boy – there was no one in all the huge church but herself. This strange man with the blue glasses couldn't mean her. She was not a boy.

'Little boy,' repeated Dr Stalling, more sternly still, shaking his forefinger fiercely at her, 'come up here at once!'

Valancy arose as if hypnotised and walked up the aisle. She was too terrified to do anything else. What dreadful thing was going to happen to her? What had happened to her? Had she actually turned into a boy? She came to a stop in front of Dr Stalling. Dr Stalling shook his forefinger – such a long, knuckly forefinger – at her and said:

'Little boy, take off your hat.'

Valancy took off her hat. She had a scrawny little pigtail hanging down her back, but Dr Stalling was shortsighted and did not perceive it.

'Little boy, go back to your seat and always take off your hat in church. Remember!'

Valancy went back to her seat carrying her hat like an automaton. Presently her mother came in.

'Doss,' said Mrs Stirling, 'what do you mean by taking off your hat? Put it on instantly!'

Valancy put it on instantly. She was cold with fear lest Dr Stalling should immediately summon her up front again. She would have to go, of course – it never occurred to her that one could disobey the rector – and the church was full of people now. Oh, what would she do if that horrible, stabbing forefinger were shaken at her again before all those people? Valancy sat through the whole service in an agony of dread and was sick for a week afterwards. Nobody knew why – Mrs Frederick again bemoaned herself of her delicate child.

Dr Stalling found out his mistake and laughed over it to Valancy – who did not laugh. She never got over her dread of Dr Stalling. And now to be caught by him on the street corner, thinking such things!

Valancy got her John Foster book – *Magic of Wings*. 'His latest – all about birds,' said Miss Clarkson. She had almost decided that she would go home, instead of going to see Dr Trent. Her courage had failed her. She was afraid of offending Uncle James – afraid of angering her mother – afraid of facing gruff, shaggy-browed old Dr Trent, who would probably tell her, as he had told Cousin Gladys, that her trouble was entirely imaginary and that she only had it because she liked to have it. No, she would not go; she would get a bottle of Redfern's Purple Pills instead. Redfern's Purple Pills were the standard medicine of the Stirling clan. Had they not cured Second Cousin Geraldine when five doctors had given her up? Valancy always felt very sceptical concerning the virtues of the Purple Pills; but there might be something in them; and it was easier to take them than to face Dr Trent alone. She would glance over the magazines in the reading room a few minutes and then go home.

Valancy tried to read a story, but it made her furious. On every page was a picture of the heroine surrounded by adoring men. And here was she, Valancy Stirling, who could not get a solitary beau! Valancy slammed the magazine shut; she opened *Magic of Wings*. Her eyes fell on the paragraph that changed her life.

'Fear is the original sin,' wrote John Foster. 'Almost all the evil in the world has its origin in the fact that someone is afraid of something. It is a cold, slimy serpent coiling about you. It is horrible to live with fear; and it is of all things degrading.'

Valancy shut *Magic of Wings* and stood up. She would go and see Dr Trent.

SIX

The ordeal was not so dreadful, after all. Dr Trent was as gruff and abrupt as usual, but he did not tell her her ailment was imaginary. After he had listened to her symptoms and asked a few questions and made a quick examination, he sat for a moment looking at her quite intently. Valancy thought he looked as if he were sorry for her. She caught her breath for a moment. Was the trouble serious? Oh, it couldn't be, surely – it really hadn't bothered her much – only lately it had got a little worse.

Dr Trent opened his mouth – but before he could speak the telephone at his elbow rang sharply. He picked up the receiver. Valancy, watching him, saw his face change suddenly as he listened,

'Lo – yes – yes – what? – yes – yes' – a brief interval – 'My God!'

Dr Trent dropped the receiver, dashed out of the room and upstairs without even a glance at Valancy. She heard him rushing madly about overhead, barking out a few remarks to somebody – presumably his housekeeper. Then he came tearing downstairs with a club bag in his hand, snatched his hat and coat from the rack, jerked open the street door and rushed down the street in the direction of the station.

Valancy sat alone in the little office, feeling more absolutely foolish than she had ever felt before in her life. Foolish – and humiliated. So this was all that had come of her heroic determination to live up to John Foster and cast fear aside. Not only was she a failure as a relative and non-existent as a sweetheart or friend, but she was not even of any importance as a patient. Dr Trent had forgotten her very presence in his excitement over whatever message had come by the telephone. She had gained nothing by ignoring Uncle James and flying in the face of family tradition.

For a moment she was afraid she was going to cry. It was all so – ridiculous. Then she heard Dr Trent's housekeeper coming down the stairs. Valancy rose and went to the office door.

'The doctor forgot all about me,' she said with a twisted smile.

'Well, that's too bad,' said Mrs Patterson sympathetically. 'But it wasn't much wonder, poor man. That was a telegram they 'phoned over from the Port. His son has been terribly injured in an auto accident in Montreal. The doctor had just ten minutes to catch the train. I don't know what he'll do if anything happens to Ned – he's just bound up in the boy. You'll have to come again, Miss Stirling. I hope it's nothing serious.'

'Oh, no, nothing serious,' agreed Valancy. She felt a little less humiliated. It was no wonder poor Dr Trent had forgotten her at such a moment. Nevertheless, she felt very flat and discouraged as she went down the street.

Valancy went home by the short-cut of Lover's Lane. She did not often go through Lover's Lane – but it was getting near suppertime and it would never do to be late. Lover's Lane wound around the back of the village, under great elms and maples, and deserved its name. It was hard to go there at any time and not find some canoodling couple – or young girls in pairs, arms intertwined, earnestly talking over their secrets. Valancy didn't know which made her feel more self-conscious and uncomfortable.

This evening she encountered both. She met Connie Hale and Kate Bayley, in new pink organdy dresses with flowers stuck coquettishly in their glossy, bare hair. Valancy had never had a pink dress or worn flowers in her hair. Then she passed a young couple she didn't know, dandering along, oblivious to everything but themselves. The young man's arm was around the girl's waist quite shamelessly. Valancy had never walked with a man's arm about her. She felt that she ought to be shocked – they might leave that sort of thing for the screening twilight, at least – but she wasn't shocked. In another flash of desperate, stark honesty she owned to herself that she was merely envious. When she passed them she felt quite sure they were laughing at her – pitying her – 'there's that queer little old maid, Valancy Stirling. They say she never had a beau in her whole life' – Valancy fairly ran to get out of Lover's Lane. Never had she felt so utterly colourless and skinny and insignificant.

Just where Lover's Lane debouched on the street, an old car was parked. Valancy knew that car well – by sound, at least – and everybody in Deerwood knew it. This was before the phrase 'tin Lizzie' had come into circulation – in Deerwood, at least; but if it had been known, this car was the tinniest of Lizzies – though it was not a Ford but an old Grey Slosson. Nothing more battered and disreputable could be imagined.

It was Barney Snaith's car and Barney himself was just scrambling up from under it, in overalls plastered with mud. Valancy gave him a swift, furtive look as she hurried by. This was only the second time she had ever seen the notorious Barney Snaith, though she had heard enough about him in the five years that he had been living 'up back' in Muskoka. The first time had been nearly a year ago, on the Muskoka road. He had been crawling out from under his car then, too, and he had given her a cheerful grin as she went by – a little, whimsical grin that gave him the look of an amused gnome. He didn't look bad – she didn't believe he was bad, in spite of the wild yarns that were always being told of him. Of course he went tearing in that terrible old Grey Slosson through Deerwood at hours when all decent people were in bed – often with old 'Roaring Abel', who made the night hideous with his howls – 'both of them dead drunk, my dear'. And everyone knew that he was an escaped convict and a defaulting bank clerk and a murderer in hiding and an infidel and an illegitimate son of old Roaring Abel Gay and the father of Roaring Abel's illegitimate grandchild and a counterfeiter and a forger and a few other awful things. But still Valancy didn't believe he was bad. Nobody with a smile like that could be bad, no matter what he had done.

It was that night the Prince of the Blue Castle changed from a being of grim jaw and hair with a dash of premature grey to a rakish individual with overlong, tawny hair, dashed with red, dark-brown eyes, and ears that stuck out just enough to give him an alert look but not enough to be called flying jibs. But he still retained something a little grim about the jaw.

Barney Snaith looked even more disreputable than usual just now. It was very evident that he hadn't shaved for days, and his hands and arms, bare to the shoulders, were black with grease. But he was whistling gleefully to himself and he seemed so happy that Valancy envied him. She envied him his light-heartedness and his irresponsibility and his mysterious little cabin up on an island in Lake Mistawis – even his rackety old Grey Slosson. Neither he nor his car had to be respectable and live up to traditions. When he rattled past her a few minutes later, bareheaded, leaning back in his Lizzie at a rakish angle, his longish hair blowing in the wind, a villainous-looking old black pipe in his mouth, she envied him again. Men had the best of it, no doubt about that. This outlaw was happy, whatever he was or wasn't. She, Valancy Stirling, respectable, well-behaved to the last degree, was unhappy and had always been unhappy. So there you were.

Valancy was just in time for supper. The sun had clouded over, and a dismal, drizzling rain was falling again. Cousin Stickles had the neuralgia. Valancy had to do the family darning and there was no time for Magic of Wings.

'Can't the darning wait till tomorrow?' she pleaded.

'Tomorrow will bring its own duties,' said Mrs Frederick inexorably.

Valancy darned all the evening and listened to Mrs Frederick and Cousin Stickles talking the eternal, niggling gossip of the clan, as they knitted drearily at interminable black stockings. They discussed Second Cousin Lilian's approaching wedding in all its bearings. On the whole, they approved. Second Cousin Lilian was doing well for herself.

'Though she hasn't hurried,' said Cousin Stickles. 'She must be twenty-five.'

'There have not – fortunately – been many old maids in our connection,' said Mrs Frederick bitterly.

Valancy flinched. She had run the darning needle into her finger.

Third Cousin Aaron Gray had been scratched by a cat and had blood-poisoning in his finger. 'Cats are most dangerous animals,' said Mrs Frederick. 'I would never have a cat about the house.'

She glared significantly at Valancy through her terrible glasses. Once, five years ago, Valancy had asked if she might have a cat. She had never referred to it since, but Mrs Frederick still suspected her of harbouring the unlawful desire in her heart of hearts.

Once Valancy sneezed. Now, in the Stirling code, it was very bad form to sneeze in public.

'You can always repress a sneeze by pressing your finger on your upper lip,' said Mrs Frederick rebukingly.

Half-past nine o'clock and so, as Mr Pepys would say, to bed. But First Cousin Stickles' neuralgic back must be rubbed with Redfern's Liniment. Valancy did that. Valancy always had to do it. She hated the smell of Redfern's Liniment – she hated the smug, beaming, portly, be-whiskered, be-spectacled picture of Dr Redfern on the bottle. Her fingers smelled of the horrible stuff after she got into bed, in spite of all the scrubbing she gave them.

Valancy's day of destiny had come and gone. She ended it as she had begun it, in tears.

SEVEN

⊗

There was a rosebush on the little Stirling lawn, growing beside the gate. It was called 'Doss's rosebush'. Cousin Georgiana had given it to Valancy five years ago and Valancy had planted it joyfully. She loved roses. But – of course – the rosebush never bloomed. That was her luck. Valancy did everything she could think of and took the advice of everybody in the clan, but still the rosebush would not bloom. It throve and grew luxuriantly, with great leafy branches untouched of rust or spider; but not even a bud had ever appeared on it. Valancy, looking at it two days after her birthday, was filled with a sudden, overwhelming hatred for it. The thing wouldn't bloom: very well, then, she would cut it down. She marched to the tool-room in the barn for her garden knife and she went at the rosebush viciously. A few minutes later horrified Mrs Frederick came out to the veranda and beheld her daughter slashing insanely among the rosebush boughs. Half of them were already strewn on the walk. The bush looked sadly dismantled.

'Doss, what on earth are you doing? Have you gone crazy?'

'No,' said Valancy. She meant to say it defiantly, but habit was too strong for her. She said it deprecatingly. 'I – I just made up my mind to cut this bush down. It is no good. It never blooms – never will bloom.'

'That is no reason for destroying it,' said Mrs Frederick sternly. 'It was a beautiful bush and quite ornamental. You have made a sorry-looking thing of it.'

'Rose trees should bloom,' said Valancy a little obstinately.

'Don't argue with me, Doss. Clear up that mess and leave the bush alone. I don't know what Georgiana will say when she sees how you have hacked it to pieces. Really, I'm surprised at you. And to do it without consulting me!'

'The bush is mine,' muttered Valancy.

'What's that? What did you say, Doss?'

'I only said the bush was mine,' repeated Valancy humbly.

Mrs Frederick turned without a word and marched back into the house. The mischief was done now. Valancy knew she had offended her mother deeply and would not be spoken to or noticed in any way for two or three days. Cousin Stickles would see to Valancy's bringing-up but Mrs Frederick would preserve the stony silence of outraged majesty.

Valancy sighed and put away her garden knife, hanging it precisely on its precise nail in the tool-shop. She cleared away the several branches and swept up the leaves. Her lips twitched as she looked at the straggling bush. It had an odd resemblance to its shaken, scrawny donor, little Cousin Georgiana herself.

'I certainly have made an awful-looking thing of it,' thought Valancy.

But she did not feel repentant – only sorry she had offended her mother. Things would be so uncomfortable until she was forgiven. Mrs Frederick was one of those women who can make their anger felt all over a house. Walls and doors are no protection from it.

'You'd better go uptown and git the mail,' said Cousin Stickles, when Valancy went in. 'I can't go – I feel all sorter peaky and piny this spring. I want you to stop at the drugstore and git me a bottle of Redfern's Blood Bitters. There's nothing like Redfern's Bitters for building a body up. Cousin James says the Purple Pills are the best, but I know better. My poor dear husband took Redfern's Bitters right up to the day he died. Don't let them charge you more'n ninety cents. I kin git it for that at the Port. And what have you been saying to your poor mother? Do you ever stop to think, Doss, that you kin only have one mother?'

'One is enough for me,' thought Valancy undutifully, as she went uptown.

She got Cousin Stickles' bottle of bitters and then she went to the post-office and asked for her mail at the General Delivery. Her mother did not have a box. They got too little mail to bother with it. Valancy did not expect any mail, except the Christian

Times, which was the only paper they took. They hardly ever got any letters. But Valancy rather liked to stand in the office and watch Mr Carewe, the grey-bearded, Santa-Clausy old clerk, handing out letters to the lucky people who did get them. He did it with such a detached, impersonal, Jove-like air, as if it did not matter in the least to him what supernal joys or shattering horrors might be in those letters for the people to whom they were addressed. Letters had a fascination for Valancy, perhaps because she so seldom got any. In her Blue Castle exciting epistles, bound with silk and sealed with crimson, were always being brought to her by pages in livery of gold and blue, but in real life her only letters were occasional perfunctory notes from relatives or an advertising circular.

Consequently she was immensely surprised when Mr Carewe, looking even more Jovian than usual, poked a letter out to her. Yes, it was addressed to her plainly, in a fierce, black hand: 'Miss Valancy Stirling, Elm Street, Deerwood' – and the postmark was Montreal. Valancy picked it up with a little quickening of her breath. Montreal! It must be from Doctor Trent. He had remembered her, after all.

Valancy met Uncle Benjamin coming in as she was going out and was glad the letter was safely in her bag.

'What,' said Uncle Benjamin, 'is the difference between a donkey and a postage-stamp?'

'I don't know. What?' answered Valancy dutifully.

'One you lick with a stick and the other you stick with a lick. Ha, ha!'

Uncle Benjamin passed in, tremendously pleased with himself.

Cousin Stickles pounced on the *Times* when Valancy got home, but it did not occur to her to ask if there were any letters. Mrs Frederick would have asked it, but Mrs Frederick's lips at present were sealed. Valancy was glad of this. If her mother had asked if there were any letters Valancy would have had to admit there was. Then she would have had to let her mother and Cousin Stickles read the letter and all would be discovered.

Her heart acted strangely on the way upstairs, and she sat down by her window for a few minutes before opening her letter. She felt very guilty and deceitful. She had never before kept a letter secret from her mother. Every letter she had ever written or received had been read by Mrs Frederick. That had never mattered. Valancy had never had anything to hide. But this did matter. She could not have anyone see this letter. But her fingers trembled with a consciousness of wickedness and unfilial conduct as she opened it – trembled a little, too, perhaps, with apprehension. She felt quite sure there was nothing seriously wrong with her heart but – one never knew.

Dr Trent's letter was like himself – blunt, abrupt, concise, wasting no words. Dr Trent never beat about the bush. 'Dear Miss Sterling' – and then a page of black, positive writing. Valancy seemed to read it at a glance; she dropped it on her lap, her face ghost-white.

Dr Trent told her that she had a very dangerous and fatal form of heart disease – angina pectoris – evidently complicated with an aneurism – whatever that was – and in the last stages. He said, without mincing matters, that nothing could be done for her. If she took great care of herself she might live a year – but she might also die at any moment – Dr Trent never troubled himself about euphemisms. She must be careful to avoid all excitement and all severe muscular efforts. She must eat and drink moderately, she must never run, she must go upstairs and uphill with great care. Any sudden jolt or shock might be fatal. She was to get the prescription he enclosed filled and carry it with her always, taking a dose whenever her attacks came on. And he was hers truly, H.B. Trent.

Valancy sat for a long while by her window. Outside was a world drowned in the light of a spring afternoon – skies entrancingly blue, winds perfumed and free, lovely, soft, blue hazes at the end of every street. Over at the railway station a group of young girls was waiting for a train; she heard their gay laughter as they chattered and joked. The train roared in and roared out again. But none of these things had any reality. Nothing had any reality except the fact that she had only another year to live.

When she was tired of sitting at the window she went over and lay down on her bed, staring at the cracked, discoloured ceiling.

The curious numbness that follows on a staggering blow possessed her. She did not feel anything except a boundless surprise and incredulity – behind which was the conviction that Dr Trent knew his business and that she, Valancy Stirling, who had never lived, was about to die.

When the gong rang for supper Valancy got up and went downstairs mechanically, from force of habit. She wondered that she had been let alone so long. But of course her mother would not pay any attention to her just now. Valancy was thankful for this. She thought the quarrel over the rosebush had been really, as Mrs Frederick herself might have said, Providential. She could not eat anything, but both Mrs Frederick and Cousin Stickles thought this was because she was deservedly unhappy over her mother's attitude, and her lack of appetite was not commented on. Valancy forced herself to swallow a cup of tea and then sat and watched the others eat, with an odd feeling that years had passed since she had sat with them at the dinner-table. She found herself smiling inwardly to think what a commotion she could make if she chose. Let her merely tell them what was in Dr Trent's letter and there would be as much fuss made as if – Valancy thought bitterly – they really cared two straws about her.

'Dr Trent's housekeeper got word from him today,' said Cousin Stickles, so suddenly that Valancy jumped guiltily. Was there anything in thought waves? 'Mrs Judd was talking to her uptown. They think his son will recover, but Dr Trent wrote that if he did he was going to take him abroad as soon as he was able to travel and wouldn't be back here for a year at least.'

'That will not matter much to us,' said Mrs Frederick majestically. 'He is not our doctor. I would not' – here she looked or seemed to look accusingly right through Valancy – 'have him to doctor a sick cat.'

'May I go upstairs and lie down?' said Valancy faintly. 'I – I have a headache.'

'What has given you a headache?' asked Cousin Stickles, since Mrs Frederick would not. The question has to be asked. Valancy could not be allowed to have headaches without interference.

'You ain't in the habit of having headaches. I hope you're not taking the mumps. Here, try a spoonful of vinegar.'

'Piffle!' said Valancy rudely, getting up from the table. She did not care just then if she were rude. She had had to be so polite all her life.

If it had been possible for Cousin Stickles to turn pale she would have. As it was not, she turned yellower.

'Are you sure you ain't feverish, Doss? You sound like it. You go and get right into bed,' said Cousin Stickles, thoroughly alarmed, 'and I'll come up and rub your forehead and the back of your neck with Redfern's Liniment.'

Valancy had reached the door, but she turned. 'I won't be rubbed with Redfern's Liniment!' she said.

Cousin Stickles stared and gasped. 'What – what do you mean?'

'I said I wouldn't be rubbed with Redfern's Liniment,' repeated Valancy. 'Horrid, sticky stuff! And it has the vilest smell of any liniment I ever saw. It's no good. I want to be left alone, that's all.'

Valancy went out, leaving Cousin Stickles aghast.

'She's feverish – she must be feverish,' ejaculated Cousin Stickles.

Mrs Frederick went on eating her supper. It did not matter whether Valancy was or was not feverish. Valancy had been guilty of impertinence to her.

EIGHT

Valancy did not sleep that night. She lay awake all through the long dark, hours – thinking – thinking. She made a discovery that surprised her: she, who had been afraid of almost everything in life, was not afraid of death. It did not seem in the least terrible to her. And she need not now be afraid of anything else. Why had she been afraid of things? Because of life. Afraid of Uncle Benjamin because of the menace of poverty in old age. But now she would never be old – neglected – tolerated. Afraid of being an old maid all her life. But now she would not be an old maid very long. Afraid of offending her mother and her clan because she had to live with and among them and couldn't live peaceably if she didn't give in to them. But now she hadn't. Valancy felt a curious freedom.

But she was still horribly afraid of one thing – the fuss the whole jamfry of them would make when she told them. Valancy shuddered at the thought of it. She couldn't endure it. Oh, she knew so well how it would be. First there would be indignation – yes, indignation on the part of Uncle James because she had gone to a doctor – any doctor – without consulting HIM. Indignation on the part of her mother for being so sly and deceitful – 'to your own mother, Doss'. Indignation on the part of the whole clan because she had not gone to Dr Marsh.

Then would come the solicitude. She would be taken to Dr Marsh, and when Dr Marsh confirmed Dr Trent's diagnosis she would be taken to specialists in Toronto and Montreal. Uncle Benjamin would foot the bill with a splendid gesture of munificence in thus assisting the widow and orphan, and talk forever after of the shocking fees specialists charged for looking wise and saying they couldn't do anything. And when the specialists could do nothing for her Uncle James would insist on her taking Purple Pills – 'I've known them to effect a cure when all the doctors had given up' – and her mother would insist on Redfern's Blood Bitters, and Cousin Stickles would insist on rubbing her over the heart every night with Redfern's Liniment on the grounds that it might do good and couldn't do harm; and everybody else would have some pet dope for her to take. Dr Stalling would come to her and say solemnly, 'You are very ill. Are you prepared for what may be before you?' – almost as if he were going to shake his forefinger at her, the forefinger that had not grown any shorter or less knobbly with age. And she would be watched and checked like a baby and never let do anything or go anywhere alone. Perhaps she would not even be allowed to sleep alone lest she die in her sleep. Cousin Stickles or her mother would insist on sharing her room and bed. Yes, undoubtedly they would.

It was this last thought that really decided Valancy. She could not put up with it and she wouldn't. As the clock in the hall below struck twelve Valancy suddenly and definitely made up her mind that she would not tell anybody. She had always been told, ever since she could remember, that she must hide her feelings. 'It is not ladylike to have feelings,' Cousin Stickles had once told her disapprovingly. Well, she would hide them with a vengeance.

But though she was not afraid of death she was not indifferent to it. She found that she resented it; it was not fair that she should have to die when she had never lived. Rebellion flamed up in her soul as the dark hours passed by – not because she had no future but because she had no past.

'I'm poor – I'm ugly – I'm a failure – and I'm near death,' she thought. She could see her own obituary notice in the Deerwood Weekly Times, copied into the Port Lawrence Journal. 'A deep gloom was cast over Deerwood, etc., etc.' – 'leaves a large circle of friends to mourn, etc., etc., etc.' – lies, all lies. Gloom, forsooth! Nobody would miss her. Her death would not matter a straw to anybody. Not even her mother loved her – her mother who had been so disappointed that she was not a boy – or at least, a pretty girl.

Valancy reviewed her whole life between midnight and the early spring dawn. It was a very drab existence, but here and there an incident loomed out with a significance out of all proportion to its real importance. These incidents were all unpleasant in one way or another. Nothing really pleasant had every happened to Valancy.

'I've never had one wholly happy hour in my life – not one,' she thought. 'I've just been a colourless nonentity. I remember reading somewhere once that there is an hour in which a woman might be happy all her life if she could but find it. I've never found my hour – never, never. And I never will now. If I could only have had that hour I'd be willing to die.'

Those significant incidents kept bobbing up in her mind like unbidden ghosts, without any sequence of time or place. For instance, that time when, at sixteen, she had blued a tubful of clothes too deeply. And the time when, at eight, she had 'stolen' some raspberry jam from Aunt Wellington's pantry. Valancy never heard the last of those two misdemeanours. At almost every clan gathering they were raked up against her as jokes. Uncle Benjamin hardly ever missed re-telling the raspberry jam incident – he had been the one to catch her, her face all stained and streaked.

'I have really done so few bad things that they have to keep harping on the old ones,' thought Valancy. 'Why, I've never even had a quarrel with anyone. I haven't an enemy. What a spineless thing I must be not to have even one enemy!'

There was that incident of the dust-pile at school when she was seven. Valancy always recalled it when Dr Stalling referred to the text, 'To him that hath shall be given and from him that hath not shall be taken even that which he hath.' Other people might puzzle over that text but it never puzzled Valancy. The whole relationship between herself and Olive, dating from the day of the dust-pile, was a commentary on it.

She had been going to school a year, but Olive, who was a year younger, had just begun and had about her all the glamour of 'a new girl' and an exceedingly pretty girl at that. It was at recess and all the girls, big and little, were out on the road in front of the school making dust-piles. The aim of each girl was to have the biggest pile. Valancy was good at making dust-piles – there was an art in it – and she had secret hopes of leading. But Olive, working off by herself, was suddenly discovered to have a larger dust-pile than anybody. Valancy felt no jealousy. Her dust-pile was quite big enough to please her. Then one of the older girls had an inspiration.

'Let's put all our dust on Olive's pile and make a tremendous one,' she exclaimed.

A frenzy seemed to seize the girls. They swooped down on the dust-piles with pails and shovels and in a few seconds Olive's pile was a veritable pyramid. In vain Valancy, with scrawny, outstretched little arms, tried to protect hers. She was ruthlessly swept aside, her dust-pile scooped up and poured on Olive's. Valancy turned away resolutely and began building another dust-pile. Again a bigger girl pounced on it. Valancy stood before it, flushed, indignant, arms outspread.

'Don't take it,' she pleaded. 'Please don't take it.'

'But why?' demanded the older girl. 'Why won't you help to build Olives bigger?'

'I want my own little dust-pile,' said Valancy piteously.

Her plea went unheeded. While she argued with one girl another scraped up her dust-pile. Valancy turned away, her heart swelling, her eyes full of tears.

'Jealous – you're jealous!' said the girls mockingly.

'You were very selfish,' said her mother coldly, when Valancy told her about it at night. That was the first and last time Valancy had ever taken any of her troubles to her mother.

Valancy was neither jealous nor selfish. It was only that she wanted a dust-pile of her own – small or big mattered not. A team of horses came down the street – Olive's dust pile was scattered over the roadway – the bell rang – the girls trooped into school and had forgotten the whole affair before they reached their seats. Valancy never forgot it. To this day she resented it in her secret soul. But was it not symbolical of her life?

'I've never been able to have my own dust-pile,' thought Valancy.

The enormous red moon she had seen rising right at the end of the street one autumn evening of her sixth year. She had been sick and cold with the awful, uncanny horror of it. So near to her. So big. She had run in trembling to her mother and her mother had laughed at her. She had gone to bed and hidden her face under the clothes in terror lest she might look at the window and see that horrible moon glaring in at her through it.

The boy who had tried to kiss her at a party when she was fifteen. She had not let him – she had evaded him and run. He was the only boy who had ever tried to kiss her. Now, fourteen years later, Valancy found herself wishing that she had let him.

The time she had been made to apologise to Olive for something she hadn't done. Olive had said that Valancy had pushed her into the mud and spoiled her new shoes on purpose. Valancy knew she hadn't. It had been an accident – and even that wasn't her fault – but nobody would believe her. She had to apologise – and kiss Olive to 'make up'. The injustice of it burned in her soul tonight.

That summer when Olive had the most beautiful hat, trimmed with creamy yellow net, with a wreath of red roses and little ribbon bows under the chin. Valancy had wanted a hat like that more than she had ever wanted anything. She pleaded for one and had been laughed at – all summer she had to wear a horrid little brown sailor with elastic that cut behind her ears. None of the girls would go around with her because she was so shabby – nobody but Olive. People had thought Olive so sweet and unselfish.

'I was an excellent foil for her,' thought Valancy. 'Even then she knew that.'

Valancy had tried to win a prize for attendance in Sunday School once. But Olive won it. There were so many Sundays Valancy had to stay home because she had colds. She had once tried to 'say a piece' in school one Friday afternoon and had broken down in it. Olive was a good reciter and never got stuck.

The night she had spent in Port Lawrence with Aunt Isabel when she was ten. Byron Stirling was there; from Montreal, twelve years old, conceited, clever. At family prayers in the morning Byron had reached across and given Valancy's thin arm such a savage pinch that she screamed out with pain. After prayers were over she was summoned to Aunt Isabel's bar of judgment. But when she said

Byron had pinched her Byron denied it. He said she cried out because the kitten scratched her. He said she had put the kitten up on her chair and was playing with it when she should have been listening to Uncle David's prayer. He was believed. In the Stirling clan the boys were always believed before the girls. Valancy was sent home in disgrace because of her exceeding bad behavior during family prayers and she was not asked to Aunt Isabel's again for many moons.

The time Cousin Betty Stirling was married. Somehow Valancy got wind of the fact that Betty was going to ask her to be one of her bridesmaids. Valancy was secretly uplifted. It would be a delightful thing to be a bridesmaid. And of course she would have to have a new dress for it – a pretty new dress – a pink dress. Betty wanted her bridesmaids to dress in pink.

But Betty had never asked her, after all. Valancy couldn't guess why, but long after her secret tears of disappointment had been dried Olive told her. Betty, after much consultation and reflection, had decided that Valancy was too insignificant – she would 'spoil the effect'. That was nine years ago. But tonight Valancy caught her breath with the old pain and sting of it.

That day in her eleventh year when her mother had badgered her into confessing something she had never done. Valancy had denied it for a long time but eventually for peace' sake she had given in and pleaded guilty. Mrs Frederick was always making people lie by pushing them into situations where they had to lie. Then her mother had made her kneel down on the parlour floor, between herself and Cousin Stickles, and say, 'O God, please forgive me for not speaking the truth.' Valancy had said it, but as she rose from her knees she muttered, 'But O God, you know I did speak the truth.' Valancy had not then heard of Galileo but her fate was similar to his. She was punished just as severely as if she hadn't confessed and prayed.

The winter she went to dancing-school. Uncle James had decreed she should go and had paid for her lessons. How she had looked forward to it! And how she had hated it! She had never had a voluntary partner. The teacher always had to tell some boy to dance with her, and generally he had been sulky about it. Yet Valancy was a good dancer, as light on her feet as thistledown. Olive, who never lacked eager partners, was heavy.

The affair of the button-string, when she was ten. All the girls in school had button-strings. Olive had a very long one with a great many beautiful buttons. Valancy had one. Most of the buttons on it were very commonplace, but she had six beauties that had come off Grandmother Stirling's wedding-gown – sparkling buttons of gold and glass, much more beautiful than any Olive had. Their possession conferred a certain distinction on Valancy. She knew every little girl in school envied her the exclusive possession of those beautiful buttons. When Olive saw them on the button-string she had looked at them narrowly but said nothing – then. The next day Aunt Wellington had come to Elm Street and told Mrs Frederick that she thought Olive should have some of those buttons – Grandmother Stirling was just as much Wellington's mother as Frederick's. Mrs Frederick had agreed amiably. She could not afford to fall out with Aunt Wellington. Moreover, the matter was of no importance whatever. Aunt Wellington carried off four of the buttons, generously leaving two for Valancy. Valancy had torn these from her string and flung them on the floor – she had not yet learned that it was unladylike to have feelings – and had been sent supperless to bed for the exhibition.

The night of Margaret Blunt's party. She had made such pathetic efforts to be pretty that night. Rob Walker was to be there; and two nights before, on the moonlit veranda of Uncle Herbert's cottage at Mistawis, Rob had really seemed attracted to her. At Margaret's party Rob never even asked her to dance – did not notice her at all. She was a wallflower, as usual. That, of course, was years ago. People in Deerwood had long since given up inviting Valancy to dances. But to Valancy its humiliation and disappointment were of the other day. Her face burned in the darkness as she recalled herself, sitting there with her pitifully crimped, thin hair and the cheeks she had pinched for an hour before coming, in an effort to make them red. All that came of it was a wild story that Valancy Stirling was rouged at Margaret Blunt's party. In those days in

Deerwood that was enough to wreck your character forever. It did not wreck Valancy's, or even damage it. People knew she couldn't be fast if she tried. They only laughed at her.

'I've had nothing but a second-hand existence,' decided Valancy. 'All the great emotions of life have passed me by. I've never even had a grief. And have I ever really loved anybody? Do I really love Mother? No, I don't. That's the truth, whether it is disgraceful or not. I don't love her – I've never loved her. What's worse, I don't even like her. So I don't know anything about any kind of love. My life has been empty – empty. Nothing is worse than emptiness. Nothing!' Valancy ejaculated the last 'nothing' aloud passionately. Then she moaned and stopped thinking about anything for a while. One of her attacks of pain had come on.

When it was over something had happened to Valancy – perhaps the culmination of the process that had been going on in her mind ever since she had read Dr Trent's letter. It was three o'clock in the morning – the wisest and most accursed hour of the clock. But sometimes it sets us free.

'I've been trying to please other people all my life and failed,' she said. 'After this I shall please myself. I shall never pretend anything again. I've breathed an atmosphere of fibs and pretences and evasions all my life. What a luxury it will be to tell the truth! I may not be able to do much that I want to do but I won't do another thing that I don't want to do. Mother can pout for weeks – I shan't worry over it. "Despair is a free man – hope is a slave."'

Valancy got up and dressed, with a deepening of that curious sense of freedom. When she had finished with her hair she opened the window and hurled the jar of potpourri over into the next lot. It smashed gloriously against the schoolgirl complexion on the old carriage-shop.

'I'm sick of fragrance of dead things,' said Valancy.

NINE

Uncle Herbert and Aunt Alberta's silver wedding was delicately referred to among the Stirlings during the following weeks as 'the time we first noticed poor Valancy was – a little – you understand?'

Not for words would any of the Stirlings have said out and out at first that Valancy had gone mildly insane or even that her mind was slightly deranged. Uncle Benjamin was considered to have gone entirely too far when he had ejaculated, 'She's dippy – I tell you, she's dippy,' and was only excused because of the outrageousness of Valancy's conduct at the aforsaid wedding dinner.

But Mrs Frederick and Cousin Stickles had noticed a few things that made them uneasy before the dinner. It had begun with the rosebush, of course; and Valancy never was really 'quite right' again. She did not seem to worry in the least over the fact that her mother was not speaking to her. You would never suppose she noticed it at all. She had flatly refused to take either Purple Pills or Redfern's Bitters. She had announced coolly that she did not intend to answer to the name of 'Doss' any longer. She had told Cousin Stickles that she wished she would give up wearing that brooch with Cousin Artemas Stickles' hair in it. She had moved her bed in her room to the opposite corner. She had read *Magic of Wings* Sunday afternoon. When Cousin Stickles had rebuked her Valancy had said indifferently, 'Oh, I forgot it was Sunday' – and had gone on reading it.

Cousin Stickles had seen a terrible thing – she had caught Valancy sliding down the bannister. Cousin Stickles did not tell Mrs Frederick this – poor Amelia was worried enough as it was. But it was Valancy's announcement on Saturday night that she was not going to go to the Anglican church any more that broke through Mrs Frederick's stony silence.

'Not going to church any more! Doss, have you absolutely taken leave –'

'Oh, I'm going to church,' said Valancy airily. 'I'm going to the Presbyterian church. But to the Anglican church I will not go.'

This was even worse. Mrs Frederick had recourse to tears, having found outraged majesty had ceased to be effective.

'What have you got against the Anglican church?' she sobbed.

'Nothing – only just that you've always made me go there. If you'd made me go to the Presbyterian church I'd want to go to the Anglican.'

'Is that a nice thing to say to your mother? Oh, how true it is that it is sharper than a serpent's tooth to have a thankless child.'

'Is that a nice thing to say to your daughter?' said unrepentant Valancy.

So Valancy's behaviour at the silver wedding was not quite the surprise to Mrs Frederick and Christine Stickles that it was to the rest. They were doubtful about the wisdom of taking her, but concluded it would 'make talk' if they didn't. Perhaps she would behave herself, and so far no outsider suspected there was anything queer about her. By a special mercy of Providence it had poured torrents Sunday morning, so Valancy had not carried out her hideous threat of going to the Presbyterian church.

Valancy would not have cared in the least if they had left her at home. These family celebrations were all hopelessly dull. But the Stirlings always celebrated everything. It was a long-established custom. Even Mrs Frederick gave a dinner party on her wedding anniversary and Cousin Stickles had friends in to supper on her birthday. Valancy hated these entertainments because they had to pinch and save and contrive for weeks afterwards to pay for them. But she wanted to go to the silver wedding. It would hurt Uncle Herbert's feelings if she stayed away, and she rather liked Uncle Herbert. Besides, she wanted to look over all her relatives from her new angle. It would be an excellent place to make public her declaration of independence if occasion offered.

'Put on your brown silk dress,' said Mrs Stirling.

As if there were anything else to put on! Valancy had only the one festive dress – that snuffy-brown silk Aunt Isabel had given her. Aunt Isabel had decreed that Valancy should never wear colours. They did not become her. When she was young they allowed her to wear white, but that had been tacitly dropped for some years. Valancy put on the brown silk. It had a high collar and long sleeves. She had never had a dress with low neck and elbow sleeves, although they had been worn, even in Deerwood, for over a year. But she did not do her hair pompadour. She knotted it on her neck and pulled it out over her ears. She thought it became her – only the little knot was so absurdly small. Mrs Frederick resented the hair but decided it was wisest to say nothing on the eve of the party. It was so important that Valancy should be kept in good humour, if possible, until it was over. Mrs Frederick did not reflect that this was the first time in her life that she had thought it necessary to consider Valancy's humours. But then Valancy had never been 'queer' before.

On their way to Uncle Herbert's – Mrs Frederick and Cousin Stickles walking in front, Valancy trotting meekly along behind – Roaring Abel drove past them. Drunk as usual but not in the roaring stage. Just drunk enough to be excessively polite. He raised his disreputable old tartan cap with the air of a monarch saluting his subjects and swept them a grand bow, Mrs Frederick and Cousin Stickles dared not cut Roaring Abel altogether. He was the only person in Deerwood who could be got to do odd jobs of carpentering and repairing when they needed to be done, so it would not do to offend him. But they responded with only the stiffest, slightest of bows. Roaring Abel must be kept in his place.

Valancy, behind them, did a thing they were fortunately spared seeing. She smiled gaily and waved her hand to Roaring Abel. Why not? She had always liked the old sinner. He was such a jolly, picturesque, unashamed reprobate and stood out against the drab respectability of Deerwood and its customs like a flame-red flag of revolt and protest. Only a few nights ago Abel had gone through Deerwood in the wee sma's, shouting oaths at the top of his stentorian voice which could be heard for miles, and lashing his horse into a furious gallop as he tore along prim, proper Elm Street.

'Yelling and blaspheming like a fiend,' shuddered Cousin Stickles at the breakfast-table.

'I cannot understand why the judgment of the Lord has not fallen upon that man long ere this,' said Mrs Frederick petulantly, as if she thought Providence was very dilatory and ought to have a gentle reminder.

'He'll be picked up dead some morning – he'll fall under his horse's hoofs and be trampled to death,' said Cousin Stickles reassuringly.

Valancy had said nothing, of course; but she wondered to herself if Roaring Abel's periodical sprees were not his futile protest against the poverty and drudgery and monotony of his existence. She went on dream sprees in her Blue Castle. Roaring Abel, having no imagination, could not do that. His escapes from reality had to be concrete. So she waved at him today with a sudden fellow feeling, and Roaring Abel, not too drunk to be astonished, nearly fell off his seat in his amazement.

By this time they had reached Maple Avenue and Uncle Herbert's house, a large, pretentious structure peppered with meaningless bay windows and excrescent porches. A house that always looked like a stupid, prosperous, self-satisfied man with warts on his face.

'A house like that,' said Valancy solemnly, 'is a blasphemy.'

Mrs Frederick was shaken to her soul. What had Valancy said? Was it profane? Or only just queer? Mrs Frederick took off her hat in Aunt Alberta's spare-room with trembling hands. She made one more feeble attempt to avert disaster. She held Valancy back on the landing as Cousin Stickles went downstairs.

'Won't you try to remember you're a lady?' she pleaded.

'Oh, if there were only any hope of being able to forget it!' said Valancy wearily.

Mrs Frederick felt that she had not deserved this from Providence.

TEN

'Bless this food to our use and consecrate our lives to Thy service,' said Uncle Herbert briskly.

Aunt Wellington frowned. She always considered Herbert's graces entirely too short and 'flippant'. A grace, to be a grace in Aunt Wellington's eyes, had to be at least three minutes long and uttered in an unearthly tone, between a groan and a chant. As a protest she kept her head bent a perceptible time after all the rest had been lifted. When she permitted herself to sit upright she found Valancy looking at her. Ever afterwards Aunt Wellington averred that she had known from that moment that there was something wrong with Valancy. In those queer, slanted eyes of hers – 'we should always have known she was not entirely right with eyes like that' – there was an odd gleam of mockery and amusement – as if Valancy were laughing at her. Such a thing was unthinkable, of course. Aunt Wellington at once ceased to think it.

Valancy was enjoying herself. She had never enjoyed herself at a 'family reunion' before. In social functions, as in childish games, she had only 'filled in'. Her clan had always considered her very dull. She had no parlour tricks. And she had been in the habit of taking refuge from the boredom of family parties in her Blue Castle, which resulted in an absent-mindedness that increased her reputation for dullness and vacuity.

'She has no social presence whatever,' Aunt Wellington had decreed once and for all. Nobody dreamed that Valancy was dumb in their presence merely because she was afraid of them. Now she was no longer afraid of them. The shackles had been stricken off her soul. She was quite prepared to talk if occasion offered. Meanwhile she was giving herself such freedom of thought as she had never dared to take before. She let herself go with a wild, inner exultation, as Uncle Herbert carved the turkey. Uncle Herbert gave Valancy a second look that day. Being a man, he didn't know what she had done to her hair, but he thought surprisedly that Doss was not such a bad-looking girl, after all; and he put an extra piece of white meat on her plate.

'What herb is most injurious to a young lady's beauty?' propounded Uncle Benjamin by way of starting conversation – 'loosening things up a bit' as he would have said.

Valancy, whose duty it was to say, 'What?' did not say it. Nobody else said it, so Uncle Benjamin, after an expectant pause, had to answer, 'Thyme', and felt that his riddle had fallen flat. He looked resentfully at Valancy, who had never failed him before, but Valancy did not seem even to be aware of him. She was gazing around the table, examining relentlessly everyone in this depressing assembly of sensible people and watching their little squirms with a detached, amused smile.

So these were the people she had always held in reverence and fear. She seemed to see them with new eyes.

Big, capable, patronising, voluble Aunt Mildred, who thought herself the cleverest woman in the clan, her husband a little lower than the angels and her children wonders. Had not her son, Howard, been all through teething at eleven months? And could she not tell you the best way to do everything, from cooking mushrooms to picking up a snake? What a bore she was! What ugly moles she had on her face!

Cousin Gladys, who was always praising her son, who had died young, and always fighting with her living one. She had neuritis – or what she called neuritis. It jumped about from one part of her body to another. It was a convenient thing. If anybody wanted her to go somewhere she didn't want to go she had neuritis in her legs. And always if any mental effort was required she could have neuritis in her head. You can't think with neuritis in your head, my dear.

'What an old humbug you are!' thought Valancy impiously.

Aunt Isabel. Valancy counted her chins. Aunt Isabel was the critic of the clan. She had always gone about squashing people flat. More members of it than Valancy were afraid of her. She had, it was conceded, a biting tongue.

'I wonder what would happen to your face if you ever smiled,' speculated Valancy, unblushingly.

Second Cousin Sarah Taylor, with her great, pale, expressionless eyes, who was noted for the variety of her pickle recipes and for nothing else. So afraid of saying something indiscreet that she never said anything worth listening to. So proper that she blushed when she saw the advertisement picture of a corset and had put a dress on her Venus de Milo statuette which made it look 'real tasty'.

Little Cousin Georgiana. Not such a bad little soul. But dreary – very. Always looking as if she had just been starched and ironed. Always afraid to let herself go. The only thing she really enjoyed was a funeral. You knew where you were with a corpse. Nothing more could happen to it. But while there was life there was fear.

Uncle James. Handsome, black, with his sarcastic, trap-like mouth and iron-grey side-burns, whose favourite amusement was to write controversial letters to the Christian Times, attacking Modernism. Valancy always wondered if he looked as solemn when he was asleep as he did when awake. No wonder his wife had died young. Valancy remembered her. A pretty, sensitive thing. Uncle James had denied her everything she wanted and showered on her everything she didn't want. He had killed her – quite legally. She had been smothered and starved.

Uncle Benjamin, wheezy, pussy-mouthed. With great pouches under his eyes that held nothing in reverence.

Uncle Wellington. Long, pallid face, thin, pale-yellow hair – 'one of the fair Stirlings' – thin, stooping body, abominably high forehead with such ugly wrinkles, and 'eyes about as intelligent as a fish's', thought Valancy. 'Looks like a cartoon of himself.'

Aunt Wellington. Named Mary but called by her husband's name to distinguish her from Great-aunt Mary. A massive, dignified, permanent lady. Splendidly arranged, iron-grey hair. Rich, fashionable beaded dress. Had her moles removed by electrolysis – which Aunt Mildred thought was a wicked evasion of the purposes of God.

Uncle Herbert, with his spiky grey hair. Aunt Alberta, who twisted her mouth so unpleasantly in talking and had a great reputation for unselfishness because she was always giving up a lot of things she didn't want. Valancy let them off easily in her judgment because she liked them, even if they were in Milton's expressive phrase, 'stupidly good'. But she wondered for what inscrutable reason Aunt Alberta had seen fit to tie a black velvet ribbon around each of her chubby arms above the elbow.

Then she looked across the table at Olive. Olive, who had been held up to her as a paragon of beauty, behaviour and success as long as she could remember. 'Why can't you hold yourself like Olive, Doss? Why can't you stand correctly like Olive, Doss? Why can't you speak prettily like Olive, Doss? Why can't you make an effort, Doss?'

Valancy's elfin eyes lost their mocking glitter and became pensive and sorrowful. You could not ignore or disdain Olive. It was quite impossible to deny that she was beautiful and effective and sometimes she was a little intelligent. Her mouth might be a trifle heavy – she might show her fine, white, regular teeth rather too lavishly when she smiled. But when all was said and done, Olive justified Uncle Benjamin's summing up – 'a stunning girl'. Yes, Valancy agreed in her heart, Olive was stunning.

Rich, golden-brown hair, elaborately dressed, with a sparkling bandeau holding its glossy puffs in place; large, brilliant blue eyes and thick silken lashes; face of rose and bare neck of snow, rising above her gown; great pearl bubbles in her ears; the blue-white diamond flame on her long, smooth, waxen finger with its rosy, pointed nail. Arms of marble, gleaming through green chiffon and shadow lace. Valancy felt suddenly thankful that her own scrawny arms were decently swathed in brown silk. Then she resumed her tabulation of Olive's charms.

Tall. Queenly. Confident. Everything that Valancy was not. Dimples, too, in cheeks and chin. 'A woman with dimples always gets her own way,' thought Valancy, in a recurring spasm of bitterness at the fate which had denied her even one dimple.

Olive was only a year younger than Valancy, though a stranger would have thought that there was at least ten years between them. But nobody ever dreaded old maidenhood for her. Olive had been surrounded by a crowd of eager beaus since her early teens, just as her mirror was always surrounded by a fringe of cards, photographs, programmes and invitations. At eighteen, when she had graduated from Havergal College, Olive had been engaged to Will Desmond, lawyer in embryo. Will Desmond had died and Olive had mourned for him properly for two years. When she was twenty-three she had a hectic affair with Donald Jackson. But Aunt and Uncle Wellington disapproved of that and in the end Olive dutifully gave him up. Nobody in the Stirling clan – whatever outsiders might say – hinted that she did so because Donald himself was cooling off. However that might be, Olive's third venture met with everybody's approval. Cecil Price was clever and handsome and 'one of the Port Lawrence Prices'. Olive had been engaged to him for three years. He had just graduated in civil engineering and they were to be married as soon as he landed a contract. Olive's hope chest was full to overflowing with exquisite things and Olive had already confided to Valancy what her wedding-dress was to be. Ivory silk draped with lace, white satin court train, lined with pale green georgette, heirloom veil of Brussels lace. Valancy knew also – though Olive had not told her – that the bridesmaids were selected and that she was not among them.

Valancy had, after a fashion, always been Olive's confidante – perhaps because she was the only girl in the connection who could not bore Olive with return confidences. Olive always told Valancy all the details of her love affairs, from the days when the little boys in school used to 'persecute' her with love letters. Valancy could not comfort herself by thinking these affairs mythical. Olive really had them. Many men had gone mad over her besides the three fortunate ones.

'I don't know what the poor idiots see in me, that drives them to make such double idiots of themselves,' Olive was wont to say. Valancy would have liked to say, 'I don't either,' but truth and diplomacy both restrained her. She did know, perfectly well.

Olive Stirling was one of the girls about whom men do go mad just as indubitably as she, Valancy, was one of the girls at whom no man ever looked twice.

'And yet,' thought Valancy, summing her up with a new and merciless conclusiveness, 'she's like a dewless morning. There's something lacking.'

ELEVEN
∞

Meanwhile the dinner in its earlier stages was dragging its slow length along true to Stirling form. The room was chilly, in spite of the calendar, and Aunt Alberta had the gas-logs lighted. Everybody in the clan envied her those gas-logs except Valancy. Glorious open fires blazed in every room of her Blue Castle when autumnal nights were cool, but she would have frozen to death in it before she would have committed the sacrilege of a gas-log. Uncle Herbert made his hardy perennial joke when he helped Aunt Wellington to the cold meat – 'Mary, will you have a little lamb?' Aunt Mildred told the same old story of once finding a lost ring in a turkey's crop. Uncle Benjamin told his favourite prosy tale of how he had once chased and punished a now famous man for stealing apples. Second Cousin Jane described all her sufferings with an ulcerating tooth. Aunt Wellington admired the pattern of Aunt Alberta's silver teaspoons and lamented the fact that one of her own had been lost.

'It spoiled the set. I could never get it matched. And it was my wedding-present from dear old Aunt Matilda.'

Aunt Isabel thought the seasons were changing and couldn't imagine what had become of our good, old-fashioned springs. Cousin Georgiana, as usual, discussed the last funeral and wondered, audibly, 'which of us will be the next to pass away'. Cousin Georgiana could never say anything as blunt as 'die'. Valancy thought she could tell her, but didn't. Cousin Gladys, likewise as usual, had a grievance. Her visiting nephews had nipped all the buds off her house-plants and chivied her brood of fancy chickens – 'squeezed some of them actually to death, my dear'.

'Boys will be boys,' reminded Uncle Herbert tolerantly.

'But they needn't be ramping, rampageous animals,' retorted Cousin Gladys, looking round the table for appreciation of her wit. Everybody smiled except Valancy. Cousin Gladys remembered that. A few minutes later, when Ellen Hamilton was being discussed, Cousin Gladys spoke of her as 'one of those shy, plain girls who can't get husbands', and glanced significantly at Valancy.

Uncle James thought the conversation was sagging to a rather low plane of personal gossip. He tried to elevate it by starting an abstract discussion on 'the greatest happiness'. Everybody was asked to state his or her idea of 'the greatest happiness'.

Aunt Mildred thought the greatest happiness – for a woman – was to be 'a loving and beloved wife and mother'. Aunt Wellington thought it would be to travel in Europe. Olive thought it would be to be a great singer like Tetrazzini. Cousin Gladys remarked mournfully that her greatest happiness would be to be free – absolutely free – from neuritis. Cousin Georgiana's greatest happiness would be 'to have her dear, dead brother Richard back'. Aunt Alberta remarked vaguely that the greatest happiness was to be found in 'the poetry of life' and hastily gave some directions to her maid to prevent anyone asking her what she meant. Mrs Frederick said the greatest happiness was to spend your life in loving service for others, and Cousin Stickles and Aunt Isabel agreed with her – Aunt Isabel with a resentful air, as if she thought Mrs Frederick had taken the wind out of her sails by saying it first. 'We are all too prone,' continued Mrs Frederick, determined not to lose so good an opportunity, 'to live in selfishness, worldliness and sin.' The other women all felt rebuked for their low ideals, and Uncle James had a conviction that the conversation had been uplifted with a vengeance.

'The greatest happiness,' said Valancy suddenly and distinctly, 'is to sneeze when you want to.'

Everybody stared. Nobody felt it safe to say anything. Was Valancy trying to be funny? It was incredible. Mrs Frederick, who had been breathing easier since the dinner had progressed so far without any outbreak on the part of Valancy began to tremble again. But she deemed it the part of prudence to say nothing. Uncle Benjamin was not so prudent. He rashly rushed in where Mrs Frederick feared to tread.

'Doss,' he chuckled, 'what is the difference between a young girl and an old maid?'

'One is happy and careless and the other is cappy and hairless,' said Valancy. 'You have asked that riddle at least fifty times in my recollection, Uncle Ben. Why don't you hunt up some new riddles if riddle you must? It is such a fatal mistake to try to be funny if you don't succeed.'

Uncle Benjamin stared foolishly. Never in his life had he, Benjamin Stirling, of Stirling and Frost, been spoken to so. And by Valancy of all people! He looked feebly around the table to see what the others thought of it. Everybody was looking rather blank. Poor Mrs Frederick had shut her eyes. And her lips moved tremblingly – as if she were praying. Perhaps she was. The situation was so unprecedented that nobody knew how to meet it. Valancy went on calmly eating her salad as if nothing out of the usual had occurred.

Aunt Alberta, to save her dinner, plunged into an account of how a dog had bitten her recently. Uncle James, to back her up, asked where the dog had bitten her.

'Just a little below the Catholic church,' said Aunt Alberta.

At that point Valancy laughed. Nobody else laughed. What was there to laugh at?

'Is that a vital part?' asked Valancy.

'What do you mean?' said bewildered Aunt Alberta, and Mrs Frederick was almost driven to believe that she had served God all her years for naught.

Aunt Isabel concluded that it was up to her to suppress Valancy.

'Doss, you are horribly thin,' she said. 'You are all corners. Do you ever try to fatten up a little?'

'No.' Valancy was not asking quarter or giving it. 'But I can tell you where you'll find a beauty parlour in Port Lawrence where they can reduce the number of your chins.'

'Val-an-cy!' The protest was wrung from Mrs Frederick. She meant her tone to be stately and majestic, as usual, but it sounded more like an imploring whine. And she did not say 'Doss.'

'She's feverish,' said Cousin Stickles to Uncle Benjamin in an agonised whisper. 'We've thought she's seemed feverish for several days.'

'She's gone dippy, in my opinion,' growled Uncle Benjamin. 'If not, she ought to be spanked. Yes, spanked.'

'You can't spank her.' Cousin Stickles was much agitated. 'She's twenty-nine years old.'

'So there is that advantage, at least, in being twenty-nine,' said Valancy, whose ears had caught this aside.

'Doss,' said Uncle Benjamin, 'when I am dead you may say what you please. As long as I am alive I demand to be treated with respect.'

'Oh, but you know we're all dead,' said Valancy, 'the whole Stirling clan. Some of us are buried and some aren't – yet. That is the only difference.'

'Doss,' said Uncle Benjamin, thinking it might cow Valancy, 'do you remember the time you stole the raspberry jam?'

Valancy flushed scarlet – with suppressed laughter, not shame. She had been sure Uncle Benjamin would drag that jam in somehow.

'Of course I do,' she said. 'It was good jam. I've always been sorry I hadn't time to eat more of it before you found me. Oh, look at Aunt Isabel's profile on the wall. Did you ever see anything so funny?'

Everybody looked, including Aunt Isabel herself which of course, destroyed it. But Uncle Herbert said kindly, 'I – I wouldn't eat any more if I were you, Doss. It isn't that I grudge it – but don't you think it would be better for yourself? Your – your stomach seems a little out of order.'

'Don't worry about my stomach, old dear,' said Valancy. 'It is all right. I'm going to keep right on eating. It's so seldom I get the chance of a satisfying meal.'

It was the first time anyone had been called 'old dear' in Deerwood. The Stirlings thought Valancy had invented the phrase and they were afraid of her from that moment. There was something so uncanny about such an expression. But in poor Mrs Frederick's opinion the reference to a satisfying meal was the worst thing Valancy had said yet. Valancy had always been a disappointment to her. Now she was a disgrace. She thought she would have to get up and go away from the table. Yet she dared not leave Valancy there.

Aunt Alberta's maid came in to remove the salad plates and bring in the dessert. It was a welcome diversion. Everybody brightened up with a determination to ignore Valancy and talk as if she wasn't there. Uncle Wellington mentioned Barney Snaith. Eventually somebody did mention Barney Snaith at every Stirling function, Valancy reflected. Whatever he was, he was an individual that could not be ignored. She resigned herself to listen. There was a subtle fascination in the subject for her, though she had not yet faced this fact. She could feel her pulses beating to her fingertips.

Of course they abused him. Nobody ever had a good word to say of Barney Snaith. All the old, wild tales were canvassed – the defaulting cashier-counterfeiter-infidel-murderer-in-hiding legends were thrashed out. Uncle Wellington was very indignant that such a creature should be allowed to exist at all in the neighbourhood of Deerwood. He didn't know what the police at Port Lawrence were thinking of. Everybody would be murdered in their beds some night. It was a shame that he should be allowed to be at large after all that he had done.

'What has he done?' asked Valancy suddenly.

Uncle Wellington stared at her, forgetting that she was to be ignored.

'Done! Done! He's done everything.'

'What has he done?' repeated Valancy inexorably. 'What do you know that he has done? You're always running him down. And what has ever been proved against him?'

'I don't argue with women,' said Uncle Wellington. 'And I don't need proof. When a man hides himself up there on an island in Muskoka, year in and year out, and nobody can find out where he came from or how he lives, or what he does there, that's proof enough. Find a mystery and you find a crime.'

'The very idea of a man named Snaith!' said Second Cousin Sarah. 'Why, the name itself is enough to condemn him!'

'I wouldn't like to meet him in a dark lane,' shivered Cousin Georgiana.

'What do you suppose he would do to you?' asked Valancy.

'Murder me,' said Cousin Georgiana solemnly.

'Just for the fun of it?' suggested Valancy.

'Exactly,' said Cousin Georgiana unsuspiciously. 'When there is so much smoke there must be some fire. I was afraid he was a criminal when he came here first. I felt he had something to hide. I am not often mistaken in my intuitions.'

'Criminal! Oh course he's a criminal,' said Uncle Wellington. 'Nobody doubts it' – glaring at Valancy. 'Why, they say he served a term in the penitentiary for embezzlement. I don't doubt it. And they say he's in with that gang that are perpetrating all those bank robberies round the country.'

'Who say?' asked Valancy.

Uncle Wellington knotted his ugly forehead at her. What had got into this confounded girl, anyway? He ignored the question.

'He has the identical look of a jailbird,' snapped Uncle Benjamin. 'I noticed it the first time I saw him.'

A fellow by the hand of nature marked,
Quoted and sighed to do a deed of shame,

declaimed Uncle James. He looked enormously pleased over managing to work that quotation in at last. He had been waiting all his life for the chance.

'One of his eyebrows is an arch and the other is a triangle,' said Valancy. 'Is that why you think him so villainous?'

Uncle James lifted his eyebrows. Generally when Uncle

James lifted his eyebrows the world came to an end. This time it continued to function.

'How do you know his eyebrows so well, Doss?' asked Olive, a trifle maliciously. Such a remark would have covered Valancy with confusion two weeks ago, and Olive knew it.

'Yes, how?' demanded Aunt Wellington.

'I've seen him twice and I looked at him closely,' said Valancy composedly. 'I thought his face the most interesting one I ever saw.'

'There is no doubt there is something fishy in the creature's past life,' said Olive, who began to think she was decidedly out of the conversation, which had centred so amazingly around Valancy. 'But he can hardly be guilty of everything he's accused of, you know.'

Valancy felt annoyed with Olive. Why should she speak up in even this qualified defence of Barney Snaith? What had she to do with him? For that matter, what had Valancy? But Valancy did not ask herself this question.

'They say he keeps dozens of cats in that hut up back on Mistawis,' said Second Cousin Sarah Taylor, by way of appearing not entirely ignorant of him.

Cats. It sounded quite alluring to Valancy, in the plural. She pictured an island in Muskoka haunted by pussies.

'That alone shows there is something wrong with him,' decreed Aunt Isabel.

'People who don't like cats,' said Valancy, attacking her dessert with a relish, 'always seem to think that there is some peculiar virtue in not liking them.'

'The man hasn't a friend except Roaring Abel,' said Uncle Wellington. 'And if Roaring Abel had kept away from him, as everybody else did, it would have been better for – for some members of his family.'

Uncle Wellington's rather lame conclusion was due to a marital glance from Aunt Wellington reminding him of what he had almost forgotten – that there were girls at the table.

'If you mean,' said Valancy passionately, 'that Barney Snaith is the father of Cecily Gay's child, he isn't. It's a wicked lie.'

In spite of her indignation Valancy was hugely amused at the expression of the faces around that festal table. She had not seen anything like it since the day, seventeen years ago, when at Cousin Gladys' thimble party, they discovered that she had got – *something* – in her head at school. Lice in her head! Valancy was done with euphemisms.

Poor Mrs Frederick was almost in a state of collapse. She had believed – or pretended to believe – the Valancy still supposed that children were found in parsley beds.

'Hush – hush!' implored Cousin Stickles.

'I don't mean to hush,' said Valancy perversely. 'I've hush-hushed all my life. I'll scream if I want to. Don't make me want to. And stop talking nonsense about Barney Snaith.'

Valancy didn't exactly understand her own indignation. What did Barney Snaith's imputed crimes and misdemeanours matter to her? And why, out of them all, did it seem most intolerable that he should have been poor, pitiful little Cecily Gay's false lover? For it did seem intolerable to her. She did not mind when they called him a thief and a counterfeiter and jailbird; but she could not endure to think that he had loved and ruined Cecily Gay. She recalled his face on the two occasions of their chance meetings – his twisted, enigmatic, engaging smile, his twinkle, his thin, sensitive, almost ascetic lips, his general air of frank daredevilry. A man with such a smile and lips might have murdered or stolen but he could not have betrayed. She suddenly hated everyone who said it or believed it of him.

'When I was a young girl I never thought or spoke about such matters, Doss,' said Aunt Wellington, crushingly.

'But I'm not a young girl" retorted Valancy, uncrushed. 'Aren't you always rubbing that into me? And you are all evil-minded, senseless gossips. Can't you leave poor Cissy Gay alone? She's dying. Whatever she did, God or the Devil has punished her enough for it. You needn't take a hand, too. As for Barney Snaith, the only crime he has been guilty of is living to himself and minding his own business. He can, it seems, get along without you. Which is an unpardonable sin, of course, in your little snobocracy.' Valancy coined that concluding word suddenly and felt that it was an inspiration. That was exactly what they were and not one of them was fit to mend another.

'Valancy, your poor father would turn over in his grave if he could hear you,' said Mrs Frederick.

'I dare say he would like that for a change,' said Valancy brazenly.

'Doss,' said Uncle James heavily, 'the Ten Commandments are fairly up to date still – especially the fifth. Have you forgotten that?'

'No,' said Valancy, 'but I thought you had – especially the ninth. Have you ever thought, Uncle James, how dull life would be without the Ten Commandments? It is only when things are forbidden that they become fascinating.'

But her excitement had been too much for her. She knew, by certain unmistakable warnings, that one of her attacks of pain was coming on. It must not find her there. She rose from her chair.

'I am going home now. I only came for the dinner. It was very good, Aunt Alberta, although your salad-dressing is not salt enough and a dash of cayenne would improve it.'

None of the flabbergasted silver wedding guests could think of anything to say until the lawn gate clanged behind Valancy in the dusk. Then –

'She's feverish – I've said right along she was feverish,' moaned Cousin Stickles.

Uncle Benjamin punished his pudgy left hand fiercely with his pudgy right.

'She's dippy – I tell you she's gone dippy,' he snorted angrily. 'That's all there is about it. Clean dippy.'

'Oh, Benjamin,' said Cousin Georgiana soothingly, 'don't condemn her too rashly. We must remember what dear old Shakespeare says – that charity thinketh no evil.'

'Charity! Poppy-cock!' snorted Uncle Benjamin. 'I never heard a young woman talk such stuff in my life as she just did. Talking about things she ought to be ashamed to think of, much less mention. Blaspheming! Insulting us! What she wants is a generous dose of spank-weed and I'd like to be the one to administer it.

H-uh-h-h-h!' Uncle Benjamin gulped down the half of a scalding cup of coffee.

'Do you suppose that the mumps could work on a person that way?' wailed Cousin Stickles.

'I opened an umbrella in the house yesterday,' sniffed Cousin Georgiana. 'I knew it betokened some misfortune.'

'Have you tried to find out if she has a temperature?' asked Cousin Mildred.

'She wouldn't let Amelia put the thermometer under her tongue,' whimpered Cousin Stickles.

Mrs Frederick was openly in tears. All her defences were down.

'I must tell you,' she sobbed, 'that Valancy has been acting very strangely for over two weeks now. She hasn't been a bit like herself – Christine could tell you. I have hoped against hope that it was only one of her colds coming on. But it is – it must be something worse.'

'This is bringing on my neuritis again,' said Cousin Gladys, putting her hand to her head.

'Don't cry, Amelia,' said Herbert kindly, pulling nervously at his spiky grey hair. He hated 'family ructions'. Very inconsiderate of Doss to start one at his silver wedding. Who could have supposed she had it in her? 'You'll have to take her to a doctor. This may be only a – er – a brainstorm. There are such things as brainstorms nowadays, aren't there?'

'I – I suggested consulting a doctor to her yesterday,' moaned Mrs Frederick. 'And she said she wouldn't go to a doctor – wouldn't. Oh, surely I have had trouble enough!'

'And she won't take Redfern's Bitters,' said Cousin Stickles.

'Or anything,' said Mrs Frederick. 'And she's determined to go to the Presbyterian church,' said Cousin Stickles – repressing, however, to her credit be it said, the story of the bannister.

'That proves she's dippy,' growled Uncle Benjamin. 'I noticed something strange about her the minute she came in today. I noticed it before today.' (Uncle Benjamin was thinking of 'm-i-r-a-z-h'.) 'Everything she said today showed an unbalanced mind. That question – "Was it a vital part?" Was there any sense at all in that remark? None whatever! There never was anything like that in the Stirlings. It must be from the Wansbarras.'

Poor Mrs Frederick was too crushed to be indignant. 'I never heard of anything like that in the Wansbarras,' she sobbed.

'Your father was odd enough,' said Uncle Benjamin.

'Poor Pa was – peculiar,' admitted Mrs Frederick tearfully, 'but his mind was never affected.'

'He talked all his life exactly as Valancy did today,' retorted Uncle Benjamin. 'And he believed he was his own great-great grandfather born over again. I've heard him say it. Don't tell me that a man who believed a thing like that was ever in his right senses. Come, come, Amelia, stop sniffling. Of course Doss has made a terrible exhibition of herself today, but she's not responsible. Old maids are apt to fly off at a tangent like that. If she had been married when she should have been she wouldn't have got like this.'

'Nobody wanted to marry her,' said Mrs Frederick, who felt that, somehow, Uncle Benjamin was blaming her.

'Well, fortunately there's no outsider here,' snapped Uncle Benjamin. 'We may keep it in the family yet. I'll take her over to see Dr Marsh tomorrow. I know how to deal with pig-headed people. Won't that be best, James?'

'We must have medical advice certainly,' agreed Uncle James.

'Well, that's settled. In the meantime, Amelia, act as if nothing had happened and keep an eye on her. Don't let her be alone. Above all, don't let her sleep alone.'

Renewed whimpers from Mrs Frederick.

'I can't help it. Night before last I suggested she'd better have Christine sleep with her. She positively refused – and locked her door. Oh, you don't know how she's changed. She won't work. At least, she won't sew. She does her usual housework, of course. But she wouldn't sweep the parlour yesterday morning, though we always sweep it on Thursdays. She said she'd wait till it was dirty. "Would you rather sweep a dirty room than a clean one?" I asked her. She said, "Of course. I'd see something for my labour then." Think of it!'

Uncle Benjamin thought of it.

'The jar of potpourri' – Cousin Stickles pronounced it as spelled – 'has disappeared from her room. I found the pieces in the next lot. She won't tell us what happened to it.'

'I should never have dreamed it of Doss,' said Uncle Herbert. 'She has always seemed such a quiet, sensible girl. A bit backward – but sensible.'

'The only thing you can be sure of in this world is the multiplication table,' said Uncle James, feeling cleverer than ever.

'Well, let's cheer up,' suggested Uncle Benjamin. 'Why are chorus girls like fine stock raisers?'

'Why?' asked Cousin Stickles, since it had to be asked and Valancy wasn't there to ask it.

'Like to exhibit calves,' chuckled Uncle Benjamin.

Cousin Stickles thought Uncle Benjamin a little indelicate. Before Olive, too. But then, he was a man.

Uncle Herbert was thinking that things were rather dull now that Doss had gone.

TWELVE
❦

Valancy hurried home through the faint blue twilight – hurried too fast perhaps. The attack she had when she thankfully reached the shelter of her own room was the worst yet. It was really very bad. She might die in one of those spells. It would be dreadful to die in such pain. Perhaps – perhaps this was death. Valancy felt pitifully alone. When she could think at all she wondered what it would be like to have someone with her who could sympathise – someone who really cared – just to hold her hand tight, if nothing else – someone just to say, 'Yes, I know. It's dreadful – be brave – you'll soon be better'; not someone merely fussy and alarmed. Not her mother or Cousin Stickles. Why did the thought of Barney Snaith come into her mind? Why did she suddenly feel, in the midst of this hideous loneliness of pain, that he would be sympathetic – sorry for anyone that was suffering? Why did he seem to her like an old, well-known friend? Was it because she had been defending him – standing up to her family for him?

She was so bad at first that she could not even get herself a dose of Dr Trent's prescription. But eventually she managed it, and soon after relief came. The pain left her and she lay on her bed, spent, exhausted, in a cold perspiration. Oh, that had been horrible! She could not endure many more attacks like that. One didn't mind dying if death could be instant and painless. But to be hurt so in dying!

Suddenly she found herself laughing. That dinner had been fun. And it had all been so simple. She had merely said the things she had always thought. Their faces! Uncle Benjamin – poor, flabbergasted Uncle Benjamin! Valancy felt quite sure he would make a new will that very night. Olive would get Valancy's share of his fat hoard. Olive had always got Valancy's share of everything. Remember the dust-pile.

To laugh at her clan as she had always wanted to laugh was all the satisfaction she could get out of life now. But she thought it was rather pitiful that it should be so. Might she not pity herself a little when nobody else did?

Valancy got up and went to her window. The moist, beautiful wind blowing across groves of young-leafed wild trees touched her face with the caress of a wise, tender, old friend. The lombardies in Mrs Tredgold's lawn, off to the left – Valancy could just see them between the stable and the old carriage-shop – were in dark purple silhouette against a clear sky and there was a milk-white, pulsating star just over one of them, like a living pearl on a silver-green lake. Far beyond the station were the shadowy, purple-hooded woods around Lake Mistawis. A white, filmy mist hung over them and just above it was a faint, young crescent. Valancy looked at it over her thin left shoulder.

'I wish,' she said whimsically, 'that I may have one little dust-pile before I die.'

THIRTEEN

Uncle Benjamin found he had reckoned without his host when he promised so airily to take Valancy to a doctor. Valancy would not go. Valancy laughed in his face.

'Why on earth should I go to Dr Marsh? There's nothing the matter with my mind. Though you all think I've suddenly gone crazy. Well, I haven't. I've simply grown tired of living to please other people and have decided to please myself. It will give you something to talk about besides my stealing the raspberry jam. So that's that.'

'Doss,' said Uncle Benjamin, solemnly and helplessly, 'you are not – like yourself.'

'Who am I like, then?' asked Valancy.

Uncle Benjamin was rather posed.

'Your Grandfather Wansbarra,' he answered desperately.

'Thanks.' Valancy looked pleased. 'That's a real compliment. I remember Grandfather Wansbarra. He was one of the few human beings I have known – almost the only one. Now, it is of no use to scold or entreat or command, Uncle Benjamin – or exchange anguished glances with Mother and Cousin Stickles. I am not going to any doctor. And if you bring any doctor here I won't see him. So what are you going to do about it?'

What indeed! It was not seemly – or even possible – to hale Valancy doctorwards by physical force. And in no other way could it be done, seemingly. Her mother's tears and imploring entreaties availed not.

'Don't worry, Mother,' said Valancy, lightly but quite respectfully. 'It isn't likely I'll do anything very terrible. But I mean to have a little fun.'

'Fun!' Mrs Frederick uttered the word as if Valancy had said she was going to have a little tuberculosis.

Olive, sent by her mother to see if she had any influence over Valancy, came away with flushed cheeks and angry eyes. She told her mother that nothing could be done with Valancy. After she, Olive, had talked to her just like a sister, tenderly and wisely, all Valancy had said, narrowing her funny eyes to mere slips, was, 'I don't show my gums when I laugh.'

'More as if she were talking to herself than to me. Indeed, Mother, all the time I was talking to her she gave me the impression of not really listening. And that wasn't all. When I finally decided that what I was saying had no influence over her I begged her, when Cecil came next week, not to say anything queer before him, at least. Mother, what do you think she said?'

'I'm sure I can't imagine,' groaned Aunt Wellington, prepared for anything.

'She said, "I'd rather like to shock Cecil. His mouth is too red for a man's." Mother, I can never feel the same to Valancy again.'

'Her mind is affected, Olive,' said Aunt Wellington solemnly. 'You must not hold her responsible for what she says.'

When Aunt Wellington told Mrs Frederick what Valancy had said to Olive, Mrs Frederick wanted Valancy to apologise.

'You made me apologise to Olive fifteen years ago for something I didn't do,' said Valancy. 'That old apology will do for now.'

Another solemn family conclave was held. They were all there except Cousin Gladys, who had been suffering such tortures of neuritis in her head 'ever since poor Doss went queer' that she couldn't undertake any responsibility. They decided – that is, they accepted a fact that was thrust in their faces – that the wisest thing was to leave Valancy alone for a while – 'give her her head' as Uncle Benjamin expressed it – 'keep a careful eye on her but let her pretty much alone'. The term of 'watchful waiting' had not been invented then, but that was practically the policy Valancy's distracted relatives decided to follow.

'We must be guided by developments,' said Uncle Benjamin. 'It is' – solemnly – 'easier to scramble eggs than unscramble them. Of course – if she becomes violent –'

Uncle James consulted Dr Ambrose Marsh. Dr Ambrose Marsh approved their decision. He pointed out to irate Uncle James – who would have liked to lock Valancy up somewhere, out of hand – that Valancy had not, as yet, really done or said anything that could be constructed as proof of lunacy – and without proof you cannot lock people up in this degenerate age. Nothing that Uncle James had reported seemed very alarming to Dr Marsh, who put up his hand to conceal a smile several times. But then he himself was not a Stirling. And he knew very little about the old Valancy. Uncle James stalked out and drove back to Deerwood, thinking that Ambrose Marsh wasn't much of a doctor, after all, and that Adelaide Stirling might have done better for herself.

FOURTEEN

Life cannot stop because tragedy enters it. Meals must be made ready though a son dies and porches must be repaired even if your only daughter is going out of her mind. Mrs Frederick, in her systematic way, had long ago appointed the second week in June for the repairing of the front porch, the roof of which was sagging dangerously. Roaring Abel had been engaged to do it many moons before and Roaring Abel promptly appeared on the morning of the first day of the second week, and fell to work. Of course he was drunk. Roaring Abel was never anything but drunk. But he was only in the first stage, which made him talkative and genial. The odour of whisky on his breath nearly drove Mrs Frederick and Cousin Stickles wild at dinner. Even Valancy, with all her emancipation, did not like it. But she liked Abel and she liked his vivid, eloquent talk, and after she washed the dinner dishes she went out and sat on the steps and talked to him.

Mrs Frederick and Cousin Stickles thought it a terrible proceeding, but what could they do? Valancy only smiled mockingly at them when they called her in, and did not go. It was so easy to defy once you got started. The first step was the only one that really counted. They were both afraid to say anything more to her lest she might make a scene before Roaring Abel, who would spread it all over the country with his own characteristic comments and exaggerations. It was too cold a day, in spite of the June sunshine, for Mrs Frederick to sit at the dining-room window and listen to what was said. She had to shut the window and Valancy and Roaring Abel had their talk to themselves. But if Mrs Frederick had known what the outcome of that talk was to be she would have prevented it, if the porch was never repaired.

Valancy sat on the steps, defiant of the chill breeze of this cold June which had made Aunt Isabel aver the seasons were changing. She did not care whether she caught a cold or not. It was delightful to sit there in that cold, beautiful, fragrant world and feel free. She filled her lungs with the clean, lovely wind and held out her arms to it and let it tear her hair to pieces while she listening to Roaring Abel, who told her his troubles between intervals of hammering gaily in time to his Scotch songs. Valancy liked to hear him. Every stroke of his hammer fell true to the note.

Old Abel Gay, in spite of his seventy years, was handsome still, in a stately, patriarchal manner. His tremendous beard, falling down over his blue flannel shirt, was still a flaming, untouched red, though his shock of hair was white as snow, and his eyes were a fiery, youthful blue. His enormous, reddish-white eyebrows were more like moustaches than eyebrows. Perhaps this was why he always kept his upper lip scrupulously shaved. His cheeks were red and his nose ought to have been, but wasn't. It was a fine, upstanding, aquiline nose, such as the noblest Roman of them all might have rejoiced in. Abel was six feet two in his stockings, broad-shouldered, lean-hipped. In his youth he had been a famous lover, finding all women too charming to bind himself to one. His years had been a wild, colourful panorama of follies and adventures, gallantries, fortunes and misfortunes. He had been forty-five before he married – a pretty slip of a girl whom his goings-on killed in a few years. Abel was piously drunk at her funeral and insisted on repeating the fifty-fifth chapter of Isaiah – Abel knew most of the Bible and all the Psalms by heart – while the minister, whom he disliked, prayed or tried to pray. Thereafter his house was run by an untidy old cousin who cooked his meals and kept things going after a fashion. In this unpromising environment little Cecilia Gay had grown up.

Valancy had known 'Cissy Gay' fairly well in the democracy of the public school, though Cissy had been three years younger than she. After they left school their paths diverged and she had seen nothing of her. Old Abel was a Presbyterian. That is, he got a Presbyterian preacher to marry him, baptise his child and bury his wife; and he knew more about Presbyterian theology than most ministers, which made him a terror to them in arguments. But Roaring Abel never went to church. Every Presbyterian minister who had been in Deerwood had tried his hand – once – at reforming Roaring Abel. But he had not been pestered of late. Rev. Mr Bently had been in Deerwood for eight years, but he had not sought out Roaring Abel since the first three months of his pastorate. He had called on Roaring Abel then and found him in the theological stage of drunkenness – which always followed the sentimental maudlin one, and preceded the roaring, blasphemous one. The eloquently prayerful one, in which he realised himself temporarily and intensely as a sinner in the hands of an angry God, was the final one. Abel never went beyond it. He generally fell asleep on his knees and awakened sober, but he had never been 'dead drunk' in his life. He told Mr Bently that he was a sound Presbyterian and sure of his election. He had no sins – that he knew of – to repent of.

'Have you never done anything in your life that you are sorry for?' asked Mr Bently.

Roaring Abel scratched his bushy white head and pretended to reflect.

'Well, yes,' he said finally. 'There were some women I might have kissed and didn't. I've always been sorry for that.'

Mr Bently went out and went home.

Abel had seen that Cissy was properly baptised – jovially drunk at the same time himself. He made her go to church and Sunday School regularly. The church people took her up and she was in turn a member of the Mission Band, the Girls' Guild and the Young Women's Missionary Society. She was a faithful, unobtrusive, sincere, little worker. Everybody liked Cissy Gay and was sorry for her. She was so modest and sensitive and pretty in that delicate, elusive fashion of beauty which fades so quickly if life is not kept in it by love and tenderness. But then liking and pity did not prevent them from tearing her in pieces like hungry cats when the catastrophe came. Four years previously Cissy Gay had gone up to a Muskoka hotel as a summer waitress. And when she had come back in the fall she was a changed creature. She hid herself away and went nowhere. The reason soon leaked out and scandal raged. That winter Cissy's baby was born. Nobody ever knew who the father was. Cecily kept her poor pale lips tightly locked on her sorry secret. Nobody dared ask Roaring Abel any questions about it. Rumour and surmise laid the guilt at Barney Snaith's door because diligent inquiry among the other maids at the hotel revealed the fact that nobody there had ever seen Cissy Gay 'with a fellow'. She had 'kept herself to herself' they said, rather resentfully. 'Too good for our dances. And now look!'

The baby had lived for a year. After its death Cissy faded away. Two years ago Dr Marsh had given her only six months to live – her lungs were hopelessly diseased. But she was still alive. Nobody went to see her. Women would not go to Roaring Abel's house. Mr Bently had gone once, when he knew Abel was away, but the dreadful old creature who was scrubbing the kitchen floor told him Cissy wouldn't see anyone. The old cousin had died and Roaring Abel had had two or three disreputable housekeepers – the only kind who could be prevailed on to go to a house where a girl was dying of consumption. But the last one had left and Roaring Abel had now no one to wait on Cissy and 'do' for him. This was the burden of his plaint to Valancy and he condemned the 'hypocrites' of Deerwood and its surrounding communities with some rich, meaty oaths that happened to reach Cousin

Stickles' ears as she passed through the hall and nearly finished the poor lady. Was Valancy listening to that?

Valancy hardly noticed the profanity. Her attention was focussed on the horrible thought of poor, unhappy, disgraced little Cissy Gay, ill and helpless in that forlorn old house out on the Mistawis road, without a soul to help or comfort her. And this in a nominally Christian community in the year of grace nineteen and some odd!

'Do you mean to say that Cissy is all alone there now, with nobody to do anything for her – nobody?'

'Oh, she can move about a bit and get a bite and sup when she wants it. But she can't work. It's d – – d hard for a man to work hard all day and go home at night tired and hungry and cook his own meals. Sometimes I'm sorry I kicked old Rachel Edwards out.' Abel described Rachel picturesquely.

'Her face looked as if it had wore out a hundred bodies. And she moped. Talk about temper! Temper's nothing to moping. She was too slow to catch worms, and dirty – d – – d dirty. I ain't unreasonable – I know a man has to eat his peck before he dies – but she went over the limit. What d'ye sp'ose I saw that lady do? She'd made some punkin jam – had it on the table in glass jars with the tops off. The dawg got up on the table and stuck his paw into one of them. What did she do? She jest took holt of the dawg and wrung the syrup off his paw back into the jar! Then screwed the top on and set it in the pantry. I sets open the door and says to her, "Go!" The dame went, and I fired the jars of punkin after her, two at a time. Thought I'd die laughing to see old Rachel run – with them punkin jars raining after her. She's told everywhere I'm crazy, so nobody'll come for love or money.'

'But Cissy must have someone to look after her,' insisted Valancy, whose mind was centred on this aspect of the case. She did not care whether Roaring Abel had anyone to cook for him or not. But her heart was wrung for Cecilia Gay.

'Oh, she gits on. Barney Snaith always drops in when he's passing and does anything she wants done. Brings her oranges and flowers and things. There's a Christian for you. Yet that sanctimonious, snivelling parcel of St Andrew's people wouldn't be seen on the same side of the road with him. Their dogs'll go to heaven before they do. And their minister – slick as if the cat had licked him!'

'There are plenty of good people, both in St Andrew's and St George's, who would be kind to Cissy if you would behave yourself,' said Valancy severely. 'They're afraid to go near your place.'

'Because I'm such a sad old dog? But I don't bite – never bit anyone in my life. A few loose words spilled around don't hurt anyone. And I'm not asking people to come. Don't want 'em poking and prying about. What I want is a housekeeper. If I shaved every Sunday and went to church I'd get all the housekeepers I'd want. I'd be respectable then. But what's the use of going to church when it's all settled by predestination? Tell me that, Miss.'

'Is it?' said Valancy.

'Yes. Can't git around it nohow. Wish I could. I don't want either heaven or hell for steady. Wish a man could have 'em mixed in equal proportions.'

'Isn't that the way it is in this world?' said Valancy thoughtfully – but rather as if her thought was concerned with something else than theology.

'No, no,' boomed Abel, striking a tremendous blow on a stubborn nail. 'There's too much hell here – entirely too much hell. That's why I get drunk so often. It sets you free for a little while – free from yourself – yes, by God, free from predestination. Ever try it?'

'No, I've another way of getting free,' said Valancy absently. 'But about Cissy now. She must have someone to look after her –'

'What are you harping on Sis for? Seems to me you ain't bothered much about her up to now. You never even come to see her. And she used to like you so well.'

'I should have,' said Valancy. 'But never mind. You couldn't understand. The point is – you must have a housekeeper.'

'Where am I to get one? I can pay decent wages if I could get a decent woman. D'ye think I like old hags?'

'Will I do?' said Valancy.

FIFTEEN
❧

'Let us be calm,' said Uncle Benjamin. 'Let us be perfectly calm.'

'Calm!' Mrs Frederick wrung her hands. 'How can I be calm – how could anybody be calm under such a disgrace as this?'

'Why in the world did you let her go?' asked Uncle James.

'Let her! How could I stop her, James? It seems she packed the big valise and sent it away with Roaring Abel when he went home after supper, while Christine and I were out in the kitchen. Then Doss herself came down with her little satchel, dressed in her green serge suit. I felt a terrible premonition. I can't tell you how it was, but I seemed to know that Doss was going to do something dreadful.'

'It's a pity you couldn't have had your premonition a little sooner,' said Uncle Benjamin drily.

'I said, "Doss, where are you going?" and she said, "I am going to look for my Blue Castle."'

'Wouldn't you think that would convince Marsh that her mind is affected?' interjected Uncle James.

'And I said, "Valancy, what do you mean?" And she said, "I am going to keep house for Roaring Abel and nurse Cissy. He will pay me thirty dollars a month." I wonder I didn't drop dead on the spot.'

'You shouldn't have let her go – you shouldn't have let her out of the house,' said Uncle James. 'You should have locked the door – anything –'

'She was between me and the front door. And you can't realise how determined she was. She was like a rock. That's the strangest thing of all about her. She used to be so good and obedient, and now she's neither to hold nor bind. But I said everything I could think of to bring her to her senses. I asked her if she had no regard for her reputation. I said to her solemnly, "Doss, when a woman's reputation is once smirched nothing can ever make it spotless again. Your character will be gone forever if you go to Roaring Abel's to wait on a bad girl like Sis Gay." And she said, "I don't believe Cissy was a bad girl, but I don't care if she was." Those were her very words, "I don't care if she was."'

'She has lost all sense of decency,' exploded Uncle Benjamin.

'"Cissy Gay is dying," she said, "and it's a shame and disgrace that she is dying in a Christian community with no one to do anything for her. Whatever she's been or done, she's a human being."'

'Well, you know, when it comes to that, I suppose she is,' said Uncle James with the air of one making a splendid concession.

'I asked Doss if she had no regard for appearances. She said, "I've been keeping up appearances all my life. Now I'm going in for realities. Appearances can go hang!" Go hang!'

'An outrageous thing!' said Uncle Benjamin violently. 'An outrageous thing!'

Which relieved his feelings, but didn't help anyone else.

Mrs Frederick wept. Cousin Stickles took up the refrain between her moans of despair.

'I told her – we both told her – that Roaring Abel had certainly killed his wife in one of his drunken rages and would kill her. She laughed and said, "I'm not afraid of Roaring Abel. He won't kill me, and he's too old for me to be afraid of his gallantries." What did she mean? What are gallantries?'

Mrs Frederick saw that she must stop crying if she wanted to regain control of the conversation.

'I said to her, "Valancy, if you have no regard for your own reputation and your family's standing, have you none for my feelings?" She said, "None." Just like that, "None!"'

'Insane people never do have any regard for other people's feelings,' said Uncle Benjamin. 'That's one of the symptoms.'

'I broke out into tears then, and she said, "Come now, Mother, be a good sport. I'm going to do an act of Christian charity, and as for the damage it will do my reputation, why, you know I haven't any matrimonial chances anyhow, so what does it matter?" And with that she turned and went out.'

'The last words I said to her,' said Cousin Stickles pathetically, 'were, "Who will rub my back at nights now?" And she said – she said – but no, I cannot repeat it.'

'Nonsense,' said Uncle Benjamin. 'Out with it. This is no time to be squeamish.'

'She said' – Cousin Stickles' voice was little more than a whisper – 'she said – "Oh, darn!"'

'To think I should have lived to hear my daughter swearing!' sobbed Mrs Frederick,

'It – it was only imitation swearing,' faltered Cousin Stickles, desirous of smoothing things over now that the worst was out. But she had never told about the bannister.

'It will be only a step from that to real swearing,' said Uncle James sternly.

'The worst of this' – Mrs Frederick hunted for a dry spot on her handkerchief – 'is that everyone will know now that she is deranged. We can't keep it a secret any longer. Oh, I cannot bear it!'

'You should have been stricter with her when she was young,' said Uncle Benjamin.

'I don't see how I could have been,' said Mrs Frederick – truthfully enough.

'The worst feature of the case is that that Snaith scoundrel is always hanging around Roaring Abel's,' said Uncle James. 'I shall be thankful if nothing worse comes of this mad freak than a few weeks at Roaring Abel's. Cissy Gay can't live much longer.'

'And she didn't even take her flannel petticoat!' lamented Cousin Stickles.

'I'll see Ambrose Marsh again about this,' said Uncle Benjamin – meaning Valancy, not the flannel petticoat.

'I'll see Lawyer Ferguson,' said Uncle James.

'Meanwhile,' added Uncle Benjamin, 'let us be calm.'

SIXTEEN

Valancy had walked out to Roaring Abel's house on the Mistawis road under a sky of purple and amber, with a queer exhilaration and expectancy in her heart. Back there, behind her, her mother and Cousin Stickles were crying – over themselves, not over her. But here the wind was in her face, soft, dew-wet, cool, blowing along the grassy roads. Oh, she loved the wind! The robins were whistling sleepily in the firs along the way and the moist air was fragrant with the tang of balsam. Big cars went purring past in the violet dusk – the stream of summer tourists to Muskoka had already begun – but Valancy did not envy any of their occupants. Muskoka cottages might be charming, but beyond, in the sunset skies, among the spires of the firs, her Blue Castle towered. She brushed the old years and habits and inhibitions away from her like dead leaves. She would not be littered with them.

Roaring Abel's rambling, tumble-down old house was situated about three miles from the village, on the very edge of 'up back', as the sparsely settled, hilly, wooded country around Mistawis was called vernacularly. It did not, it must be confessed, look much like a Blue Castle.

It had once been a snug place enough in the days when Abel Gay had been young and prosperous, and the punning, arched sign over the gate – 'A. Gay, Carpenter', had been fine and freshly painted. Now it was a faded, dreary old place, with a leprous, patched roof and shutters hanging askew. Abel never seemed to do any carpenter jobs about his own house. It had a listless air, as if tired of life. There was a dwindling grove of ragged, crone-like old spruces behind it. The garden, which Cissy used to keep neat and pretty, had run wild. On two sides of the house were fields full of nothing but mulleins. Behind the house was a long stretch of useless barrens, full of scrub pines and spruces, with here and there a blossoming bit of wild cherry, running back to a belt of timber on the shores of Lake Mistawis, two miles away. A rough, rocky, boulder-strewn lane ran through it to the woods – a lane white with pestiferous, beautiful daisies.

Roaring Abel met Valancy at the door.

'So you've come,' he said incredulously. 'I never s'posed that ruck of Stirlings would let you.'

Valancy showed all her pointed teeth in a grin.

'They couldn't stop me.'

'I didn't think you'd so much spunk,' said Roaring Abel admiringly. 'And look at the nice ankles of her,' he added, as he stepped aside to let her in.

If Cousin Stickles had heard this she would have been certain that Valancy's doom, earthly and unearthly, was sealed. But Abel's superannuated gallantry did not worry Valancy. Besides, this was the first compliment she had ever received in her life and she found herself liking it. She sometimes suspected she had nice ankles, but nobody had ever mentioned it before. In the Stirling clan ankles were among the unmentionables.

Roaring Abel took her into the kitchen, where Cissy Gay was lying on the sofa, breathing quickly, with little scarlet spots on her hollow cheeks. Valancy had not seen Cecilia Gay for years. Then she had been such a pretty creature, a slight blossom-like girl, with soft, golden hair, clear-cut, almost waxen features, and large, beautiful blue eyes. She was shocked at the change in her. Could this be sweet Cissy – this pitiful little thing that looked like a tired broken flower? She had wept all the beauty out of her eyes; they looked too big – enormous – in her wasted face. The last time Valancy had seen Cecilia Gay those faded, piteous eyes had been limpid, shadowy blue pools aglow with mirth. The contrast was so terrible that Valancy's own eyes filled with tears. She knelt down by Cissy and put her arms about her.

'Cissy dear, I've come to look after you. I'll stay with you till – till – as long as you want me.'

'Oh!' Cissy put her thin arms about Valancy's neck. 'Oh – will you? It's been so – lonely. I can wait on myself – but it's been so lonely. It – would just be like – heaven – to have someone here – like you. You were always – so sweet to me – long ago.'

Valancy held Cissy close. She was suddenly happy. Here was someone who needed her – someone she could help. She was no longer a superfluity. Old things had passed away; everything had become new.

'Most things are predestinated, but some are just darn sheer luck,' said Roaring Abel, complacently smoking his pipe in the corner.

SEVENTEEN

When Valancy had lived for a week at Roaring Abel's she felt as if years had separated her from her old life and all the people she had known in it. They were beginning to seem remote – dream-like – far-away – and as the days went on they seemed still more so, until they ceased to matter altogether.

She was happy. Nobody ever bothered her with conundrums or insisted on giving her Purple Pills. Nobody called her Doss or worried her about catching cold. There were no quilts to piece, no abominable rubber-plant to water, no ice-cold maternal tantrums to endure. She could be alone whenever she liked, go to bed when she liked, sneeze when she liked. In the long, wondrous, northern twilights, when Cissy was asleep and Roaring Abel away, she could sit for hours on the shaky back veranda steps, looking out over the barrens to the hills beyond, covered with their fine, purple bloom, listening to the friendly wind singing wild, sweet melodies in the little spruces, and drinking in the aroma of the sunned grasses, until darkness flowed over the landscape like a cool, welcome wave.

Sometimes of an afternoon, when Cissy was strong enough, the two girls went into the barrens and looked at the wood-flowers. But they did not pick any. Valancy had read to Cissy the gospel thereof according to John Foster: 'It is a pity to gather wood-flowers. They lose half their witchery away from the green and the flicker. The way to enjoy wood-flowers is to track them down to their remote haunts – gloat over them – and then leave them with backward glances, taking with us only the beguiling memory of their grace and fragrance.'

Valancy was in the midst of realities after a lifetime of unrealities. And busy – very busy. The house had to be cleaned. Not for nothing had Valancy been brought up in the Stirling habits of neatness and cleanliness. If she found satisfaction in cleaning dirty rooms she got her fill of it there. Roaring Abel thought she was foolish to bother doing so much more than she was asked to do, but he did not interfere with her. He was very well satisfied with his bargain. Valancy was a good cook. Abel said she got a flavour into things. The only fault he found with her was that she did not sing at her work.

'Folk should always sing at their work,' he insisted. 'Sounds cheerful-like.'

'Not always,' retorted Valancy. 'Fancy a butcher singing at his work. Or an undertaker.'

Abel burst into his great broad laugh.

'There's no getting the better of you. You've got an answer every time. I should think the Stirlings would be glad to be rid of you. They don't like being sassed back.'

During the day Abel was generally away from home – if not working, then shooting or fishing with Barney Snaith. He generally came home at nights – always very late and often very drunk. The first night they heard him come howling into the yard, Cissy had told Valancy not to be afraid.

'Father never does anything – he just makes a noise.'

Valancy, lying on the sofa in Cissy's room, where she had elected to sleep, lest Cissy should need attention in the night – Cissy would never have called her – was not at all afraid, and said so. By the time Abel had got his horses put away, the roaring stage had passed and he was in his room at the end of the hall crying and praying. Valancy could still hear his dismal moans when she went calmly to sleep. For the most part, Abel was a good-natured creature, but occasionally he had a temper. Once Valancy asked him coolly:

'What is the use of getting in a rage?'

'It's such a d – – d relief,' said Abel.

They both burst out laughing together.

'You're a great little sport,' said Abel admiringly. 'Don't mind my bad French. I don't mean a thing by it. Jest habit. Say, I like a woman that ain't afraid to speak to me. Sis there was always too meek – too meek. That's why she got adrift. I like you.'

'All the same,' said Valancy determinedly, 'there is no use in sending things to hell as you're always doing. And I'm not going to have you tracking mud all over a floor I've just scrubbed. You must use the scraper whether you consign it to perdition or not.'

Cissy loved the cleanness and neatness. She had kept it so, too, until her strength failed. She was very pitifully happy because she had Valancy with her. It had been so terrible – the long, lonely days and nights with no companionship save those dreadful old women who came to work. Cissy had hated and feared them. She clung to Valancy like a child.

There was no doubt that Cissy was dying. Yet at no time did she seem alarmingly ill. She did not even cough a great deal. Most days she was able to get up and dress – sometimes even to work about in the garden or the barrens for an hour or two. For a few weeks after Valancy's coming she seemed so much better that Valancy began to hope she might get well. But Cissy shook her head.

'No, I can't get well. My lungs are almost gone. And I – don't want to. I'm so tired, Valancy. Only dying can rest me. But it's lovely to have you here – you'll never know how much it means to me. But Valancy – you work too hard. You don't need to – Father only wants his meals cooked. I don't think you are strong yourself. You turn so pale sometimes. And those drops you take. Are you well, dear?'

'I'm all right,' said Valancy lightly. She would not have Cissy worried. 'And I'm not working hard. I'm glad to have some work to do – something that really wants to be done.'

'Then' – Cissy slipped her hand wistfully into Valancy's – 'don't let's talk any more about my being sick. Let's just forget it. Let's pretend I'm a little girl again – and you have come here to play with me. I used to wish that long ago – wish that you could come. I knew you couldn't, of course. But how I did wish it! You always seemed so different from the other girls – so kind and sweet – and as if you had something in yourself nobody knew about – some dear, pretty secret. Had you, Valancy?'

'I had my Blue Castle,' said Valancy, laughing a little. She was pleased that Cissy had thought of her like this. She had never suspected that anybody liked or admired or wondered about her. She told Cissy all about her Blue Castle. She had never told anyone about it before.

'Everyone has a Blue Castle, I think,' said Cissy softly. 'Only everyone has a different name for it. I had mine – once.'

She put her two thin little hands over her face. She did not tell Valancy – then – who had destroyed her Blue Castle. But Valancy knew that, whoever it was, it was not Barney Snaith.

EIGHTEEN
∞

Valancy was acquainted with Barney by now – well acquainted, it seemed, though she had spoken to him only a few times. But then she had felt just as well acquainted with him the first time they had met. She had been in the garden at twilight, hunting for a few stalks of white narcissus for Cissy's room when she heard that terrible old Grey Slosson coming down through the woods from Mistawis – one could hear it miles away. Valancy did not look up as it drew near, thumping over the rocks in that crazy lane. She had never looked up, though Barney had gone racketting past every evening since she had been at Roaring Abel's. This time he did not racket past. The old Grey Slosson stopped with even more terrible noises than it made going. Valancy was conscious that Barney had sprung from it and was leaning over the ramshackle gate. She suddenly straightened up and looked into his face. Their eyes met – Valancy was suddenly conscious of a delicious weakness. Was one of her heart attacks coming on? But this was a new symptom.

His eyes, which she had always thought brown, now seen close, were deep violet – translucent and intense. Neither of his eyebrows looked like the other. He was thin – too thin – she wished she could feed him up a bit – she wished she could sew the buttons on his coat – and make him cut his hair – and shave every day. There was something in his face – one hardly knew what it was. Tiredness? Sadness? Disillusionment? He had dimples in his thin cheeks when he smiled. All these thoughts flashed through Valancy's mind in that one moment while his eyes looked into hers.

'Good evening, Miss Stirling.'

Nothing could be more commonplace and conventional. Anyone might have said it. But Barney Snaith had a way of saying things that gave them poignancy. When he said good evening you felt that it was a good evening and that it was partly his doing that it was. Also, you felt that some of the credit was yours. Valancy felt all this vaguely, but she couldn't imagine why she was trembling from head to foot – it must be her heart. If only he didn't notice it!

'I'm going over to the Port,' Barney was saying. 'Can I acquire merit by getting or doing anything there for you or Cissy?'

'Will you get some salt codfish for us?' said Valancy. It was the only thing she could think of. Roaring Abel had expressed a desire that day for a dinner of boiled salt codfish. When her knights came riding to the Blue Castle, Valancy had sent them on many a quest, but she had never asked any of them to get her salt codfish.

'Certainly. You're sure there's nothing else? Lots of room in Lady Jane Grey Slosson. And she always gets back some time, does Lady Jane.'

'I don't think there's anything more,' said Valancy. She knew he would bring oranges for Cissy anyhow – he always did.

Barney did not turn away at once. He was silent for a little. Then he said, slowly and whimsically:

'Miss Stirling, you're a brick! You're a whole cartload of bricks. To come here and look after Cissy – under the circumstances.'

'There's nothing so bricky about that,' said Valancy. 'I'd nothing else to do. And – I like it here. I don't feel as if I'd done anything specially meritorious. Mr Gay is paying me fair wages. I never earned any money before – and I like it.' It seemed so easy to talk to Barney Snaith, someway – this terrible Barney Snaith of the lurid tales and mysterious past – as easy and natural as if talking to herself.

'All the money in the world couldn't buy what you're doing for Cissy Gay,' said Barney. 'It's splendid and fine of you. And if there's anything I can do to help you in any way, you have only to let me know. If Roaring Abel ever tries to annoy you –'

'He doesn't. He's lovely to me. I like Roaring Abel,' said Valancy frankly.

'So do I. But there's one stage of his drunkenness – perhaps you haven't encountered it yet – when he sings ribald songs –'

'Oh, yes. He came home last night like that. Cissy and I just went to our room and shut ourselves in where we couldn't hear him. He apologised this morning. I'm not afraid of any of Roaring Abel's stages.'

'Well, I'm sure he'll be decent to you, apart from his inebriated yowls,' said Barney. 'And I've told him he's got to stop damning things when you're around.'

'Why?' asked Valancy slyly, with one of her odd, slanted glances and a sudden flake of pink on each cheek, born of the thought that Barney Snaith had actually done so much for her. 'I often feel like damning things myself.'

For a moment Barney stared. Was this elfin girl the little, old-maidish creature who had stood there two minutes ago? Surely there was magic and devilry going on in that shabby, weedy old garden.

Then he laughed.

'It will be a relief to have someone to do it for you, then. So you don't want anything but salt codfish?'

'Not tonight. But I dare say I'll have some errands for you very often when you go to Port Lawrence. I can't trust Mr Gay to remember to bring all the things I want.'

Barney had gone away, then, in his Lady Jane, and Valancy stood in the garden for a long time.

Since then he had called several times, walking down through the barrens, whistling. How that whistle of his echoed through the spruces on those June twilights! Valancy caught herself listening for it every evening – rebuked herself – then let herself go. Why shouldn't she listen for it?

He always brought Cissy fruit and flowers. Once he brought Valancy a box of candy – the first box of candy she had ever been given. It seemed sacrilege to eat it.

She found herself thinking of him in season and out of season. She wanted to know if he ever thought about her when she wasn't before his eyes, and, if so, what. She wanted to see that mysterious house of his back on the Mistawis island. Cissy had never seen it. Cissy, though she talked freely of Barney and had known him for five years, really knew little more of him than Valancy herself.

'But he isn't bad,' said Cissy. 'Nobody need ever tell me he is. He can't have done a thing to be ashamed of.'

'Then why does he live as he does?' asked Valancy – to hear somebody defend him.

'I don't know. He's a mystery. And of course there's something behind it, but I know it isn't disgrace. Barney Snaith simply couldn't do anything disgraceful, Valancy.'

Valancy was not so sure. Barney must have done something – sometime. He was a man of education and intelligence. She had soon discovered that, in listening to his conversations and wrangles with Roaring Abel – who was surprisingly well read and could discuss any subject under the sun when sober. Such a man wouldn't bury himself for five years in Muskoka and live and look like a tramp if there were not too good – or bad – a reason for it. But it didn't matter. All that mattered was that she was sure now that he had never been Cissy Gay's lover. There was nothing like that between them. Though he was very fond of Cissy and she of him, as anyone could see. But it was a fondness that didn't worry Valancy.

'You don't know what Barney has been to me, these past two years,' Cissy had said simply. 'Everything would have been unbearable without him.'

'Cissy Gay is the sweetest girl I ever knew – and there's a man somewhere I'd like to shoot if I could find him,' Barney had said savagely.

Barney was an interesting talker, with a knack of telling a great deal about his adventures and nothing at all about himself. There was one glorious rainy day when Barney and Abel swapped yarns all the afternoon while Valancy mended tablecloths and listened. Barney told weird tales of his adventures with 'shacks' on trains while hoboing it across the continent. Valancy thought she ought to think his stealing rides quite dreadful, but didn't. The story of his working his way to England on a cattle-ship sounded more legitimate. And his yarns of the Yukon enthralled her – especially the one of the night he was lost on the divide between the Gold Run and Sulphur Valley. He had spent two years out there. Where in all this was there room for the penitentiary and the other things?

If he were telling the truth. But Valancy knew he was.

'Found no gold,' he said. 'Came away poorer than when I went. But such a place to live! Those silences at the back of the north wind got me. I've never belonged to myself since.'

Yet he was not a great talker. He told a great deal in a few well-chosen words – how well-chosen Valancy did not realise. And he had a knack of saying things without opening his mouth at all.

'I like a man whose eyes say more than his lips,' thought Valancy.

But then she liked everything about him – his tawny hair – his whimsical smiles – the little glints of fun in his eyes – his loyal affection for that unspeakable Lady Jane – his habit of sitting with his hands in his pockets, his chin sunk on his breast, looking up from under his mismatched eyebrows. She liked his nice voice which sounded as if it might become caressing or wooing with very little provocation. She was at times almost afraid to let herself think these thoughts. They were so vivid that she felt as if the others must know what she was thinking.

'I've been watching a woodpecker all day,' he said one evening on the shaky old back veranda. His account of the woodpecker's doings was satisfying. He had often some gay or cunning little anecdote of the wood folk to tell them. And sometimes he and

Roaring Abel smoked fiercely the whole evening and never said a word, while Cissy lay in the hammock swung between the veranda posts and Valancy sat idly on the steps, her hands clasped over her knees, and wondered dreamily if she were really Valancy Stirling and if it were only three weeks since she had left the ugly old house on Elm Street.

The barrens lay before her in a white moon splendour, where dozens of little rabbits frisked. Barney, when he liked, could sit down on the edge of the barrens and lure those rabbits right to him by some mysterious sorcery he possessed. Valancy had once seen a squirrel leap from a scrub pine to his shoulder and sit there chattering to him. It reminded her of John Foster.

It was one of the delights of Valancy's new life that she could read John Foster's books as often and as long as she wanted to. She read them all to Cissy, who loved them. She also tried to read them to Abel and Barney, who did not love them. Abel was bored and Barney politely refused to listen at all.

'Piffle,' said Barney.

NINETEEN

Of course, the Stirlings had not left the poor maniac alone all this time or refrained from heroic efforts to rescue her perishing soul and reputation. Uncle James, whose lawyer had helped him as little as his doctor, came one day and, finding Valancy alone in the kitchen, as he supposed, gave her a terrible talking to – told her she was breaking her mother's heart and disgracing her family.

'But why?' said Valancy, not ceasing to scour her porridge pot decently. 'I'm doing honest work for honest pay. What is there in that that is disgraceful?'

'Don't quibble, Valancy,' said Uncle James solemnly. 'This is no fit place for you to be, and you know it. Why, I'm told that that jailbird, Snaith, is hanging around here every evening.'

'Not every evening,' said Valancy reflectively. 'No, not quite every evening.'

'It's – it's insufferable!' said Uncle James violently. 'Valancy, you must come home. We won't judge you harshly. I assure you we won't. We will overlook all this.'

'Thank you,' said Valancy.

'Have you no sense of shame?' demanded Uncle James.

'Oh, yes. But the things I am ashamed of are not the things you are ashamed of.' Valancy proceeded to rinse her dishcloth meticulously.

Still was Uncle James patient. He gripped the sides of his chair and ground his teeth.

'We know your mind isn't just right. We'll make allowances. But you must come home. You shall not stay here with that drunken, blasphemous old scoundrel –'

'Were you by any chance referring to me, Mister Stirling?' demanded Roaring Abel, suddenly appearing in the doorway of the back veranda where he had been smoking a peaceful pipe and listening to "old Jim Stirling's" tirade with huge enjoyment. His red beard fairly bristled with indignation and his huge eyebrows quivered. But cowardice was not among James Stirling's shortcomings.

'I was. And, furthermore, I want to tell you that you have acted an iniquitous part in luring this weak and unfortunate girl away from her home and friends, and I will have you punished yet for it –'

James Stirling got no further. Roaring Abel crossed the kitchen at a bound, caught him by his collar and his trousers, and hurled him through the doorway and over the garden paling with as little apparent effort as he might have employed in whisking a troublesome kitten out of the way.

'The next time you come back here,' he bellowed, 'I'll throw you through the window – and all the better if the window is shut! Coming here, thinking yourself God to put the world to rights!'

Valancy candidly and unashamedly owned to herself that she had seen few more satisfying sights than Uncle James' coat-tails flying out into the asparagus bed. She had once been afraid of this man's judgment. Now she saw clearly that he was nothing but a rather stupid little village tin-god.

Roaring Abel turned with his great broad laugh.

'He'll think of that for years when he wakes up in the night. The Almighty made a mistake in making so many Stirlings. But since they are made, we've got to reckon with them. Too many to kill out. But if they come here bothering you I'll shoo 'em off before a cat could lick its ear.'

The next time they sent Dr Stalling. Surely Roaring Abel would not throw him into asparagus beds. Dr Stalling was not so sure of this and had no great liking for the task. He did not believe Valancy Stirling was out of her mind. She had always been queer. He, Dr Stalling, had never been able to understand her. Therefore, beyond doubt, she was queer. She was only just a little queerer than usual now. And Dr Stalling had his own reasons for disliking Roaring Abel. When Dr Stalling had first come to Deerwood he had had a liking for long hikes around Mistawis and Muskoka. On one of these occasions he had got lost and after much wandering had fallen in with Roaring Abel with his gun over his shoulder.

Dr Stalling had contrived to ask his question in about the most idiotic manner possible. He said, 'Can you tell me where I'm going?'

'How the devil should I know where you're going, gosling?' retorted Abel contemptuously.

Dr Stalling was so enraged that he could not speak for a moment or two and in that moment Abel had disappeared in the woods. Dr Stalling had eventually found his way home, but he had never hankered to encounter Abel Gay again.

Nevertheless he came now to do his duty. Valancy greeted him with a sinking heart. She had to own to herself that she was terribly afraid of Dr Stalling still. She had a miserable conviction that if he shook his long, bony finger at her and told her to go home, she dared not disobey.

'Mr Gay,' said Dr Stalling politely and condescendingly, 'may I see Miss Stirling alone for a few minutes?' Roaring Abel was a little drunk – just drunk enough to be excessively polite and very cunning. He had been on the point of going away when Dr Stalling arrived, but now he sat down in a corner of the parlour and folded his arms.

'No, no, mister,' he said solemnly. 'That wouldn't do – wouldn't do at all. I've got the reputation of my household to keep up. I've got to chaperone this young lady. Can't have any sparkin' going on here behind my back.'

Outraged Dr Stalling looked so terrible that Valancy wondered how Abel could endure his aspect. But Abel was not worried at all.

'D'ye know anything about it, anyway?' he asked genially.

'About what?'

'Sparking,' said Abel coolly.

Poor Dr Stalling, who had never married because he believed in a celibate clergy, would not notice this ribald remark. He turned his back on Abel and addressed himself to Valancy.

'Miss Stirling, I am here in response to your mother's wishes. She begged me to come. I am charged with some messages from her. Will you' – he wagged his forefinger – 'will you hear them?'

'Yes,' said Valancy faintly, eyeing the forefinger. It had a hypnotic effect on her.

'The first is this. If you will leave this – this –'

'House,' interjected Roaring Abel. 'H-o-u-s-e. Troubled with an impediment in your speech, ain't you, Mister?'

' – this place and return to your home, Mr James Stirling will himself pay for a good nurse to come here and wait on Miss Gay.'

Back of her terror Valancy smiled in secret. Uncle James must indeed regard the matter as desperate when he would loosen his purse-strings like that. At any rate, her clan no longer despised her or ignored her. She had become important to them.

'That's my business, Mister,' said Abel. 'Miss Stirling can go if she pleases, or stay if she pleases. I made a fair bargain with her, and she's free to conclude it when she likes. She gives me meals that stick to my ribs. She don't forget to put salt in the porridge. She never slams doors, and when she has nothing to say she don't talk. That's uncanny in a woman, you know, Mister. I'm satisfied. If she isn't, she's free to go. But no woman comes here in Jim

Stirling's pay. If anyone does' – Abel's voice was uncannily bland and polite – 'I'll spatter the road with her brains. Tell him that with A. Gay's compliments.'

'Dr Stalling, a nurse is not what Cissy needs,' said Valancy earnestly. 'She isn't so ill as that, yet. What she wants is companionship – somebody she knows and likes just to live with her. You can understand that, I'm sure.'

'I understand that your motive is quite – ahem – commendable.' Dr Stalling felt that he was very broad-minded indeed – especially as in his secret soul he did not believe Valancy's motive was commendable. He hadn't the least idea what she was up to, but he was sure her motive was not commendable. When he could not understand a thing he straightway condemned it. Simplicity itself! 'But your first duty is to your mother. She needs you. She implores you to come home – she will forgive everything if you will only come home.'

'That's a pretty little thought,' remarked Abel meditatively, as he ground some tobacco up in his hand.

Dr Stalling ignored him.

'She entreats, but I, Miss Stirling,' – Dr Stalling remembered that he was an ambassador of Jehovah – 'I command. As your pastor and spiritual guide, I command you to come home with me – this very day. Get your hat and coat and come now.'

Dr Stalling shook his finger at Valancy. Before that pitiless finger she drooped and wilted visibly.

'She's giving in,' thought Roaring Abel. 'She'll go with him. Beats all, the power these preacher fellows have over women.'

Valancy was on the point of obeying Dr Stalling. She must go home with him – and give up. She would lapse back to Doss Stirling again and for her few remaining days or weeks be the cowed, futile creature she had always been. It was her fate – typified by that relentless, uplifted forefinger. She could no more escape from it than Roaring Abel from his predestination. She eyed it as the fascinated bird eyes the snake. Another moment –

'Fear is the original sin,' suddenly said a still, small voice away back – back – back of Valancy's consciousness. 'Almost all the evil in the world has its origin in the fact that someone is afraid of something.'

Valancy stood up. She was still in the clutches of fear, but her soul was her own again. She would not be false to that inner voice.

'Dr Stalling,' she said slowly, 'I do not at present owe any duty to my mother. She is quite well; she has all the assistance and companionship she requires; she does not need me at all. I am needed here. I am going to stay here.'

'There's spunk for you,' said Roaring Abel admiringly.

Dr Stalling dropped his forefinger. One could not keep on shaking a finger forever.

'Miss Stirling, is there nothing that can influence you? Do you remember your childhood days –'

'Perfectly. And hate them.'

'Do you realise what people will say? What they are saying?'

'I can imagine it,' said Valancy, with a shrug of her shoulders. She was suddenly free of fear again. 'I haven't listened to the gossip of Deerwood tea parties and sewing circles twenty years for nothing. But, Dr Stalling, it doesn't matter in the least to me what they say – not in the least.'

Dr Stalling went away then. A girl who cared nothing for public opinion! Over whom sacred family ties had no restraining influence! Who hated her childhood memories!

Then Cousin Georgiana came – on her own initiative, for nobody would have thought it worthwhile to send her. She found Valancy alone, weeding the little vegetable garden she had planted, and she made all the platitudinous pleas she could think of. Valancy heard her patiently. Cousin Georgiana wasn't such a bad old soul. Then she said:

'And now that you have got all that out of your system, Cousin Georgiana, can you tell me how to make creamed codfish so that it will not be as thick as porridge and as salt as the Dead Sea?'

———•◆•———

'We'll just have to wait,' said Uncle Benjamin. 'After all, Cissy Gay can't live long. Dr Marsh tells me she may drop off any day.'

Mrs Frederick wept. It would really have been so much easier to bear if Valancy had died. She could have worn mourning then.

TWENTY

When Abel Gay paid Valancy her first month's wages – which he did promptly, in bills reeking with the odour of tobacco and whiskey – Valancy went into Deerwood and spent every cent of it. She got a pretty green crêpe dress with a girdle of crimson beads, at a bargain sale, a pair of silk stockings, to match, and a little crinkled green hat with a crimson rose in it. She even bought a foolish little beribboned and belaced nightgown.

She passed the house on Elm Street twice – Valancy never even thought about it as 'home' – but saw no one. No doubt her mother was sitting in the room this lovely June evening playing solitaire – and cheating. Valancy knew that Mrs Frederick always cheated. She never lost a game. Most of the people Valancy met looked at her seriously and passed her with a cool nod. Nobody stopped to speak to her.

Valancy put on her green dress when she got home. Then she took it off again. She felt so miserably undressed in its low neck and short sleeves. And that low, crimson girdle around the hips seemed positively indecent. She hung it up in the closet, feeling flatly that she had wasted her money. She would never have the courage to wear that dress. John Foster's arraignment of fear had no power to stiffen her against this. In this one thing habit and custom were still all-powerful. Yet she sighed as she went down to meet Barney Snaith in her old snuff-brown silk. That green thing had been very becoming – she had seen so much in her one ashamed glance. Above it her eyes had looked like odd brown jewels and the girdle had given her flat figure an entirely different appearance. She wished she could have left it on. But there were some things John Foster did not know.

Every Sunday evening Valancy went to the little Free Methodist church in a valley on the edge of 'up back' – a spireless little grey building among the pines, with a few sunken graves and mossy gravestones in the small, paling-encircled, grass-grown square beside it. She liked the minister who preached there. He was so simple and sincere. An old man, who lived in Port Lawrence and came out by the lake in a little disappearing propeller boat to give a free service to the people of the small, stony farms back of the hills, who would otherwise never have heard any gospel message. She liked the simple service and the fervent singing. She liked to sit by the open window and look out into the pine woods. The congregation was always small. The Free Methodists were few in number, poor and generally illiterate. But Valancy loved those Sunday evenings. For the first time in her life she liked going to church. The rumour reached Deerwood that she had 'turned Free Methodist' and sent Mrs Frederick to bed for a day. But Valancy had not turned anything. She went to the church because she liked it and because in some inexplicable way it did her good. Old Mr Towers believed exactly what he preached and somehow it made a tremendous difference.

Oddly enough, Roaring Abel disapproved of her going to the hill church as strongly as Mrs Frederick herself could have done. He had 'no use for Free Methodists. He was a Presbyterian.' But Valancy went in spite of him.

'We'll hear something worse than that about her soon,' Uncle Benjamin predicted gloomily.

They did.

Valancy could not quite explain, even to herself, just why she wanted to go to that party. It was a dance 'up back' at Chidley Corners; and dances at Chidley Corners were not, as a rule, the sort of assemblies where well-brought-up young ladies were found. Valancy knew it was coming off, for Roaring Abel had been engaged as one of the fiddlers.

But the idea of going had never occurred to her until Roaring Abel himself broached it at supper.

'You come with me to the dance,' he ordered. 'It'll do you good – put some colour in your face. You look peaked – you want something to liven you up.'

Valancy found herself suddenly wanting to go. She knew nothing at all of what dances at Chidley Corners were apt to be like. Her idea of dances had been fashioned on the correct affairs that went by that name in Deerwood and Port Lawrence. Of course she knew the Corners' dance wouldn't be just like them. Much more informal, of course. But so much the more interesting. Why shouldn't she go? Cissy was in a week of apparent health and improvement. She wouldn't mind staying alone in the least. She entreated Valancy to go if she wanted to. And Valancy did want to go.

She went to her room to dress. A rage against the snuff-brown silk seized her. Wear that to a party! Never. She pulled her green crêpe from its hanger and put in on feverishly. It was nonsense to feel so – so – naked – just because her neck and arms were bare. That was just her old maidishness. She would not be ridden by it. On went the dress – the slippers.

It was the first time she had worn a pretty dress since the organdies of her early teens. And they had never made her look like this.

If she only had a necklace or something. She wouldn't feel so bare then. She ran down to the garden. There were clovers there – great crimson things growing in the long grass. Valancy gathered handfuls of them and strung them on a cord. Fastened above her neck they gave her the comfortable sensation of a collar and were oddly becoming. Another circlet of them went round her hair, dressed in the low puffs that became her. Excitement brought those faint pink stains to her face. She flung on her coat and pulled the little, twisty hat over her hair.

'You look so nice and – and – different, dear,' said Cissy. 'Like a green moonbeam with a gleam of red in it, if there could be such a thing.'

Valancy stooped to kiss her.

'I don't feel right about leaving you alone, Cissy.'

'Oh, I'll be all right. I feel better tonight than I have for a long while. I've been feeling badly to see you sticking here so closely on my account. I hope you'll have a nice time. I never was at a party at the Corners, but I used to go sometimes, long ago, to dances up back. We always had good times. And you needn't be afraid of Father being drunk tonight. He never drinks when he engages to play for a party. But – there may be – liquor. What will you do if it gets rough?'

'Nobody would molest me.'

'Not seriously, I suppose. Father would see to that. But it might be noisy and – and unpleasant.'

'I won't mind. I'm only going as a looker-on. I don't expect to dance. I just want to see what a party up back is like. I've never seen anything except decorous Deerwood.'

Cissy smiled rather dubiously. She knew much better than Valancy what a party 'up back' might be like if there should be liquor. But again there mightn't be.

'I hope you'll enjoy it,' she repeated.

Valancy enjoyed the drive there. They went early, for it was twelve miles to Chidley Corners, and they had to go in Abel's old, ragged top-buggy. The road was rough and rocky, like most Muskoka roads, but full of the austere charm of northern woods. It wound through beautiful, purring pines that were ranks of enchantment in the June sunset, and over the curious jade-green rivers of Muskoka, fringed by aspens that were always quivering with some supernal joy.

Roaring Abel was excellent company, too. He knew all the stories and legends of the wild, beautiful 'up back', and he told them to Valancy as they drove along. Valancy had several fits of inward laughter over what Uncle Benjamin and Aunt Wellington, et al., would feel and think and say if they saw her driving with Roaring Abel in that terrible buggy to a dance at Chidley Corners.

At first the dance was quiet enough, and Valancy was amused and entertained. She even danced twice herself, with a couple of nice 'up back' boys who danced beautifully and told her she did, too.

Another compliment came her way – not a very subtle one, perhaps, but Valancy had had too few compliments in her life to be over-nice on that point. She overheard two of the 'up back' young men talking about her in the dark 'lean-to' behind her.

"Know who that girl in green is?'

'Nope. Guess she's from out front. The Port, maybe. Got a stylish look to her.'

'No beaut but cute-looking, I'll say. 'Jever see such eyes?'

The big room was decorated with pine and fir boughs, and lighted by Chinese lanterns. The floor was waxed, and Roaring Abel's fiddle, purring under his skilled touch, worked magic. The 'up back' girls were pretty and prettily dressed. Valancy thought it the nicest party she had ever attended.

By eleven o'clock she had changed her mind. A new crowd had arrived – a crowd unmistakably drunk. Whiskey began to circulate freely. Very soon almost all the men were partly drunk. Those in the porch and outside around the door began howling 'come-all-ye's' and continued to howl them. The room grew noisy and reeking. Quarrels started up here and there. Bad language and obscene songs were heard. The girls, swung rudely in the dances, became dishevelled and tawdry. Valancy, alone in her corner, was feeling disgusted and repentant. Why had she ever come to such a place? Freedom and independence were all very well, but one should not be a little fool. She might have known what it would be like – she might have taken warning from Cissy's guarded sentences. Her head was aching – she was sick of the whole thing. But what could she do? She must stay to the end. Abel could not leave till then. And that would probably be not till three or four in the morning.

The new influx of boys had left the girls far in the minority and partners were scarce. Valancy was pestered with invitations to dance. She refused them all shortly, and some of her refusals were not well taken. There were muttered oaths and sullen looks. Across the room she saw a group of the strangers talking together and glancing meaningly at her. What were they plotting?

It was at this moment that she saw Barney Snaith looking in over the heads of the crowds at the doorway. Valancy had two distinct convictions – one was that she was quite safe now; the other was that this was why she had wanted to come to the dance. It had been such an absurd hope that she had not recognised it before, but now she knew she had come because of the possibility that Barney might be there, too. She thought that perhaps she ought to be ashamed for this, but she wasn't. After her feeling of relief her next feeling was one of annoyance with Barney for coming there unshaved. Surely he might have enough self-respect to groom himself up decently when he went to a party. There he was, bareheaded, bristly-chinned, in his old trousers and his blue homespun shirt. Not even a coat. Valancy could have shaken him in her anger. No wonder people believed everything bad of him.

But she was not afraid any longer. One of the whispering group left his comrades and came across the room to her, through the whirling couples that now filled it uncomfortably. He was a tall, broad-shouldered fellow, not ill-dressed or ill-looking but unmistakably half drunk. He asked Valancy to dance. Valancy declined civilly. His face turned livid. He threw his arm about her and pulled her to him. His hot, whiskied breath burned her face.

'We won't have fine-lady airs here, my girl. If you ain't too good to come here you ain't too good to dance with us. Me and my pals have been watching you. You're got to give us each a turn and a kiss to boot.'

Valancy tried desperately and vainly to free herself. She was being dragged out into the maze of shouting, stamping, yelling dancers. The next moment the man who held her went staggering across the room from a neatly planted blow on the jaw, knocking down whirling couples as he went. Valancy felt her arm grasped.

'This way – quick,' said Barney Snaith. He swung her out through the open window behind him, vaulted lightly over the sill and caught her hand.

'Quick – we must run for it – they'll be after us.'

Valancy ran as she had never run before, clinging tight to Barney's hand, wondering why she did not drop dead in such a mad scamper. Suppose she did! What a scandal it would make for her poor people. For the first time Valancy felt a little sorry for them. Also, she felt glad that she had escaped from that horrible row. Also, glad that she was holding tight to Barney's hand. Her feelings were badly mixed and she had never had so many in such a brief time in her life.

They finally reached a quiet corner in the pine woods. The pursuit had taken a different direction and the whoops and yells behind them were growing faint. Valancy, out of breath, with a crazily beating heart, collapsed on the trunk of a fallen pine.

'Thanks,' she gasped.

'What a goose you were to come to such a place!' said Barney.

'I – didn't – know – it – would – be like this,' protested Valancy.

'You should have known. Chidley Corners!'

'It – was – just – a name – to me.'

Valancy knew Barney could not realise how ignorant she was of the regions 'up back'. She had lived in Deerwood all her life and of course he supposed she knew. He didn't know how she had been brought up. There was no use trying to explain.

'When I drifted in at Abel's this evening and Cissy told me you'd come here I was amazed. And downright scared. Cissy told me she was worried about you but hadn't liked to say anything to dissuade you for fear you'd think she was thinking selfishly about herself. So I came on up here instead of going to Deerwood.'

Valancy felt a sudden delightful glow irradiating soul and body under the dark pines. So he had actually come up to look after her.

'As soon as they stop hunting for us we'll sneak around to the Muskoka road. I left Lady Jane down there. I'll take you home. I suppose you've had enough of your party.'

'Quite,' said Valancy meekly. The first half of the way home neither of them said anything. It would not have been much use. Lady Jane made so much noise they could not have heard each other. Anyway, Valancy did not feel conversationally inclined. She was ashamed of the whole affair – ashamed of her folly in going – ashamed of being found in such a place by Barney Snaith. By Barney Snaith, reputed jail-breaker, infidel, forger and defaulter. Valancy's lips twitched in the darkness as she thought of it. But she was ashamed.

And yet she was enjoying herself – was full of a strange exultation – bumping over that rough road beside Barney Snaith. The big trees shot by them. The tall mulleins stood up along the road in stiff, orderly ranks like companies of soldiers. The thistles looked like drunken fairies or tipsy elves as their car-lights passed over them. This was the first time she had even been in a car. After all, she liked it. She was not in the least afraid, with Barney at the wheel. Her spirits rose rapidly as they tore along. She ceased to feel ashamed. She ceased to feel anything except that she was part of a comet rushing gloriously through the night of space.

All at once, just where the pine woods frayed out to the scrub barrens, Lady Jane became quiet – too quiet. Lady Jane slowed down quietly – and stopped.

Barney uttered an aghast exclamation. Got out. Investigated. Came apologetically back.

'I'm a doddering idiot. Out of gas. I knew I was short when I left home, but I meant to fill up in Deerwood. Then I forgot all about it in my hurry to get to the Corners.'

'What can we do?' asked Valancy coolly.

'I don't know. There's no gas nearer than Deerwood, nine miles away. And I don't dare leave you here alone. There are always tramps on this road – and some of those crazy fools back at the Corners may come straggling along presently. There were boys there from the Port. As far as I can see, the best thing to do is for us just to sit patiently here until some car comes along and lends us enough gas to get to Roaring Abel's with.'

'Well, what's the matter with that?' said Valancy.

'We may have to sit here all night,' said Barney.

'I don't mind,' said Valancy.

Barney gave a short laugh. 'If you don't, I needn't. I haven't any reputation to lose.'

'Nor I,' said Valancy comfortably.

TWENTY-ONE

'We'll just sit here,' said Barney, 'and if we think of anything worthwhile saying we'll say it. Otherwise, not. Don't imagine you're bound to talk to me.'

'John Foster says,' quoted Valancy, '"If you can sit in silence with a person for half an hour and yet be entirely comfortable, you and that person can be friends. If you cannot, friends you'll never be and you need not waste time in trying."'

'Evidently John Foster says a sensible thing once in a while,' conceded Barney.

They sat in silence for a long while. Little rabbits hopped across the road. Once or twice an owl laughed out delightfully. The road beyond them was fringed with the woven shadow lace of trees. Away off to the southwest the sky was full of silvery little cirrus clouds above the spot where Barney's island must be.

Valancy was perfectly happy. Some things dawn on you slowly. Some things come by lightning flashes. Valancy had had a lightning flash.

She knew quite well now that she loved Barney. Yesterday she had been all her own. Now she was this man's. Yet he had done nothing – said nothing. He had not even looked at her as a woman. But that didn't matter. Nor did it matter what he was or what he had done. She loved him without any reservations. Everything in her went out wholly to him. She had no wish to stifle or disown her love. She seemed to be his so absolutely that thought apart from him – thought in which he did not predominate – was an impossibility.

She had realised, quite simply and fully, that she loved him, in the moment when he was leaning on the car door, explaining that Lady Jane had no gas. She had looked deep into his eyes in the moonlight and had known. In just that infinitesimal space of time everything was changed. Old things passed away and all things became new.

She was no longer unimportant, little old maid Valancy Stirling. She was a woman, full of love and therefore rich and significant – justified to herself. Life was no longer empty and futile, and death could cheat her of nothing. Love had cast out her last fear.

Love! What a searing, torturing, intolerably sweet thing it was – this possession of body, soul and mind! With something at its core as fine and remote and purely spiritual as the tiny blue spark in the heart of the unbreakable diamond. No dream had ever been like this. She was no longer solitary. She was one of a vast sisterhood – all the women who had ever loved in the world.

Barney need never know it – though she would not in the least have minded his knowing. But she knew it and it made a tremendous difference to her. Just to love! She did not ask to be loved. It was rapture enough just to sit there beside him in silence, alone in the summer night in the white splendour of moonshine, with the wind blowing down on them out of the pine woods. She had always envied the wind. So free. Blowing where it listed. Through the hills. Over the lakes. What a tang, what a zip it had! What a magic of adventure! Valancy felt as if she had exchanged her shop-worn soul for a fresh one, fire-new from the workshop of the gods. As far back as she could look, life had been dull – colourless – savourless. Now she had come to a little patch of violets, purple and fragrant – hers for the plucking. No matter who or what had been in Barney's past – no matter who or what might be in his future – no one else could ever have this perfect hour. She surrendered herself utterly to the charm of the moment.

'Ever dream of ballooning?' said Barney suddenly.

'No,' said Valancy.

'I do – often. Dream of sailing through the clouds – seeing the glories of sunset – spending hours in the midst of a terrific storm with lightning playing above and below you – skimming above a silver cloud floor under a full moon – wonderful!'

'It does sound so,' said Valancy. 'I've stayed on earth in my dreams.'

She told him about her Blue Castle. It was so easy to tell Barney things. One felt he understood everything – even the things you didn't tell him. And then she told him a little of her existence before she came to Roaring Abel's. She wanted him to see why she had gone to the dance 'up back'.

'You see – I've never had any real life,' she said. 'I've just – breathed. Every door has always been shut to me.'

'But you're still young,' said Barney.

'Oh, I know. Yes, I'm "still young" – but that's so different from young,' said Valancy bitterly. For a moment she was tempted to tell Barney why her years had nothing to do with her future; but she did not. She was not going to think of death tonight.

'Though I never was really young,' she went on – 'until tonight', she added in her heart. 'I never had a life like other girls. You couldn't understand. Why,' – she had a desperate desire that Barney should know the worst about her – 'I didn't even love my mother. Isn't it awful that I don't love my mother?'

'Rather awful – for her,' said Barney drily.

'Oh, she didn't know it. She took my love for granted. And I wasn't any use or comfort to her or anybody. I was just a – a – vegetable. And I got tired of it. That's why I came to keep house for Mr Gay and look after Cissy.'

'And I suppose your people thought you'd gone mad.'

'They did – and do – literally,' said Valancy. 'But it's a comfort to them. They'd rather believe me mad than bad. There's no other alternative. But I've been living since I came to Mr Gay's. It's been a delightful experience. I suppose I'll pay for it when I have to go back – but I'll have had it.'

'That's true,' said Barney. 'If you buy your experience it's your own. So it's no matter how much you pay for it. Somebody else's experience can never be yours. Well, it's a funny old world.'

'Do you think it really is old?' asked Valancy dreamily. 'I never believe that in June. It seems so young tonight – somehow. In that quivering moonlight – like a young, white girl – waiting.'

'Moonlight here on the verge of up back is different from moonlight anywhere else,' agreed Barney. 'It always makes me feel so clean, somehow – body and soul. And of course the age of gold always comes back in spring.'

It was ten o'clock now. A dragon of black cloud ate up the moon. The spring air grew chill – Valancy shivered. Barney reached back into the innards of Lady Jane and clawed up an old, tobacco-scented overcoat.

'Put that on,' he ordered.

'Don't you want it yourself?' protested Valancy.

'No. I'm not going to have you catching cold on my hands.'

'Oh, I won't catch cold. I haven't had a cold since I came to Mr Gay's – though I've done the foolishest things. It's funny, too – I used to have them all the time. I feel so selfish taking your coat.'

'You've sneezed three times. No use winding up your "experience" up back with grippe or pneumonia.'

He pulled it up tight about her throat and buttoned it on her. Valancy submitted with secret delight. How nice it was to have someone look after you so! She snuggled down into the tobaccoey folds and wished the night could last forever.

Ten minutes later a car swooped down on them from 'up back'. Barney sprang from Lady Jane and waved his hand. The car came to a stop beside them. Valancy saw Uncle Wellington and Olive gazing at her in horror from it.

So Uncle Wellington had got a car! And he must have been spending the evening up at Mistawis with Cousin Herbert. Valancy almost laughed aloud at the expression on his face as he recognised her. The pompous, be-whiskered old humbug!

'Can you let me have enough gas to take me to Deerwood?' Barney was asking politely. But Uncle Wellington was not attending to him.

'Valancy, how came you here!' he said sternly.

'By chance or God's grace,' said Valancy.

'With this jailbird – at ten o'clock at night!' said Uncle Wellington.

Valancy turned to Barney. The moon had escaped from its dragon and in its light her eyes were full of deviltry.

'Are you a jailbird?'

'Does it matter?' said Barney, gleams of fun in his eyes.

'Not to me. I only asked out of curiosity,' continued Valancy.

'Then I won't tell you. I never satisfy curiosity.' He turned to Uncle Wellington and his voice changed subtly.

'Mr Stirling, I asked you if you could let me have some gas. If you can, well and good. If not, we are only delaying you unnecessarily.'

Uncle Wellington was in a horrible dilemma. To give gas to this shameless pair! But not to give it to them! To go away and leave them there in the Mistawis woods – until daylight, likely. It was better to give it to them and let them get out of sight before anyone else saw them.

'Got anything to get gas in?' he grunted surlily.

Barney produced a two-gallon measure from Lady Jane. The two men went to the rear of the Stirling car and began manipulating the tap. Valancy stole sly glances at Olive over the collar of Barney's coat. Olive was sitting grimly staring straight ahead with an outraged expression. She did not mean to take any notice of Valancy. Olive had her own secret reasons for feeling outraged. Cecil had been in Deerwood lately and of course had heard all about Valancy. He agreed that her mind was changed and was exceedingly anxious to find out whence the derangement had been inherited. It was a serious thing to have in the family – a very serious thing. One had to think of one's – descendants.

'She got it from the Wansbarras,' said Olive positively. 'There's nothing like that in the Stirlings – nothing!'

'I hope not – I certainly hope not,' Cecil had responded dubiously. 'But then – to go out as a servant – for that is what it practically amounts to. Your cousin!'

Poor Olive felt the implication. The Port Lawrence Prices were not accustomed to ally themselves with families whose members 'worked out'.

Valancy could not resist temptation. She leaned forward.

'Olive, does it hurt?'

Olive bit – stiffly.

'Does what hurt?'

'Looking like that.'

For a moment Olive resolved she would take no further notice of Valancy. Then duty came uppermost. She must not miss the opportunity.

'Doss,' she implored, leaning forward also, 'won't you come home – come home tonight?'

Valancy yawned.

'You sound like a revival meeting,' she said. 'You really do.'

'If you will come back –'

'All will be forgiven.'

'Yes,' said Olive eagerly. Wouldn't it be splendid if she could induce the prodigal daughter to return? 'We'll never cast it up to you. Doss, there are nights when I cannot sleep for thinking of you.'

'And me having the time of my life,' said Valancy, laughing.

'Doss, I can't believe you're bad. I've always said you couldn't be bad –'

'I don't believe I can be,' said Valancy. 'I'm afraid I'm hopelessly proper. I've been sitting here for three hours with Barney Snaith and he hasn't even tried to kiss me. I wouldn't have minded if he had, Olive.'

Valancy was still leaning forward. Her little hat with its crimson rose was tilted down over one eye – Valancy's smile – what had happened to Valancy! She looked – not pretty – Doss couldn't be pretty – but provocative, fascinating – yes, abominably so. Olive drew back. It was beneath her dignity to say more. After all, Valancy must be both mad and bad.

'Thanks – that's enough,' said Barney behind the car. 'Much obliged, Mr Stirling. Two gallons – seventy cents. Thank you.'

Uncle Wellington climbed foolishly and feebly into his car. He wanted to give Snaith a piece of his mind, but dared not. Who knew what the creature might do if provoked? No doubt he carried firearms.

Uncle Wellington looked indecisively at Valancy. But Valancy had turned her back on him and was watching Barney pour the gas into Lady Jane's maw.

'Drive on,' said Olive decisively. 'There's no use in waiting here. Let me tell you what she said to me.'

'The little hussy! The shameless little hussy!' said Uncle Wellington.

TWENTY-TWO

The next thing the Stirlings heard was that Valancy had been seen with Barney Snaith in a movie theatre in Port Lawrence and after it at supper in a Chinese restaurant there. This was quite true – and no one was more surprised at it than Valancy herself. Barney had come along in Lady Jane one dim twilight and told Valancy unceremoniously if she wanted a drive to hop in.

'I'm going to the Port. Will you go there with me?'

His eyes were teasing and there was a bit of defiance in his voice. Valancy, who did not conceal from herself that she would have gone anywhere with him to any place, 'hopped in' without more ado. They tore into and through Deerwood. Mrs Frederick and Cousin Stickles, taking a little air on the veranda, saw them whirl by in a cloud of dust and sought comfort in each other's eye. Valancy, who in some dim pre-existence had been afraid of a car, was hatless and her hair was blowing wildly round her face. She would certainly come down with bronchitis – and die at Roaring Abel's. She wore a low-neck dress and her arms were bare. That Snaith creature was in his shirt-sleeves, smoking a pipe. They were going at the rate of forty miles an hour – sixty, Cousin Stickles averred. Lady Jane could hit the pike when she wanted to. Valancy waved her hand gaily to her relatives. As for Mrs Frederick, she was wishing she knew how to go into hysterics.

'Was it for this,' she demanded in hollow tones, 'that I suffered the pangs of motherhood?'

'I will not believe,' said Cousin Stickles solemnly, 'that our prayers will not yet be answered.'

'Who – who will protect that unfortunate girl when I am gone?' moaned Mrs Frederick.

As for Valancy, she was wondering if it could really be only a few weeks since she had sat there with them on that veranda.

Hating the rubberplant. Pestered with teasing questions like black flies. Always thinking of appearances. Cowed because of Aunt Wellington's teaspoons and Uncle Benjamin's money. Poverty-stricken. Afraid of everybody. Envying Olive. A slave to moth-eaten traditions. Nothing to hope for or expect.

And now every day was a gay adventure.

Lady Jane flew over the fifteen miles between Deerwood and the Port – through the Port. The way Barney went past traffic policemen was not holy. The lights were beginning to twinkle out like stars in the clear, lemon-hued twilight air. This was the only time Valancy ever really liked the town, and she was crazy with the delight of speeding. Was it possible she had ever been afraid of a car? She was perfectly happy, riding beside Barney. Not that she deluded herself into thinking it had any significance. She knew quite well that Barney had asked her to go on the impulse of the moment – an impulse born of a feeling of pity for her and her starved little dreams. She was looking tired after a wakeful night with a heart attack, followed by a busy day. She had so little fun. He'd give her an outing for once. Besides, Abel was in the kitchen, at the point of drunkenness where he was declaring he did not believe in God and beginning to sing ribald songs. It was just as well she should be out of the way for a while. Barney knew Roaring Abel's repertoire.

They went to the movie – Valancy had never been to a movie. And then, finding a nice hunger upon them, they went and had fried chicken – unbelievable delicious – in the Chinese restaurant. After which they rattled home again, leaving a devastating trail of scandal behind them. Mrs Frederick gave up going to church altogether. She could not endure her friends' pitying glances and questions. But Cousin Stickles went every Sunday. She said they had been given a cross to bear.

TWENTY-THREE

On one of Cissy's wakeful nights, she told Valancy her poor little story. They were sitting by the open window. Cissy could not get her breath lying down that night. An inglorious gibbous moon was hanging over the wooded hills and in its spectral light Cissy looked frail and lovely and incredibly young. A child. It did not seem possible that she could have lived through all the passion and pain and shame of her story.

'He was stopping at the hotel across the lake. He used to come over in his canoe at night – we met in the pines down the shore. He was a young college student – his father was a rich man in Toronto. Oh, Valancy, I didn't mean to be bad – I didn't, indeed. But I loved him so – I love him yet – I'll always love him. And I – didn't know – some things. I didn't understand. Then his father came and took him away. And – after a little – I found out – oh, Valancy, – I was so frightened. I didn't know what to do. I wrote him – and he came. He – he said he would marry me, Valancy.'

'And why – and why?'

'Oh, Valancy, he didn't love me any more. I saw that at a glance. He – he was just offering to marry me because he thought he ought to – because he was sorry for me. He wasn't bad – but he was so young – and what was I that he should keep on loving me?'

'Never mind making excuses for him,' said Valancy a bit shortly. 'So you wouldn't marry him?'

'I couldn't – not when he didn't love me any more. Somehow – I can't explain – it seemed a worse thing to do than – the other. He – he argued a little – but he went away. Do you think I did right, Valancy?'

'Yes, I do. You did right. But he –'

'Don't blame him, dear. Please don't. Let's not talk about him at all. There's no need. I wanted to tell you how it was – I didn't want you to think me bad –'

'I never did think so.'

'Yes, I felt that – whenever you came. Oh, Valancy, what you've been to me! I can never tell you – but God will bless you for it. I know He will – "with what measure ye mete".'

Cissy sobbed for a few minutes in Valancy's arms. Then she wiped her eyes.

'Well, that's almost all. I came home. I wasn't really so very unhappy. I suppose I should have been – but I wasn't. Father wasn't hard on me. And my baby was so sweet, Valancy – with such lovely blue eyes – and little rings of pale gold hair like silk floss – and tiny dimpled hands. I used to bite his satin-smooth little face all over – softly, so as not to hurt him, you know –'

'I know,' said Valancy, wincing. 'I know – a woman always knows – and dreams –'

'And he was all mine. Nobody else had any claim on him. When he died, oh, Valancy, I thought I must die too – I didn't see how anybody could endure such anguish and live. To see his dear little eyes and know he would never open them again – to miss his warm little body nestled against mine at night and think of him sleeping alone and cold, his wee face under the hard frozen earth. It was so awful for the first year – after that it was a little easier, one didn't keep thinking "this day last year" – but I was so glad when I found out I was dying.'

'Who could endure life if it were not for the hope of death?' murmured Valancy softly – it was of course a quotation from some book of John Foster's.

'I'm glad I've told you all about it,' sighed Cissy. 'I wanted you to know.'

Cissy died a few nights after that. Roaring Abel was away. When Valancy saw the change that had come over Cissy's face she wanted to telephone for the doctor. But Cissy wouldn't let her.

'Valancy, why should you? He can do nothing for me. I've known for several days that – this – was near. Let me die in peace, dear – just holding your hand. Oh, I'm so glad you're here. Tell Father goodbye for me. He's always been as good to me as he knew how – and Barney. Somehow, I think that Barney –'

But a spasm of coughing interrupted and exhausted her. She fell asleep when it was over, still holding to Valancy's hand. Valancy sat there in the silence. She was not frightened – or even sorry. At sunrise Cissy died. She opened her eyes and looked past Valancy at something – something that made her smile suddenly and happily. And, smiling, she died.

Valancy crossed Cissy's hands on her breast and went to the open window. In the eastern sky, amid the fires of sunrise, an old moon was hanging – as slender and lovely as a new moon. Valancy had never seen an old, old moon before. She watched it pale and fade until it paled and faded out of sight in the living rose of day. A little pool in the barrens shone in the sunrise like a great golden lily.

But the world suddenly seemed a colder place to Valancy. Again nobody needed her. She was not in the least sorry Cecilia was dead. She was only sorry for all her suffering in life. But nobody could ever hurt her again. Valancy had always thought death dreadful. But Cissy had died so quietly – so pleasantly. And at the very last – something – had made up to her for everything. She was lying there now, in her white sleep, looking like a child. Beautiful! All the lines of shame and pain gone.

Roaring Abel drove in, justifying his name. Valancy went down and told him. The shock sobered him at once. He slumped down on the seat of his buggy, his great head hanging.

'Cissy dead – Cissy dead,' he said vacantly. 'I didn't think it would 'a' come so soon. Dead. She used to run down the lane to meet me with a little white rose stuck in her hair. Cissy used to be a pretty little girl. And a good little girl.'

'She has always been a good little girl,' said Valancy.

TWENTY-FOUR

Valancy herself made Cissy ready for burial. No hands but hers
should touch that pitiful, wasted little body. The old house was
spotless on the day of burial. Barney Snaith was not there. He had
done all he could to help Valancy before it – he had shrouded the
pale Cecilia in white roses from the garden – and then had gone
back to his island. But everybody else was there. All Deerwood and
'up back' came. They forgave Cissy splendidly at last. Mr Bradly
gave a very beautiful funeral address. Valancy had wanted her old
Free Methodist man, but Roaring Abel was obdurate. He was a
Presbyterian and no one but a Presbyterian minister should bury
his daughter. Mr Bradly was very tactful. He avoided all dubious
points and it was plain to be seen he hoped for the best. Six reputable
citizens of Deerwood bore Cecilia Gay to her grave in decorous
Deerwood cemetery. Among them was Uncle Wellington.

The Stirlings all came to the funeral, men and women. They had
had a family conclave over it. Surely now that Cissy Gay was dead
Valancy would come home. She simply could not stay there with
Roaring Abel. That being the case, the wisest course – decreed
Uncle James – was to attend the funeral – legitimise the whole
thing, so to speak – show Deerwood that Valancy had really done
a most creditable deed in going to nurse poor Cecilia Gay and that
her family backed her up in it. Death, the miracle worker, suddenly
made the thing quite respectable. If Valancy would return to
home and decency while public opinion was under its influence
all might yet be well. Society was suddenly forgetting all Cecilia's
wicked doings and remembering what a pretty, modest little thing
she had been – 'and motherless, you know – motherless!' It was
the psychological moment – said Uncle James.

So the Stirlings went to the funeral. Even Cousin Gladys' neuritis
allowed her to come. Cousin Stickles was there, her bonnet dripping

all over her face, crying as woefully as if Cissy had been her nearest and dearest. Funerals always brought Cousin Stickles' 'own sad bereavement' back.

And Uncle Wellington was a pallbearer.

Valancy, pale, subdued-looking, her slanted eyes smudged with purple, in her snuff-brown dress, moving quietly about, finding seats for people, consulting in undertones with minister and undertaker, marshalling the 'mourners' into the parlour, was so decorous and proper and Stirlingish that her family took heart of grace. This was not – could not be – the girl who had sat all night in the woods with Barney Snaith – who had gone tearing bareheaded through Deerwood and Port Lawrence. This was the Valancy they knew. Really, surprisingly capable and efficient. Perhaps she had always been kept down a bit too much – Amelia really was rather strict – hadn't had a chance to show what was in her. So thought the Stirlings. And Edward Beck, from the Port road, a widower with a large family who was beginning to take notice, took notice of Valancy and thought she might make a mighty fine second wife. No beauty – but a fifty-year-old widower, Mr Beck told himself very reasonably, couldn't expect everything. Altogether, it seemed that Valancy's matrimonial chances were never so bright as they were at Cecilia Gay's funeral.

What the Stirlings and Edward Beck would have thought had they known the back of Valancy's mind must be left to the imagination. Valancy was hating the funeral – hating the people who came to stare with curiosity at Cecilia's marble-white face – hating the smugness – hating the dragging, melancholy singing – hating Mr Bradly's cautious platitudes. If she could have had her absurd way, there would have been no funeral at all. She would have covered Cissy over with flowers, shut her away from prying eyes, and buried her beside her nameless little baby in the grassy burying-ground under the pines of the 'up back' church, with a bit of kindly prayer from the old Free Methodist minister. She remembered Cissy saying once, 'I wish I could be buried deep in the heart of the woods where nobody would ever come to say, "Cissy Gay is buried here" and tell over my miserable story."

But this! However, it would soon be over. Valancy knew, if the Stirlings and Edward Beck didn't, exactly what she intended to do then. She had lain awake all the preceding night thinking about it and finally deciding on it.

When the funeral procession had left the house, Mrs Frederick sought out Valancy in the kitchen.

'My child,' she said tremulously, 'you'll come home now?'

'Home,' said Valancy absently. She was getting on an apron and calculating how much tea she must put to steep for supper. There would be several guests from 'up back' – distant relatives of the Gays' who had not remembered them for years. And she was so tired she wished she could borrow a pair of legs from the cat.

'Yes, home,' said Mrs Frederick, with a touch of asperity. 'I suppose you won't dream of staying here now – alone with Roaring Abel.'

'Oh, no, I'm not going to stay here,' said Valancy. 'Of course, I'll have to stay for a day or two, to put the house in order generally. But that will be all. Excuse me, Mother, won't you? I've a frightful lot to do – all those "up back" people will be here to supper.'

Mrs Frederick retreated in considerable relief, and the Stirlings went home with lighter hearts.

'We will just treat her as if nothing had happened when she comes back,' decreed Uncle Benjamin. 'That will be the best plan. Just as if nothing had happened.'

TWENTY-FIVE
❦

On the evening of the day after the funeral Roaring Abel went off for a spree. He had been sober for four whole days and could endure it no longer. Before he went, Valancy told him she would be going away the next day. Roaring Abel was sorry, and said so. A distant cousin from 'up back' was coming to keep house for him – quite willing to do so now since there was no sick girl to wait on – but Abel was not under any delusions concerning her.

'She won't be like you, my girl. Well, I'm obliged to you. You helped me out of a bad hole and I won't forget it. And I won't forget what you did for Cissy. I'm your friend, and if you ever want any of the Stirlings spanked and put in a corner send for me. I'm going to wet my whistle. Lord, but I'm dry! Don't reckon I'll be back afore tomorrow night, so if you're going home tomorrow, goodbye now.'

'I may go home tomorrow,' said Valancy, 'but I'm not going back to Deerwood.'

'Not going –'

'You'll find the key on the woodshed nail,' interrupted Valancy, politely and unmistabably. 'The dog will be in the barn and the cat in the cellar. Don't forget to feed her till your cousin comes. The pantry is full and I made bread and pies today. Goodbye, Mr Gay. You have been very kind to me and I appreciate it.'

'We've had a d – – d decent time of it together, and that's a fact,' said Roaring Abel. 'You're the best small sport in the world, and your little finger is worth the whole Stirling clan tied together. Goodbye and good luck.'

Valancy went out to the garden. Her legs trembled a little, but otherwise she felt and looked composed. She held something tightly in her hand. The garden was lying in the magic of the warm, odorous July twilight. A few stars were out and the robins were calling through the velvety silences of the barrens. Valancy stood by the gate expectantly. Would he come? If he did not –

He was coming. Valancy heard Lady Jane Grey far back in the woods. Her breath came a little more quickly. Nearer – and nearer – she could see Lady Jane now – bumping down the lane – nearer – nearer – he was there – he had sprung from the car and leaning over the gate, looking at her.

'Going home, Miss Stirling?'

'I don't know – yet,' said Valancy slowly. Her mind was made up, with no shadow of turning, but the moment was very tremendous.

'I thought I'd run down and ask if there was anything I could do for you,' said Barney.

Valancy took it with a canter.

'Yes, there is something you can do for me,' she said, evenly and distinctly. 'Will you marry me?'

For a moment Barney was silent. There was no particular expression on his face. Then he gave an odd laugh.

'Come, now! I knew luck was just waiting around the corner for me. All the signs have been pointing that way today.'

'Wait.' Valancy lifted her hand. 'I'm in earnest – but I want to get my breath after that question. Of course, with my bringing up, I realise perfectly well that this is one of the things "a lady should not do".'

'But why – why?'

'For two reasons.' Valancy was still a little breathless, but she looked Barney straight in the eyes while all the dead Stirlings revolved rapidly in their graves and the living ones did nothing because they did not know that Valancy was at that moment proposing lawful marriage to the notorious Barney Snaith. 'The first reason is, I – I –' Valancy tried to say 'I love you' but could not. She had to take refuge in a pretended flippancy. 'I'm crazy about you. The second is – this.'

She handed him Dr Trent's letter.

Barney opened it with the air of a man thankful to find some safe, sane thing to do. As he read it his face changed. He understood – more perhaps than Valancy wanted him to.

'Are you sure nothing can be done for you?'

Valancy did not misunderstand the question.

'Yes. You know Dr Trent's reputation in regard to heart disease. I haven't long to live – perhaps only a few months – a few weeks. I want to live them. I can't go back to Deerwood – you know what my life was like there. And' – she managed it this time – 'I love you. I want to spend the rest of my life with you. That's all.'

Barney folded his arms on the gate and looked gravely enough at a white, saucy star that was winking at him just over Roaring Abel's kitchen chimney.

'You don't know anything about me. I may be a – murderer.'

'No, I don't. You may be something dreadful. Everything they say of you may be true. But it doesn't matter to me.'

'You care that much for me, Valancy?' said Barney incredulously, looking away from the star and into her eyes – her strange, mysterious eyes.

'I care – that much,' said Valancy in a low voice. She was trembling. He had called her by her name for the first time. It was sweeter than another man's caress could have been just to hear him say her name like that.

'If we are going to get married,' said Barney, speaking suddenly in a casual, matter-of-fact voice, 'some things must be understood.'

'Everything must be understood,' said Valancy.

'I have things I want to hide,' said Barney coolly. 'You are not to ask me about them.'

'I won't,' said Valancy.

'You must never ask to see my mail.'

'Never.'

'And we are never to pretend anything to each other.'

'We won't,' said Valancy. 'You won't even have to pretend you like me. If you marry me I know you're only doing it out of pity.'

'And we'll never tell a lie to each other about anything – a big lie or petty lie.'

'Especially a petty lie,' agreed Valancy.

'And you'll have to live back on my island. I won't live any-where else.'

'That's partly why I want to marry you,' said Valancy.

Barney peered at her.

'I believe you mean it. Well – let's get married, then.'

'Thank you,' said Valancy, with a sudden return of primness. She would have been much less embarrassed if he had refused her.

'I suppose I haven't any right to make conditions. But I'm going to make one. You are never to refer to my heart or my liability to sudden death. You are never to urge me to be careful. You are to forget – absolutely forget – that I'm not perfectly healthy. I have written a letter to my mother – here it is – you are to keep it. I have explained everything in it. If I drop dead suddenly – as I likely will do –'

'It will exonerate me in the eyes of your kindred from the suspicion of having poisoned you,' said Barney with a grin.

'Exactly.' Valancy laughed gaily. 'Dear me, I'm glad this is over. It has been – a bit of an ordeal. You see, I'm not in the habit of going about asking men to marry me. It is so nice of you not to refuse me – or offer to be a brother!'

'I'll go to the Port tomorrow and get a license. We can be married tomorrow evening. Dr Stalling, I suppose?'

'Heavens, no.' Valancy shuddered. 'Besides, he wouldn't do it. He'd shake his forefinger at me and I'd jilt you at the altar. No, I want my old Mr Towers to marry me.'

'Will you marry me as I stand?' demanded Barney. A passing car, full of tourists, honked loudly – it seemed derisively. Valancy looked at him. Blue homespun shirt, nondescript hat, muddy overalls. Unshaved!

'Yes,' she said.

Barney put his hands over the gate and took her little, cold ones gently in his.

'Valancy,' he said, trying to speak lightly, 'of course I'm not in love with you – never thought of such a thing as being in love. But, do you know, I've always thought you were a bit of a dear.'

TWENTY-SIX

The next day passed for Valancy like a dream. She could not make herself or anything she did seem real. She saw nothing of Barney, though she expected he must go rattling past on his way to the Port for a license.

Perhaps he had changed his mind.

But at dusk the lights of Lady Jane suddenly swooped over the crest of the wooded hill beyond the lane. Valancy was waiting at the gate for her bridegroom. She wore her green dress and her green hat because she had nothing else to wear. She did not look or feel at all bride-like – she really looked like a wild elf strayed out of the greenwood. But that did not matter. Nothing at all mattered except that Barney was coming for her.

'Ready?' said Barney, stopping Lady Jane with some new, horrible noises.

'Yes.' Valancy stepped in and sat down. Barney was in his blue shirt and overalls. But they were clean overalls. He was smoking a villainous-looking pipe and he was bareheaded. But he had a pair of oddly smart boots on under his shabby overalls. And he was shaved. They clattered into Deerwood and through Deerwood and hit the long, wooded road to the Port.

'Haven't changed your mind?' said Barney.

'No. Have you?'

'No.'

That was their whole conversation on the fifteen miles. Everything was more dream-like than ever. Valancy didn't know whether she felt happy. Or terrified. Or just plain fool.

Then the lights of Port Lawrence were about them. Valancy felt as if she were surrounded by the gleaming, hungry eyes of hundreds of great, stealthy panthers. Barney briefly asked where Mr Towers lived, and Valancy as briefly told him. They stopped before the shabby little house in an unfashionable street. They went in to the small, shabby parlour. Barney produced his license. So he had got it. Also a ring. This thing was real. She, Valancy Stirling, was actually on the point of being married.

They were standing up together before Mr Towers. Valancy heard Mr Towers and Barney saying things. She heard some other person saying things. She herself was thinking of the way she had once planned to be married – away back in her early teens when such a thing had not seemed impossible. White silk and tulle veil and orange-blossoms; no bridesmaid. But one flower girl, in a frock of cream shadow lace over pale pink, with a wreath of flowers in her hair, carrying a basket of roses and lilies-of-the-valley. And the groom, a noble-looking creature, irreproachably clad in whatever the fashion of the day decreed. Valancy lifted her eyes and saw herself and Barney in the little slanting, distorting mirror over the mantelpiece. She in her odd, unbridal green hat and dress; Barney in shirt and overalls. But it was Barney. That was all that mattered. No veil – no flowers – no guests – no presents – no wedding cake – but just Barney. For all the rest of her life there would be Barney.

'Mrs Snaith, I hope you will be very happy,' Mr Towers was saying.

He had not seemed surprised at their appearance – not even at Barney's overalls. He had seen plenty of queer weddings 'up back'. He did not know Valancy was one of the Deerwood Stirlings – he did not even know there were Deerwood Stirlings. He did not know Barney Snaith was a fugitive from justice. Really, he was an incredibly ignorant old man. Therefore he married them and gave them his blessing very gently and solemnly and prayed for them that night after they had gone away. His conscience did not trouble him at all.

'What a nice way to get married!' Barney was saying as he put Lady Jane in gear. 'No fuss and flub-dub. I never supposed it was half so easy.'

'For heaven's sake,' said Valancy suddenly, 'let's forget we are married and talk as if we weren't. I can't stand another drive like the one we had coming in.'

Barney howled and threw Lady Jane into high with an infernal noise.

'And I thought I was making it easy for you,' he said. 'You didn't seem to want to talk.'

'I didn't. But I wanted you to talk. I don't want you to make love to me, but I want you to act like an ordinary human being. Tell me about this island of yours. What sort of a place is it?'

'The jolliest place in the world. You're going to love it. The first time I saw it I loved it. Old Tom MacMurray owned it then. He built the little shack on it, lived there in winter and rented it to Toronto people in summer. I bought it from him – became by that one simple transaction a landed proprietor owning a house and an island. There is something so satisfying in owning a whole island. And isn't an uninhabited island a charming idea? I'd wanted to own one ever since I'd read Robinson Crusoe. It seemed too good to be true. And beauty! Most of the scenery belongs to the government, but they don't tax you for looking at it, and the moon belongs to everybody. You won't find my shack very tidy. I suppose you'll want to make it tidy.'

'Yes,' said Valancy honestly. 'I have to be tidy. I don't really want to be. But untidiness hurts me. Yes, I'll have to tidy up your shack.'

'I was prepared for that,' said Barney, with a hollow groan.

'But,' continued Valancy relentingly, 'I won't insist on your wiping your feet when you come in.'

'No, you'll only sweep up after me with the air of a martyr,' said Barney. 'Well, anyway, you can't tidy the lean-to. You can't even enter it. The door will be locked and I shall keep the key.'

'Bluebeard's chamber,' said Valancy. 'I shan't even think of it. I don't care how many wives you have hanging up in it. So long as they're really dead.'

'Dead as door-nails. You can do as you like in the rest of the house. There's not much of it – just one big living-room and one small bedroom. Well built, though. Old Tom loved his job. The beams of our house are cedar and the rafters fir. Our living-room windows face west and east. It's wonderful to have a room where you can see both sunrise and sunset. I have two cats there. Banjo and Good luck. Adorable animals. Banjo is a big, enchanting, grey devil-cat. Striped, of course. I don't care a hang for any cat that hasn't stripes. I never knew a cat who could swear as genteely and effectively as Banjo. His only fault is that he snores horribly when he is asleep. Luck is a dainty little cat. Always looking wistfully at you, as if he wanted to tell you something. Maybe he will pull it off sometime. Once in a thousand years, you know, one cat is allowed to speak. My cats are philosophers – neither of them ever cries over spilt milk.

'Two old crows live in a pine-tree on the point and are reasonably neighbourly. Call 'em Nip and Tuck. And I have a demure little tame owl. Name, Leander. I brought him up from a baby and he lives over on the mainland and chuckles to himself o'nights. And bats – it's a great place for bats at night. Scared of bats?'

'No; I like them.'

'So do I. Nice, queer, uncanny, mysterious creatures. Coming from nowhere – going nowhere. Swoop! Banjo likes 'em, too. Eats 'em.

I have a canoe and a disappearing propeller boat. Went to the Port in it today to get my license. Quieter than Lady Jane.'

'I thought you hadn't gone at all – that you had changed your mind,' admitted Valancy.

Barney laughed – the laugh Valancy did not like – the little, bitter, cynical laugh.

'I never change my mind,' he said shortly. They went back through Deerwood. Up the Muskoka road. Past Roaring Abel's. Over the rocky, daisied lane. The dark pine woods swallowed them up. Through the pine woods, where the air was sweet with the incense of the unseen, fragile bells of the linnaeas that carpeted the banks of the trail. Out to the shore of Mistawis. Lady Jane must be left here. They got out. Barney led the way down a little path to the edge of the lake.

'There's our island,' he said gloatingly.

Valancy looked – and looked – and looked again. There was a diaphanous, lilac mist on the lake, shrouding the island. Through it the two enormous pine-trees that clasped hands over Barney's shack loomed out like dark turrets. Behind them was a sky still rose-hued in the afterlight, and a pale young moon.

Valancy shivered like a tree the wind stirs suddenly. Something seemed to sweep over her soul.

'My Blue Castle!' she said. 'Oh, my Blue Castle!'

They got into the canoe and paddled out to it. They left behind the realm of everyday and things known and landed on a realm of mystery and enchantment where anything might happen – anything might be true. Barney lifted Valancy out of the canoe and swung her to a lichen-covered rock under a young pine-tree. His arms were about her and suddenly his lips were on hers. Valancy found herself shivering with the rapture of her first kiss.

'Welcome home, dear,' Barney was saying.

TWENTY-SEVEN

Cousin Georgiana came down the lane leading up to her little house. She lived half a mile out of Deerwood and she wanted to go in to Amelia's and find out if Doss had come home yet. Cousin Georgiana was anxious to see Doss. She had something very important to tell her. Something, she was sure, Doss would be delighted to hear. Poor Doss! She had had rather a dull life of it. Cousin Georgiana owned to herself that she would not like to live under Amelia's thumb. But that would be all changed now. Cousin Georgiana felt tremendously important. For the time being, she quite forgot to wonder which of them would go next.

And here was Doss herself, coming along the road from Roaring Abel's in such a queer green dress and hat. Talk about luck. Cousin Georgiana would have a chance to impart her wonderful secret right away, with nobody else about to interrupt. It was, you might say, a Providence.

Valancy, who had been living for four days on her enchanted island, had decided that she might as well go in to Deerwood and tell her relatives that she was married. Otherwise, finding that she had disappeared from Roaring Abel's, they might get out a search warrant for her. Barney had offered to drive her in, but she had preferred to go alone. She smiled very radiantly at Cousin Georgiana, who, she remembered, as of someone known a long time ago, had really been not a bad little creature. Valancy was so happy that she could have smiled at anybody – even Uncle James. She was not averse to Cousin Georgiana's company. Already, since the houses along the road were becoming numerous, she was conscious that curious eyes were looking at her from every window.

'I suppose you're going home, dear Doss?' said Cousin Georgiana as she shook hands – furtively eyeing Valancy's dress and wondering if she had any petticoat on at all.

'Sooner or later,' said Valancy cryptically.

'Then I'll go along with you. I've been wanting to see you very especially, Doss dear. I've something quite wonderful to tell you.'

'Yes?' said Valancy absently. What on earth was Cousin Georgiana looking so mysterious and important about? But did it matter? No. Nothing mattered but Barney and the Blue Castle up back in Mistawis.

'Who do you suppose called to see me the other day?' asked Cousin Georgiana archly.

Valancy couldn't guess.

'Edward Beck.' Cousin Georgiana lowered her voice almost to a whisper. 'Edward Beck.'

Why the italics? And was Cousin Georgiana blushing?

'Who on earth is Edward Beck?' asked Valancy indifferently.

Cousin Georgiana stared.

'Surely you remember Edward Beck,' she said reproachfully. 'He lives in that lovely house on the Port Lawrence road and he comes to our church – regularly. You must remember him.'

'Oh, I think I do now,' said Valancy, with an effort of memory. 'He's that old man with a wen on his forehead and dozens of children, who always sits in the pew by the door, isn't he?'

'Not dozens of children, dear – oh, no, not dozens. Not even one dozen. Only nine. At least only nine that count. The rest are dead. He isn't old – he's only about forty-eight – the prime of life, Doss – and what does it matter about a wen?'

'Nothing, of course,' agreed Valancy quite sincerely. It certainly did not matter to her whether Edward Beck had a wen or a dozen wens or no wen at all. But Valancy was getting vaguely suspicious. There was certainly an air of suppressed triumph about Cousin Georgiana. Could it be possible that Cousin Georgiana was thinking of marrying again? Marrying Edward Beck? Absurd. Cousin Georgiana was sixty-five if she were a day and her little anxious face was as closely covered with fine wrinkles as if she had been a hundred. But still –

'My dear,' said Cousin Georgiana, 'Edward Beck wants to marry you.'

Valancy stared at Cousin Georgiana for a moment. Then she wanted to go off into a peal of laughter. But she only said:

'Me?'

'Yes, you. He fell in love with you at the funeral. And he came to consult me about it. I was such a friend of his first wife, you know. He is very much in earnest, Dossie. And it's a wonderful chance for you. He's very well off – and you know – you – you –'

'Am not so young as I once was,' agreed Valancy. '"To her that hath shall be given." Do you really think I would make a good stepmother, Cousin Georgiana?'

'I'm sure you would. You were always so fond of children.'

'But nine is such a family to start with,' objected Valancy gravely.

'The two oldest are grown up and the third almost. That leaves only six that really count. And most of them are boys. So much easier to bring up than girls. There's an excellent book – *Health Care of the Growing Child* – Gladys has a copy, I think. It would be such a help to you. And there are books about morals. You'd manage nicely. Of course I told Mr Beck that I thought you would – would –'

'Jump at him,' supplied Valancy.

'Oh, no, no, dear. I wouldn't use such an indelicate expression. I told him I thought you would consider his proposal favourably. And you will, won't you, dearie?'

'There's only one obstacle,' said Valancy dreamily. 'You see, I'm married already.'

'Married!' Cousin Georgiana stopped stock-still and stared at Valancy. 'Married!'

'Yes. I was married to Barney Snaith last Tuesday evening in Port Lawrence.'

There was a convenient gate-post hard by. Cousin Georgiana took firm hold of it.

'Doss, dear – I'm an old woman – are you trying to make fun of me?'

'Not at all. I'm only telling you the truth. For heaven's sake, Cousin Georgiana,' – Valancy was alarmed by certain symptoms – 'don't go crying here on the public road!'

Cousin Georgiana choked back the tears and gave a little moan of despair instead.

'Oh, Doss, what have you done? What have you done?'

'I've just been telling you. I've got married,' said Valancy, calmly and patiently.

'To that – that – aw – that – Barney Snaith. Why, they say he's had a dozen wives already.'

'I'm the only one round at present,' said Valancy.

'What will your poor mother say?' moaned Cousin Georgiana.

'Come along with me and hear, if you want to know,' said Valancy. 'I'm on my way to tell her now.'

Cousin Georgiana let go the gate-post cautiously and found that she could stand alone. She meekly trotted on beside Valancy – who suddenly seemed quite a different person in her eyes. Cousin Georgiania had a tremendous respect for a married woman. But it was terrible to think of what the poor girl had done. So rash. So reckless. Of course Valancy must be stark mad. But she seemed so happy in her madness that Cousin Georgiana had a momentary conviction that it would be a pity if the clan tried to scold her back to sanity. She had never seen that look in Valancy's eyes before. But what would Amelia say? And Ben?

'To marry a man you know nothing about,' thought Cousin Georgiana aloud.

'I know more about him than I know of Edward Beck,' said Valancy.

'Edward Beck goes to church,' said Cousin Georgiana. 'Does Bar – does your husband?'

'He has promised that he will go with me on fine Sundays,' said Valancy.

When they turned in at the Stirling gate Valancy gave an exclamation of surprise.

'Look at my rosebush! Why, it's blooming!'

It was. Covered with blossoms. Great, crimson, velvety blossoms. Fragrant. Glowing. Wonderful.

'My cutting it to pieces must have done it good,' said Valancy, laughing. She gathered a handful of the blossoms – they would look well on the supper table of the veranda at Mistawis – and went, still laughing, up the walk, conscious that Olive was standing on the steps, Olive, goddess-like in loveliness, looking down with a slight frown on her forehead. Olive, beautiful, insolent. Her full form voluptuous in its swathings of rose silk and lace. Her golden-brown hair curling richly under her big, white-frilled hat. Her colour ripe and melting.

'Beautiful,' thought Valancy coolly, 'but' – as if she suddenly saw her cousin through new eyes – 'without the slightest touch of distinction.'

So Valancy had come home, thank goodness, thought Olive. But Valancy was not looking like a repentant, returned prodigal. This was the cause of Olive's frown. She was looking triumphant – graceless! That outlandish dress – that queer hat – those hands full of blood-red roses. Yet there was something about both dress and hat, as Olive instantly felt, that was entirely lacking in her own attire. This deepened the frown. She put out a condescending hand.

'So you're back, Doss? Very warm day, isn't it? Did you walk in?'

'Yes. Coming in?'

'Oh, no. I've just been in. I've come often to comfort poor Aunty. She's been so lonesome. I'm going to Mrs Bartlett's tea. I have to help pour. She's giving it for her cousin from Toronto. Such a charming girl. You'd have loved meeting her, Doss. I think Mrs Bartlett did send you a card. Perhaps you'll drop in later on.'

'No, I don't think so,' said Valancy indifferently. 'I'll have to be home to get Barney's supper. We're going for a moonlit canoe ride around Mistawa tonight.'

'Barney? Supper?' gasped Olive. 'What do you mean, Valancy Stirling?'

'Valancy Snaith, by the grace of God.'

Valancy flaunted her wedding-ring in Olive's stricken face. Then she nimbly stepped past her and into the house. Cousin Georgiana followed. She would not miss a moment of the great scene, even though Olive did look as if she were going to faint.

Olive did not faint. She went stupidly down the street to Mrs Bartlett's. What did Doss mean? She couldn't have – that ring – oh, what fresh scandal was that wretched girl bringing on her defenceless family now? She should have been – shut up – long ago.

Valancy opened the sitting-room door and stepped unexpectedly right into grim assemblage of Stirlings. They had not come together of malice prepense. Aunt Wellington and Cousin Gladys and Aunt Mildred and Cousin Sarah had just called in on their way home from a meeting of the missionary society. Uncle James had dropped in to give Amelia some information regarding a doubtful investment. Uncle Benjamin had called, apparently, to tell them it was a hot day and ask them what was the difference between a bee and a donkey. Cousin Stickles had been tactless enough to know the answer – 'one gets all the honey, the other all the whacks' – and Uncle Benjamin was in a bad humour. In all of their minds, unexpressed, was the idea of finding out if Valancy had yet come home, and, if not, what steps must be taken in the matter.

Well, here was Valancy at last, a poised, confident thing, not humble and deprecating as she should have been. And so oddly, improperly young-looking. She stood in the doorway and looked at them, Cousin Georgiana timorous, expectant, behind her. Valancy was so happy she didn't hate her people any more. She could even see a number of good qualities in them that she had never seen before. And she was sorry for them. Her pity made her quite gentle.

'Well, Mother,' she said pleasantly.

'So you've come home at last!' said Mrs Frederick, getting out a handkerchief. She dared not be outraged, but she did not mean to be cheated of her tears.

'Well, not exactly,' said Valancy. She threw her bomb. 'I thought I ought to drop in and tell you I was married. Last Tuesday night. To Barney Snaith.'

Uncle Benjamin bounced up and sat down again.

'God bless my soul,' he said dully. The rest seemed turned to stone. Except Cousin Gladys, who turned faint. Aunt Mildred and Uncle Wellington had to help her out to the kitchen.

'She would have to keep up the Victorian traditions,' said Valancy, with a grin. She sat down, uninvited, on a chair. Cousin Stickles had begun to sob.

'Is there one day in your life that you haven't cried?' asked Valancy curiously.

'Valancy,' said Uncle James, being the first to recover the power of utterance, 'did you mean what you said just now?'

'I did.'

'Do you mean to say that you have actually gone and married – married – that notorious Barney Snaith – that – that – criminal – that –'

'I have.'

'Then,' said Uncle James violently, 'you are a shameless creature, lost to all sense of propriety and virtue, and I wash my hands entirely of you. I do not want ever to see your face again.'

'What have you left to say when I commit murder?' asked Valancy.

Uncle Benjamin again appealed to God to bless his soul.

'That drunken outlaw – that –'

A dangerous spark appeared in Valancy's eyes. They might say what they liked to and of her but they should not abuse Barney.

'Say "damn" and you'll feel better,' she suggested.

'I can express my feelings without blasphemy. And I tell you you have covered yourself with eternal disgrace and infamy by marrying that drunkard –'

'You would be more endurable if you got drunk occasionally. Barney is not a drunkard.'

'He was seen drunk in Port Lawrence – pickled to the gills,' said Uncle Benjamin.

'If that is true – and I don't believe it – he had a good reason for it. Now I suggest that you all stop looking tragic and accept the situation. I'm married – you can't undo that. And I'm perfectly happy.'

'I suppose we ought to be thankful he has really married her,' said Cousin Sarah, by way of trying to look on the bright side.

'If he really has,' said Uncle James, who had just washed his hands of Valancy. 'Who married you?'

'Mr Towers, of Port Lawrence.'

'By a Free Methodist!' groaned Mrs Frederick – as if to have been married by an imprisoned Methodist would have been a shade less disgraceful. It was the first thing she had said. Mrs

Frederick didn't know what to say. The whole thing was too horrible – too horrible – too nightmarish. She was sure she must wake up soon. After all their bright hopes at the funeral!

'It makes me think of those what-d'ye-call-'ems,' said Uncle Benjamin helplessly. 'Those yarns – you know – of fairies taking babies out of their cradles.'

'Valancy could hardly be a changeling at twenty-nine,' said Aunt Wellington satirically.

'She was the oddest-looking baby I ever saw, anyway,' averted Uncle Benjamin. 'I said so at the time – you remember, Amelia? I said I had never seen such eyes in a human head.'

'I'm glad I never had any children,' said Cousin Sarah. 'If they don't break your heart in one way they do it in another.'

'Isn't it better to have your heart broken than to have it wither up?' queried Valancy. 'Before it could be broken it must have felt something splendid. That would be worth the pain.'

'Dippy – clean dippy,' muttered Uncle Benjamin, with a vague, unsatisfactory feeling that somebody had said something like that before.

'Valancy,' said Mrs Frederick solemnly, 'do you ever pray to be forgiven for disobeying your mother?'

'I should pray to be forgiven for obeying you so long,' said Valancy stubbornly. 'But I don't pray about that at all. I just thank God every day for my happiness.'

'I would rather,' said Mrs Frederick, beginning to cry rather belatedly, 'see you dead before me than listen to what you have told me today.'

Valancy looked at her mother and aunts, and wondered if they could ever have known anything of the real meaning of love. She felt sorrier for them than ever. They were so very pitiable. And they never suspected it.

'Barney Snaith is a scoundrel to have deluded you into marrying him,' said Uncle James violently.

'Oh, I did the deluding. I asked him to marry me,' said Valancy, with a wicked smile.

'Have you no pride?' demanded Aunt Wellington.

'Lots of it. I am proud that I have achieved a husband by my own unaided efforts. Cousin Georgiana here wanted to help me to Edward Beck.'

'Edward Beck is worth twenty thousand dollars and has the finest house between here and Port Lawrence,' said Uncle Benjamin.

'That sounds very fine,' said Valancy scornfully, 'but it isn't worth that' – she snapped her fingers – 'compared to feeling Barney's arms around me and his cheek against mine.'

'Oh, Doss!' said Cousin Stickles. Cousin Sarah said, 'Oh, Doss!' Aunt Wellington said, 'Valancy, you need not be indecent.'

'Why, it surely isn't indecent to like to have your husband put his arm around you? I should think it would be indecent if you didn't.'

'Why expect decency from her?' inquired Uncle James sarcastically. 'She has cut herself off from decency forevermore. She has made her bed. Let her lie on it.'

'Thanks,' said Valancy very gratefully. 'How you would have enjoyed being Torquemada! Now, I must really be getting back. Mother, may I have those three woollen cushions I worked last winter?'

'Take them – take everything!' said Mrs Frederick.

'Oh, I don't want everything – or much. I don't want my Blue Castle cluttered. Just the cushions. I'll call for them some day when we motor in.'

Valancy rose and went to the door. There she turned. She was sorrier than ever for them all. They had no Blue Castle in the purple solitudes of Mistawis.

'The trouble with you people is that you don't laugh enough,' she said.

'Doss dear,' said Cousin Georgiana mournfully, 'some day you will discover that blood is thicker than water.'

'Of course it is. But who wants water to be thick?' parried Valancy. 'We want water to be thin – sparkling – crystal-clear.'

Cousin Stickles groaned.

Valancy would not ask any of them to come and see her – she was afraid they would come out of curiosity. But she said:

'Do you mind if I drop in and see you once in a while, Mother?'

'My house will always be open to you,' said Mrs Frederick, with a mournful dignity.

'You should never recognise her again,' said Uncle James sternly, as the door closed behind Valancy.

'I cannot quite forget that I am a mother,' said Mrs Frederick. 'My poor, unfortunate girl!'

'I dare say the marriage isn't legal,' said Uncle James comfortingly. 'He has probably been married half a dozen times before. But I am through with her. I have done all I could, Amelia. I think you will admit that. Henceforth' – Uncle James was terribly solemn about it – 'Valancy is to me as one dead.'

'Mrs Barney Snaith,' said Cousin Georgiana, as if trying it out to see how it would sound.

'He has a score of aliases, no doubt,' said Uncle Benjamin. 'For my part, I believe the man is half Indian. I haven't a doubt they're living in a wigwam.' 'If he has married her under the name of Snaith and it isn't his real name wouldn't that make the marriage null and void?' asked Cousin Stickles hopefully.

Uncle James shook his head.

'No, it is the man who marries, not the name.'

'You know,' said Cousin Gladys, who had recovered and returned but was still shaky, 'I had a distinct premonition of this at Herbert's silver dinner. I remarked it at the time. When she was defending Snaith. You remember, of course. It came over me like a revelation. I spoke to David when I went home about it.'

'What – what,' demanded Aunt Wellington of the universe, 'has come over Valancy? Valancy!'

The universe did not answer but Uncle James did.

'Isn't there something coming up of late about secondary personalities cropping out? I don't hold with many of those new-fangled notions, but there may be something in this one. It would account for her incomprehensible conduct.'

'Valancy is so fond of mushrooms,' sighed Cousin Georgiana. 'I'm afraid she'll get poisoned eating toadstools by mistake living up back in the woods.'

'There are worse things than death,' said Uncle James, believing that it was the first time in the world that such statement had been made.

'Nothing can ever be the same again!' sobbed Cousin Stickles.

Valancy, hurrying along the dusty road, back to cool Mistawis and her purple island, had forgotten all about them – just as she had forgotten that she might drop dead at any moment if she hurried.

TWENTY-EIGHT

Summer passed by. The Stirling clan – with the insignificant exception of Cousin Georgiana – had tacitly agreed to follow Uncle James' example and look upon Valancy as one dead. To be sure, Valancy had an unquiet, ghostly habit of recurring resurrections when she and Barney clattered through Deerwood and out to the Port in that unspeakable car. Valancy bareheaded, with stars in her eyes. Barney, bareheaded, smoking his pipe. But shaved. Always shaved now, if any of them had noticed it. They even had the audacity to go in to Uncle Benjamin's store to buy groceries. Twice Uncle Benjamin ignored them. Was not Valancy one of the dead? While Snaith had never existed. But the third time he told Barney he was a scroundrel who should be hung for luring an unfortunate, weak-minded girl away from her home and friends.

Barney's one straight eyebrow went up.

'I have made her happy,' he said coolly, 'and she was miserable with her friends. So that's that.'

Uncle Benjamin stared. It had never occurred to him that women had to be, or ought to be, 'made happy'.

'You – you pup!' he said.

'Why be so unoriginal?' queried Barney amiably. 'Anybody could call me a pup. Why not think of something worthy of the Stirlings? Besides, I'm not a pup. I'm really quite a middle-aged dog. Thirty-five, if you're interested in knowing.'

Uncle Benjamin remembered just in time that Valancy was dead. He turned his back on Barney.

Valancy was happy – gloriously and entirely so. She seemed to be living in a wonderful house of life and every day opened a new, mysterious room. It was in a world which had nothing in common with the one she had left behind – a world where time was not – which was young with immortal youth – where there was neither past nor future but only the present. She surrendered herself utterly to the charm of it.

The absolute freedom of it all was unbelievable. They could do exactly as they liked. No Mrs Grundy. No traditions. No relatives. Or in laws. 'Peace, perfect peace, with loved ones far away,' as Barney quoted shamelessly.

Valancy had gone home once and got her cushions. And Cousin Georgiana had given her one of her famous candlewick spreads of most elaborate design. 'For your spare room bed, dear,' she said.

'But I haven't got any spare room,' said Valancy.

Cousin Georgiana looked horrified. A house without a spare-room was monstrous to her.

'But it's a lovely spread,' said Valancy, with a kiss, 'and I'm so glad to have it. I'll put it on my own bed. Barney's old patchwork quilt is getting ragged.'

'I don't see how you can be contented to live up back,' sighed Cousin Georgiana. 'It's so out of the world.'

'Contented!' Valancy laughed. What was the use of trying to explain to Cousin Georgiana. 'It is,' she agreed, 'most gloriously and entirely out of the world.'

'And you are really happy, dear?' asked Cousin Georgiana wistfully.

'I really am,' said Valancy gravely, her eyes dancing.

'Marriage is such a serious thing,' sighed Cousin Georgiana.

'When it's going to last long,' agreed Valancy.

Cousin Georgiana did not understand this at all. But it worried her and she lay awake at nights wondering what Valancy meant by it.

Valancy loved her Blue Castle and was completely satisfied with it. The big living room had three windows, all commanding exquisite views of exquisite Mistawis. The one in the end of the room was an oriel window – which Tom MacMurray, Barney explained, had got out of some little, old 'up back' church that had been sold. It faced the west and when the sunsets flooded it Valancy's whole being knelt in prayer as if in some great cathedral. The new moons always looked down through it, the lower pine boughs swayed about the top of it, and all through the nights the soft, dim silver of the lake dreamed through it.

There was a stone fireplace on the other side. No desecrating gas imitation but a real fireplace where you could burn real logs. With a big grizzly bearskin on the floor before it, and beside it a hideous, red-plush sofa of Tom MacMurray's régime. But its ugliness was hidden by silver-grey timber wolf skins, and Valancy's cushions made it gay and comfortable. In a corner a nice, tall, lazy old clock ticked – the right kind of a clock. One that did not hurry the hours away but ticked them off deliberately. It was the jolliest looking old clock. A fat, corpulent clock with a great, round, man's face painted on it, the hands stretching out of its nose and the hours encircling it like a halo.

There was a big glass case of stuffed owls and several deer heads – likewise of Tom MacMurray's vintage. Some comfortable old chairs that asked to be sat upon. A squat little chair with a cushion was prescriptively Banjo's. If anybody else dared sit on it Banjo glared him out of it with his topaz-hued, black-ringed eyes. Banjo had an adorable habit of hanging over the back of it, trying to catch his own tail. Losing his temper because he couldn't catch it. Giving it a fierce bite for spite when he did catch it. Yowling malignantly with pain. Barney and Valancy laughed at him until they ached. But it was Good Luck they loved. They were both agreed that Good Luck was so lovable that he practically amounted to an obsession.

One side of the wall was lined with rough, homemade bookshelves filled with books, and between the two side windows hung an old mirror in a faded gilt-frame, with fat cupids gamboling in the panel over the glass. A mirror, Valancy thought, that must be like the fabled mirror into which Venus had once looked and which thereafter reflected as beautiful every woman who looked into it. Valancy thought she was almost pretty in that mirror. But that may have been because she had shingled her hair.

This was before the day of bobs and was regarded as a wild, unheard-of proceeding – unless you had typhoid. When Mrs Frederick heard of it she almost decided to erase Valancy's name from the family Bible. Barney cut the hair, square off at the back of Valancy's neck, bringing it down in a short black fringe over her forehead. It gave a meaning and a purpose to her little, three-cornered face that it never had possessed before. Even her nose ceased to irritate her. Her eyes were bright, and her sallow skin had cleared to the hue of creamy ivory. The old family joke had come true – she was really fat at last – anyway, no longer skinny. Valancy might never be beautiful, but she was of the type that looks its best in the woods – elfin – mocking – alluring. Her heart bothered her very little. When an attack threatened she was generally able to head it off with Dr Trent's prescription. The only bad one she had was one night when she was temporarily out of medicine. And it was a bad one. For the time being, Valancy realised keenly that death was actually waiting to pounce on her any moment. But the rest of the time she would not – did not – let herself remember it at all.

TWENTY-NINE

Valancy toiled not, neither did she spin. There was really very little work to do. She cooked their meals on a coal-oil stove, performing all her little domestic rites carefully and exultingly, and they ate out on the veranda that almost overhung the lake. Before them lay Mistawis, like a scene out of some fairy tale of old time. And Barney smiling his twisted, enigmatical smile at her across the table.

'What a view old Tom picked out when he built this shack!' Barney would say exultantly.

Supper was the meal Valancy liked best. The faint laughter of winds was always about them and the colours of Mistawis, imperial and spiritual, under the changing clouds were something that cannot be expressed in mere words. Shadows, too. Clustering in the pines until a wind shook them out and pursued them over Mistawis. They lay all day along the shores, threaded by ferns and wild blossoms. They stole around the headlands in the glow of the sunset, until twilight wove them all into one great web of dusk.

The cats, with their wise, innocent little faces, would sit on the veranda railing and eat the tidbits Barney flung them. And how good everything tasted! Valancy, amid all the romance of Mistawis, never forgot that men had stomachs. Barney paid her no end of compliments on her cooking.

'After all,' he admitted, 'there's something to be said for square meals. I've mostly got along by boiling two or three dozen eggs hard at once and eating a few when I got hungry, with a slice of bacon once in a while and a jorum of tea.'

Valancy poured tea out of Barney's little battered old pewter teapot of incredible age. She had not even a set of dishes – only Barney's mismatched chipped bits – and a dear, big, pobby old jug of robin's-egg blue.

After the meal was over they would sit there and talk for hours – or sit and say nothing, in all the languages of the world, Barney pulling away at his pipe, Valancy dreaming idly and deliciously, gazing at the far-off hills beyond Mistawis where the spires of firs came out against the sunset. The moonlight would begin to silver the Mistawis. Bats would begin to swoop darkly against the pale, western gold. The little waterfall that came down on the high bank not far away would, by some whim of the wildwood gods, begin to look like a wonderful white woman beckoning through the spicy, fragrant evergreens. And Leander would begin to chuckle diabolically on the mainland shore. How sweet it was to sit there and do nothing in the beautiful silence, with Barney at the other side of the table, smoking!

There were plenty of other islands in sight, though none were near enough to be troublesome as neighbours. There was one little group of islets far off to the west which they called the Fortunate Isles. At sunrise they looked like a cluster of emeralds, at sunset like a cluster of amethysts. They were too small for houses; but the lights on the larger islands would bloom out all over the lake, and bonfires would be lighted on their shores, streaming up into the wood shadows and throwing great, blood-red ribbons over the waters. Music would drift to them alluringly from boats here and there, or from the verandas on the big house of the millionaire on the biggest island.

'Would you like a house like that, Moonlight?' Barney asked once, waving his hand at it. He had taken to calling her Moonlight, and Valancy loved it.

'No,' said Valancy, who had once dreamed of a mountain castle ten times the size of the rich man's 'cottage' and now pitied the poor inhabitants of palaces. 'No. It's too elegant. I would have to carry it with me everywhere I went. On my back like a snail. It would own me – possess me, body and soul. I like a house I can love and cuddle and boss. Just like ours here. I don't envy Hamilton Gossard "the finest summer residence in Canada". It is magnificent, but it isn't my Blue Castle.'

Away down at the far end of the lake they got every night a glimpse of a big, continental train rushing through a clearing. Valancy liked to watch its lighted windows flash by and wonder who was on it and what hopes and fears it carried. She also amused herself by picturing Barney and herself going to the dances and dinners in the houses on the islands, but she did not want to go in reality. Once they did go to a masquerade dance in the pavilion at one of the hotels up the lake, and had a glorious evening, but slipped away in their canoe, before unmasking time, back to the Blue Castle.

'It was lovely – but I don't want to go again,' said Valancy.

So many hours a day Barney shut himself up in Bluebeard's Chamber. Valancy never saw the inside of it. From the smells that filtered through at times she concluded he must be conducting chemical experiments – or counterfeiting money. Valancy supposed there must be smelly processes in making counterfeit money.

But she did not trouble herself about it. She had no desire to peer into the locked chambers of Barney's house of life. His past and his future concerned her not. Only this rapturous present. Nothing else mattered.

Once he went away and stayed away two days and nights. He had asked Valancy if she would be afraid to stay alone and she had said she would not. He never told her where he had been. She was not afraid to be alone, but she was horribly lonely. The sweetest sound she had ever heard was Lady Jane's clatter through the woods when Barney returned. And then his signal whistle from the shore. She ran down to the landing rock to greet him – to nestle herself into his eager arms – they did seem eager.

'Have you missed me, Moonlight?' Barney was whispering.

'It seems a hundred years since you went away,' said Valancy.

'I won't leave you again.'

'You must,' protested Valancy, 'if you want to. I'd be miserable if I thought you wanted to go and didn't, because of me. I want you to feel perfectly free.'

Barney laughed – a little cynically.

'There is no such thing as freedom on earth,' he said. 'Only different kinds of bondages. And comparative bondages. You think you are free now because you've escaped from a peculiarly unbearable kind of bondage. But are you? You love me – that's a bondage.'

'Who said or wrote that "the prison unto which we doom ourselves no prison is"?' asked Valancy dreamily, clinging to his arm as they climbed up the rock steps.

'Ah, now you have it,' said Barney. 'That's all the freedom we can hope for – the freedom to choose our prison. But, Moonlight,' – he stopped at the door of the Blue Castle and looked about him – at the glorious lake, the great, shadowy woods, the bonfires, the twinkling lights – 'Moonlight, I'm glad to be home again. When I came down through the woods and saw my home lights – mine – gleaming out under the old pines – something I'd never seen before – oh, girl, I was glad – glad!'

But in spite of Barney's doctrine of bondage, Valancy thought they were splendidly free. It was amazing to be able to sit up half the night and look at the moon if you wanted to. To be late for meals if you wanted to – she who had always been rebuked so sharply by her mother and so reproachfully by Cousin Stickles if she were one minute late. Dawdle over meals as long as you wanted to. Leave your crusts if you wanted to. Not come home at all for meals if you wanted to. Sit on a sun-warm rock and paddle your bare feet in the hot sand if you wanted to. Just sit and do nothing in the beautiful silence if you wanted to. In short, do any fool thing you wanted to whenever the notion took you. If that wasn't freedom, what was?

THIRTY

They didn't spend all their days on the island. They spent more than half of them wandering at will through the enchanted Muskoka country. Barney knew the woods as a book and he taught their lore and craft to Valancy. He could always find trail and haunt of the shy wood people. Valancy learned the different fairy-likenesses of the mosses – the charm and exquisiteness of woodland blossoms. She learned to know every bird at sight and mimic its call – though never so perfectly as Barney. She made friends with every kind of tree. She learned to paddle a canoe as well as Barney himself. She liked to be out in the rain and she never caught cold.

Sometimes they took a lunch with them and went berrying – strawberries and blueberries. How pretty blueberries were – the dainty green of the unripe berries, the glossy pinks and scarlets of the half ripes, the misty blue of the fully matured! And Valancy learned the real flavour of the strawberry in its highest perfection. There was a certain sunlit dell on the banks of Mistawis along which white birches grew on one side and on the other still, changeless ranks of young spruces. There were long grasses at the roots of the birches, combed down by the winds and wet with morning dew late into the afternoons. Here they found berries that might have graced the banquets of Lucullus, great ambrosial sweetnesses hanging like rubies to long, rosy stalks. They lifted them by the stalk and ate them from it, uncrushed and virgin, tasting each berry by itself with all its wild fragrance ensphered therein. When Valancy carried any of these berries home that elusive essence escaped and they became nothing more than the common berries of the market-place – very kitchenly good indeed, but not as they would have been, eaten in their birch dell until her fingers were stained as pink as Aurora's eyelids.

Or they went after water-lilies. Barney knew where to find them in the creeks and bays of Mistawis. Then the Blue Castle was glorious with them, every receptacle that Valancy could contrive filled with the exquisite things. If not water lilies then cardinal flowers, fresh and vivid from the swamps of Mistawis, where they burned like ribbons of flame.

Sometimes they went trouting on little nameless rivers or hidden brooks on whose banks Naiads might have sunned their white, wet limbs. Then all they took with them were some raw potatoes and salt. They roasted the potatoes over a fire and Barney showed Valancy how to cook the trout by wrapping them in leaves, coating them with mud and baking them in a bed of hot coals. Never were such delicious meals. Valancy had such an appetite it was no wonder she put flesh on her bones.

Or they just prowled and explored through woods that always seemed to be expecting something wonderful to happen. At least, that was the way Valancy felt about them. Down the next hollow – over the next hill – you would find it.

'We don't know where we're going, but isn't it fun to go?' Barney used to say.

Once or twice night overtook them, too far from their Blue Castle to get back. But Barney made a fragrant bed of bracken and fir boughs and they slept on it dreamlessly, under a ceiling of old spruces with moss hanging from them, while beyond them moonlight and the murmur of pines blended together so that one could hardly tell which was light and which was sound.

There were rainy days, of course, when Muskoka was a wet green land. Days when showers drifted across Mistawis like pale ghosts of rain and they never thought of staying in because of it. Days when it rained in right good earnest and they had to stay in. Then Barney shut himself up in Bluebeard's Chamber and Valancy read, or dreamed on the wolfskins with Good Luck purring beside her and Banjo watching them suspiciously from his own peculiar chair. On Sunday evenings they paddled across to a point of land and walked from there through the woods to the little Free Methodist church. One felt really too happy for Sunday. Valancy had never really liked Sundays before.

And always, Sundays and weekdays, she was with Barney. Nothing else really mattered. And what a companion he was! How understanding! How jolly! How – how Barney-like! That summed it all up.

Valancy had taken some of her two hundred dollars out of the bank and spent it in pretty clothes. She had a little smoke-blue chiffon which she always put on when they spent the evenings at home – smoke-blue with touches of silver about it. It was after she began wearing it that Barney began calling her Moonlight.

'Moonlight and blue twilight – that is what you look like in that dress. I like it. It belongs to you. You aren't exactly pretty, but you have some adorable beauty-spots. Your eyes. And that little kissable dent just between your collar bones. You have the wrist and ankle of an aristocrat. That little head of yours is beautifully shaped. And when you look backward over your shoulder you're maddening – especially in twilight or moonlight. An elf maiden. A wood sprite. You belong to the woods, Moonlight – you should never be out of them. In spite of your ancestry, there is something wild and remote and untamed about you. And you have such a nice, sweet, throaty, summery voice. Such a nice voice for lovemaking.'

'Shure an' ye've kissed the Blarney Stone,' scoffed Valancy. But she tasted these compliments for weeks.

She got a pale green bathing-suit, too – a garment which would have given her clan their deaths if they had ever seen her in it. Barney taught her how to swim. Sometimes she put her bathing-dress on when she got up and didn't take it off until she went to bed – running down to the water for a plunge whenever she felt like it and sprawling on the sun-warm rocks to dry.

She had forgotten all the old humiliating things that used to come up against her in the night – the injustices and the disappointments. It was as if they had all happened to some other person – not to her, Valancy Snaith, who had always been happy.

'I understand now what it means to be born again,' she told Barney.

Holmes speaks of grief 'staining backward' through the pages of life; but Valancy found her happiness had stained backward likewise and flooded with rose-colour her whole previous drab existence. She found it hard to believe that she had ever been lonely and unhappy and afraid.

'When death comes, I shall have lived,' thought Valancy. 'I shall have had my hour.'

And her dust-pile!

One day Valancy had heaped up the sand in the little island cove in a tremendous cone and stuck a gay little Union Jack on top of it.

'What are you celebrating?' Barney wanted to know.

'I'm just exorcising an old demon,' Valancy told him.

THIRTY-ONE

Autumn came. Late September with cool nights. They had to forsake the veranda; but they kindled a fire in the big fireplace and sat before it with jest and laughter. They left the doors open, and Banjo and Good Luck came and went at pleasure. Sometimes they sat gravely on the bearskin rug between Barney and Valancy; sometimes they slunk off into the mystery of the chill night outside. The stars smouldered in the horizon mists through the old oriel. The haunting, persistent croon of the pine-trees filled the air. The little waves began to make soft, sobbing splashes on the rocks below them in the rising winds. They needed no light but the firelight that sometimes leaped up and revealed them – sometimes shrouded them in shadow. When the night wind rose higher Barney would shut the door and light a lamp and read to her – poetry and essays and gorgeous, dim chronicles of ancient wars. Barney never would read novels: he vowed they bored him. But sometimes she read them herself, curled up on the wolf skins, laughing aloud in peace. For Barney was not one of those aggravating people who can never hear you smiling audibly over something you've read without inquiring placidly, 'What is the joke?'

October – with a gorgeous pageant of colour around Mistawis, into which Valancy plunged her soul. Never had she imagined anything so splendid. A great, tinted peace. Blue, wind-winnowed skies. Sunlight sleeping in the glades of that fairyland. Long dreamy purple days paddling idly in their canoe along shores and up the rivers of crimson and gold. A sleepy, red hunter's moon. Enchanted tempests that stripped the leaves from the trees and heaped them along the shores. Flying shadows of clouds. What had all the smug, opulent lands out front to compare with this?

November – with uncanny witchery in its changed trees. With murky red sunsets flaming in smoky crimson behind the westering hills. With dear days when the austere woods were beautiful and gracious in a dignified serenity of folded hands and closed eyes – days full of a fine, pale sunshine that sifted through the late, leafless gold of the juniper-trees and glimmered among the grey beeches, lighting up evergreen banks of moss and washing the colonnades of the pines. Days with a high-sprung sky of flawless turquoise. Days when an exquisite melancholy seemed to hang over the landscape and dream about the lake. But days, too, of the wild blackness of great autumn storms, followed by dank, wet, streaming nights when there was witch-laughter in the pines and fitful moans among the mainland trees. What cared they? Old Tom had built his roof well, and his chimney drew.

'Warm fire – books – comfort – safety from storm – our cats on the rug. Moonlight,' said Barney, 'would you be any happier now if you had a million dollars?'

'No – nor half so happy. I'd be bored by conventions and obligations then.'

December. Early snows and Orion. The pale fires of the Milky Way. It was really winter now – wonderful, cold, starry winter. How Valancy had always hated winter! Dull, brief, uneventful days. Long, cold, companionless nights. Cousin Stickles with her back that had to be rubbed continually. Cousin Stickles making weird noises gargling her throat in the mornings. Cousin Stickles whining over the price of coal. Her mother, probing, questioning, ignoring. Endless colds and bronchitis – or the dread of it. Redfern's Liniment and Purple Pills.

But now she loved winter. Winter was beautiful 'up back' – almost intolerably beautiful. Days of clear brilliance. Evenings that were like cups of glamour – the purest vintage of winter's wine. Nights with their fire of stars. Cold, exquisite winter sunrises. Lovely ferns of ice all over the windows of the Blue Castle. Moonlight on birches in a silver thaw. Ragged shadows on windy evenings – torn, twisted, fantastic shadows. Great silences, austere and searching. Jewelled, barbaric hills. The sun suddenly breaking through grey clouds over long, white Mistawis. Icy-grey twilights, broken by snow-squalls, when their cosy living-room, with its goblins of firelight and inscrutable cats seemed cosier than ever. Every hour brought a new revelation and wonder.

Barney ran Lady Jane into Roaring Abel's barn and taught Valancy how to snowshoe – Valancy, who ought to be laid up with bronchitis. But Valancy had not even a cold. Later on in the winter Barney had a terrible one and Valancy nursed him through it with a dread of pneumonia in her heart. But Valancy's colds seemed to have gone where old moons go. Which was luck – for she hadn't even Redfern's Liniment. She had thoughtfully bought a bottle at the Port and Barney had hurled it into frozen Mistawis with a scowl.

'Bring no more of that devilish stuff here,' he had ordered briefly. It was the first and last time he had spoken harshly to her.

They went for long tramps through the exquisite reticence of winter woods and the silver jungles of frosted trees, and found loveliness everywhere.

At times they seemed to be walking through a spellbound world of crystal and pearl, so white and radiant were clearings and lakes and sky. The air was so crisp and clear that it was half intoxicating.

Once they stood in a hesitation of ecstasy at the entrance of a narrow path between ranks of birches. Every twig and spray was outlined in snow. The undergrowth along its sides was a little fairy forest cut out of marble. The shadows cast by the pale sunshine were fine and spiritual.

'Come away,' said Barney, turning. 'We must not commit the desecration of tramping through there.'

One evening they came upon a snowdrift far back in an old clearing which was in the exact likeness of a beautiful woman's profile. Seen too close by, the resemblance was lost, as in the fairy-tale of the Castle of St John. Seen from behind, it was a shapeless oddity. But at just the right distance and angle the outline was so perfect that when they came suddenly upon it, gleaming out against the dark background of spruce in the glow of winter sunset they both exclaimed in amazement. There was a low, noble brow, a straight, classic nose, lips and chin and cheek-curve modelled as if some goddess of old time had sat to the sculptor, and a breast of such cold, swelling purity as the very spirit of the winter woods might display.

'All the beauty that old Greece and Rome, sung, painted, taught,' quoted Barney.

'And to think no human eyes save ours have seen or will see it,' breathed Valancy, who felt at times as if she were living in a book by John Foster. As she looked around her she recalled some passages she had marked in the new Foster book Barney had brought her from the Port – with an adjuration not to expect him to read or listen to it.

'All the tintings of winter woods are extremely delicate and elusive,' recalled Valancy. 'When the brief afternoon wanes and the sun just touches the tops of the hills, there seems to be all over the woods an abundance, not of colour, but of the spirit of colour. There is really nothing but pure white after all, but one has the impression of fairy-like blendings of rose and violet, opal and heliotrope on the slopes – in the dingles and along the curves of the forest-land. You feel sure the tint is there, but when you look at it directly it is gone. From the corner of your eye you are aware that it is lurking over yonder in a spot where there was nothing but pale purity a moment ago. Only just when the sun is setting is there a fleeting moment of real colour. Then the redness streams out over the snow and incarnadines the hills and rivers and smites the crest of the pines with flame. Just a few minutes of transfiguration and revelation – and it is gone.'

'I wonder if John Foster ever spent a winter in Mistawis,' said Valancy.

'Not likely,' scoffed Barney. 'People who write tosh like that generally write it in a warm house on some smug city street.'

'You are too hard on John Foster,' said Valancy severely. 'No one could have written that little paragraph I read you last night without having seen it first – you know he couldn't.'

'I didn't listen to it,' said Barney morosely. 'You know I told you I wouldn't.'

'Then you've got to listen to it now,' persisted Valancy. She made him stand still on his snowshoes while she repeated it.'She is a rare artist, this old Mother Nature, who works "for the joy of working" and not in any spirit of vain show. Today the fir woods are a symphony of greens and greys, so subtle that you cannot tell where one shade begins to be the other. Grey trunk, green bough, grey-green moss above the white, grey-shadowed floor. Yet the old gypsy doesn't like unrelieved monotones. She must have a dash of colour. See it. A broken dead fir bough, of a beautiful red-brown, swinging among the beards of moss.'

'Good Lord, do you learn all that fellow's books by heart?' was Barney's disgusted reaction as he strode off.

'John Foster's books were all that saved my soul alive the past five years,' averred Valancy. 'Oh, Barney, look at that exquisite filigree of snow in the furrows of that old elm-tree trunk.'

When they came out to the lake they changed from snowshoes to skates and skated home. For a wonder Valancy had learned, when she was a little schoolgirl, to skate on the pond behind the Deerwood school. She never had any skates of her own, but some of the other girls had lent her theirs and she seemed to have a natural knack of it. Uncle Benjamin had once promised her a pair of skates for Christmas, but when Christmas came he had given her rubbers instead. She had never skated since she grew up, but the old trick came back quickly, and glorious were the hours she and Barney spent skimming over the white lakes and past the dark islands where the summer cottages were closed and silent. Tonight they flew down Mistawis before the wind, in an exhilaration that crimsoned Valancy's cheeks under her white tam. And at the end was her dear little house, on the island of pines, with a coating of snow on its roof, sparkling in the moonlight. Its windows glinted impishly at her in the stray gleams.

'Looks exactly like a picture-book, doesn't it?' said Barney.

They had a lovely Christmas. No rush. No scramble. No niggling attempts to make ends meet. No wild effort to remember whether she hadn't given the same kind of present to the same person two Christmases before – no mob of last-minute shoppers

– no dreary family 'reunions' where she sat mute and unimportant – no attacks of 'nerves'. They decorated the Blue Castle with pine boughs, and Valancy made delightful little tinsel stars and hung them up amid the greenery. She cooked a dinner to which Barney did full justice, while Good Luck and Banjo picked the bones.

'A land that can produce a goose like that is an admirable land,' vowed Barney. 'Canada forever!' And they drank to the Union Jack a bottle of dandelion wine that Cousin Georgiana had given Valancy along with the bedspread.

'One never knows,' Cousin Georgiana had said solemnly, 'when one may need a little stimulant.'

Barney had asked Valancy what she wanted for a Christmas present.

'Something frivolous and unnecessary,' said Valancy, who had got a pair of goloshes last Christmas and two long-sleeved, woolen undervests the year before. And so on back.

To her delight, Barney gave her a necklace of pearl beads. Valancy had wanted a string of milky pearl beads – like congealed moonshine – all her life. And these were so pretty. All that worried her was that they were really too good. They must have cost a great deal – fifteen dollars, at least. Could Barney afford that? She didn't know a thing about his finances. She had refused to let him buy any of her clothes – she had enough for that, she told him, as long as she would need clothes. In a round, black jar on the chimney-piece Barney put money for their household expenses – always enough. The jar was never empty, though Valancy never caught him replenishing it. He couldn't have much, of course, and that necklace – but Valancy tossed care aside. She would wear it and enjoy it. It was the first pretty thing she had ever had.

THIRTY-TWO

New year. The old, shabby, inglorious outlived calendar came down. The new one went up. January was a month of storms. It snowed for three weeks on end. The thermometer went miles below zero and stayed there. But, as Barney and Valancy pointed out to each other, there were no mosquitoes. And the roar and crackle of their big fire drowned the howls of the north wind. Good Luck and Banjo waxed fat and developed resplendent coats of thick, silky fur. Nip and Tuck had gone.

'But they'll come back in spring,' promised Barney.

There was no monotony. Sometimes they had dramatic little private spats that never even thought of becoming quarrels. Sometimes Roaring Abel dropped in – for an evening or a whole day – with his old tartan cap and his long red beard coated with snow. He generally brought his fiddle and played for them, to the delight of all except Banjo, who would go temporarily insane and retreat under Valancy's bed. Sometimes Abel and Barney talked while Valancy made candy for them; sometimes they sat and smoked in silence à la Tennyson and Carlyle, until the Blue Castle reeked and Valancy fled to the open. Sometimes they played checkers fiercely and silently the whole night through. Sometimes they all ate the russet apples Abel had brought, while the jolly old clock ticked the delightful minutes away.

'A plate of apples, an open fire, and "a jolly goode booke" are a fair substitute for heaven,' vowed Barney. 'Anyone can have the streets of gold. Let's have another whack at Carman.'

It was easier now for the Stirlings to believe Valancy of the dead. Not even dim rumours of her having been over at the Port came to trouble them, though she and Barney used to skate there occasionally to see a movie and eat hot dogs shamelessly at the corner stand afterwards. Presumably none of the Stirlings ever thought about her – except Cousin Georgiana, who used to lie awake worrying about poor Doss. Did she have enough to eat? Was that dreadful creature good to her? Was she warm enough at nights?

Valancy was quite warm at nights. She used to wake up and revel silently in the cosiness of those winter nights on that little island in the frozen lake. The nights of other winters had been so cold and long. Valancy hated to wake up in them and think about the bleakness and emptiness of the day that had passed and the bleakness and emptiness of the day that would come. Now she almost counted that night lost on which she didn't wake up and lie awake for half an hour just being happy, while Barney's regular breathing went on beside her, and through the open door the smouldering brands in the fireplace winked at her in the gloom. It was very nice to feel a little Lucky cat jump up on your bed in the darkness and snuggle down at your feet, purring; but Banjo would be sitting dourly by himself out in front of the fire like a brooding demon. At such moments Banjo was anything but canny, but Valancy loved his uncanniness.

The side of the bed had to be right against the window. There was no other place for it in the tiny room. Valancy, lying there, could look out of the window, through the big pine boughs that actually touched it, away up Mistawis, white and lustrous as a pavement of pearl, or dark and terrible in the storm. Sometimes the pine boughs tapped against the panes with friendly signals. Sometimes she heard the little hissing whisper of snow against them right at her side. Some nights the whole outer world seemed given over to the empery of silence; then came nights when there would be a majestic sweep of wind in the pines; nights of dear starlight when it whistled freakishly and joyously around the Blue Castle; brooding nights before storm when it crept along the floor of the lake with a low, wailing cry of brooding and mystery. Valancy wasted many perfectly good sleeping hours in these delightful communings. But she could sleep as long in the morning as she wanted to. Nobody cared. Barney cooked his own breakfast of bacon and eggs and then shut himself up in Bluebeard's Chamber till suppertime. Then they had an evening of reading and talk. They talked about everything in this world and a good many things in other worlds. They laughed over their own jokes until the Blue Castle re-echoed.

'You do laugh beautifully,' Barney told her once. 'It makes me want to laugh just to hear you laugh. There's a trick about your laugh – as if there were so much more fun back of it that you wouldn't let out. Did you laugh like that before you came to Mistawis, Moonlight?'

'I never laughed at all – really. I used to giggle foolishly when I felt I was expected to. But now – the laugh just comes.'

It struck Valancy more than once that Barney himself laughed a great deal oftener than he used to and that his laugh had changed. It had become wholesome. She rarely heard the little cynical note in it now. Could a man laugh like that who had crimes on his conscience? Yet Barney must have done something. Valancy had indifferently made up her mind as to what he had done. She concluded he was a defaulting bank cashier. She had found in one of Barney's books an old clipping cut from a Montreal paper in which a vanished, defaulting cashier was described. The description applied to Barney – as well as to half a dozen other men Valancy knew – and from some casual remarks he had dropped from time to time she concluded he knew Montreal rather well. Valancy had it all figured out in the back of her mind. Barney had been in a bank. He was tempted to take some money to speculate – meaning, of course, to put it back. He had got in deeper and deeper, until he found there was nothing for it but flight. It had happened so to scores of men. He had, Valancy was absolutely certain, never meant to do wrong. Of course, the name of the man in the clipping was Bernard Craig. But Valancy had always thought Snaith was an alias. Not that it mattered.

Valancy had only one unhappy night that winter. It came in late March when most of the snow had gone and Nip and Tuck had returned. Barney had gone off in the afternoon for a long, woodland tramp, saying he would be back by dark if all went well. Soon after he had gone it had begun to snow. The wind rose and presently Mistawis was in the grip of one of the worst storms of the winter. It tore up the lake and struck at the little house. The dark angry woods on the mainland scowled at Valancy, menace in the toss of their boughs, threats in their windy gloom, terror in the roar of their hearts. The trees on the island crouched in fear. Valancy spent the night huddled on the rug before the fire, her face buried in her hands, when she was not vainly peering from the oriel in a futile effort to see through the furious smoke of wind and snow that had once been blue-dimpled Mistawis. Where was Barney? Lost on the merciless lakes? Sinking exhausted in the drifts of the pathless woods? Valancy died a hundred deaths that night and paid in full for all the happiness of her Blue Castle. When morning came the storm broke and cleared; the sun shone gloriously over Mistawis; and at noon Barney came home. Valancy saw him from the oriel as he came around a wooded point, slender and black against the glistening white world. She did not run to meet him. Something happened to her knees and she dropped down on Banjo's chair. Luckily Banjo got out from under in time, his whiskers bristling with indignation. Barney found her there, her head buried in her hands.

'Barney, I thought you were dead,' she whispered.

Barney hooted.

'After two years of the Klondike did you think a baby storm like this could get me? I spent the night in that old lumber shanty over by Muskoka. At bit cold but snug enough. Little goose! Your eyes look like burnt holes in a blanket. Did you sit up here all night worrying over an old woodsman like me?'

'Yes,' said Valancy. 'I – couldn't help it. The storm seemed so wild. Anybody might have been lost in it. When – I saw you – come round the point – there – something happened to me. I don't know what. It was as if I had died and come back to life. I can't describe it any other way.'

THIRTY-THREE

Spring. Mistawis black and sullen for a week or two, then flaming in sapphire and turquoise, lilac and rose again, laughing through the oriel, caressing its amethyst islands, rippling under winds soft as silk. Frogs, little green wizards of swamp and pool, singing everywhere in the long twilights and long into the nights; islands fairy-like in a green haze; the evanescent beauty of wild young trees in early leaf; frost-like loveliness of the new foliage of juniper-trees; the woods putting on a fashion of spring flowers, dainty, spiritual things akin to the soul of the wilderness; red mist on the maples; willows decked out with glossy silver pussies; all the forgotten violets of Mistawis blooming again; lure of April moons.

'Think how many thousands of springs have been here on Mistawis – and all of them beautiful,' said Valancy. 'Oh, Barney, look at that wild plum! I will – I must quote from John Foster. There's a passage in one of his books – I've re-read it a hundred times. He must have written it before a tree just like that:

'Behold the young wild plum-tree which has adorned herself after immemorial fashion in a wedding-veil of fine lace. The fingers of wood pixies must have woven it, for nothing like it ever came from an earthly loom. I vow the tree is conscious of its loveliness. It is bridling before our very eyes – as if its beauty were not the most ephemeral thing in the woods, as it is the rarest and most exceeding, for today it is and tomorrow it is not. Every south wind purring through the boughs will winnow away a shower of slender petals. But what matter? Today it is queen of the wild places and it is always today in the woods.'

'I'm sure you feel much better since you've got that out of your system,' said Barney heartlessly.

'Here's a patch of dandelions,' said Valancy, unsubdued. 'Dandelions shouldn't grow in the woods, though. They haven't any sense of the fitness of things at all. They are too cheerful and self-satisfied. They haven't any of the mystery and reserve of the real wood-flowers.'

'In short, they've no secrets,' said Barney. 'But wait a bit. The woods will have their own way even with those obvious dandelions. In a little while all that obtrusive yellowness and complacency will be gone and we'll find here misty, phantom-like globes hovering over those long grasses in full harmony with the traditions of the forest.'

'That sounds John Fosterish,' teased Valancy.

'What have I done that deserved a slam like that?' complained Barney.

One of the earliest signs of spring was the renaissance of Lady Jane. Barney put her on roads that no other car would look at, and they went through Deerwood in mud to the axles. They passed several Stirlings, who groaned and reflected that now spring was come they would encounter that shameless pair everywhere. Valancy, prowling about Deerwood shops, met Uncle Benjamin on the street; but he did not realise until he had gone two blocks further on that the girl in the scarlet-collared blanket coat, with cheeks reddened in the sharp April air and the fringe of black hair over laughing, slanted eyes, was Valancy. When he did realise it, Uncle Benjamin was indignant. What business had Valancy to look like – like – like a young girl? The way of the transgressor was hard. Had to be. Scriptural and proper. Yet Valancy's path couldn't be hard. She wouldn't look like that if it were. There was something wrong. It was almost enough to make a man turn modernist.

Barney and Valancy clanged on to the Port, so that it was dark when they went through Deerwood again. At her old home Valancy, seized with a sudden impulse, got out, opened the little gate and tiptoed around to the sitting-room window. There sat her mother and Cousin Stickles drearily, grimly knitting. Baffling and inhuman as ever. If they had looked the least bit lonesome Valancy would have gone in. But they did not. Valancy would not disturb them for worlds.

THIRTY-FOUR

Valancy had two wonderful moments that spring.

One day, coming home through the woods, with her arms full of trailing arbutus and creeping spruce, she met a man who she knew must be Allan Tierney. Allan Tierney, the celebrated painter of beautiful women. He lived in New York in winter, but he owned an island cottage at the northern end of Mistawis to which he always came the minute the ice was out of the lake. He was reputed to be a lonely, eccentric man. He never flattered his sitters. There was no need to, for he would not paint anyone who required flattery. To be painted by Allan Tierney was all the cachet of beauty a woman could desire. Valancy had heard so much about him that she couldn't help turning her head back over her shoulder for another shy, curious look at him. A shaft of pale spring sunlight fell through a great pine athwart her bare black head and her slanted eyes. She wore a pale green sweater and had bound a fillet of linnaea vine about her hair. The feathery fountain of trailing spruce overflower her arms and fell around her. Allan Tierney's eyes lighted up.

'I've had a caller,' said Barney the next afternoon, when Valancy had returned from another flower quest.

'Who?' Valancy was surprised but indifferent. She began filling a basket with arbutus.

'Allan Tierney. He wants to paint you, Moonlight.'

'Me!' Valancy dropped her basket and her arbutus. 'You're laughing at me, Barney.'

'I'm not. That's what Tierney came for. To ask my permission to paint my wife – as the Spirit of Muskoka, or something like that.'

'But – but –' stammered Valancy, 'Allan Tierney never paints any but – any but –'

'Beautiful women,' finished Barney. 'Conceded. Q. E. D., Mistress Barney Snaith is a beautiful woman.'

'Nonsense,' said Valancy, stooping to retrieve her arbutus. 'You know that's nonsense, Barney. I know I'm a heap better-looking than I was a year ago, but I'm not beautiful.'

'Allan Tierney never makes a mistake,' said Barney. 'You forget, Moonlight, that there are different kinds of beauty. Your imagination is obsessed by the very obvious type of your cousin Olive. Oh, I've seen her – she's a stunner – but you'd never catch Allan Tierney wanting to paint her. In the horrible but expressive slang phrase, she keeps all her goods in the shop-window. But in your subconscious mind you have a conviction that nobody can be beautiful who doesn't look like Olive. Also, you remember your face as it was in the days when your soul was not allowed to shine through it. Tierney said something about the curve of your cheek as you looked back over your shoulder. You know I've often told you it was distracting. And he's quite batty about your eyes. If I wasn't absolutely sure it was solely professional – he's really a crabbed old bachelor, you know – I'd be jealous.'

'Well, I don't want to be painted,' said Valancy. 'I hope you told him that.'

'I couldn't tell him that. I didn't know what you wanted. But I told him I didn't want my wife painted – hung up in a salon for the mob to stare at. Belonging to another man. For of course I couldn't buy the picture. So even if you had wanted to be painted, Moonlight, your tyrannous husband would not have permitted it. Tierney was a bit squiffy. He isn't used to being turned down like that. His requests are almost like royalty's.'

'But we are outlaws,' laughed Valancy. 'We bow to no decrees – we acknowledge no sovereignty.'

In her heart she thought unashamedly:

'I wish Olive could know that Allan Tierney wanted to paint me. Me! Little-old-maid-Valancy-Stirling-that-was.'

Her second wonder-moment came one evening in May. She realised that Barney actually liked her. She had always hoped he did, but sometimes she had a little, disagreeable, haunting dread that he was just kind and nice and chummy out of pity; knowing that she hadn't long to live and determined she should have a good time as long as she did live; but away back in his mind rather looking forward to freedom again, with no intrusive woman creature in his island fastness and no chattering thing beside him in his woodland prowls. She knew he could never love her. She did not even want him to. If he loved her he would be unhappy when she died – Valancy never flinched from the plain word. No 'passing away' for her. And she did not want him to be the least unhappy. But neither did she want him to be glad – or relieved. She wanted him to like her and miss her as a good chum. But she had never been sure until this night that he did.

They had walked over the hills in the sunset. They had the delight of discovering a virgin spring in a ferny hollow and had drunk together from it out of a birch-bark cup; they had come to an old tumble-down rail fence and sat on it for a long time. They didn't talk much, but Valancy had a curious sense of oneness. She knew that she couldn't have felt that if he hadn't liked her.

'You nice little thing,' said Barney suddenly. 'Oh, you nice little thing! Sometimes I feel you're too nice to be real – that I'm just dreaming you.'

'Why can't I die now – this very minute – when I am so happy!' thought Valancy.

Well, it couldn't be so very long now. Somehow, Valancy had always felt she would live out the year Dr Trent had allotted. She had not been careful – she had never tried to be. But, somehow, she had always counted on living out her year. She had not let herself think about it at all. But now, sitting here beside Barney, with her hand in his, a sudden realisation came to her. She had not had a heart attack for a long while – two months at least. The last one she had had was two or three nights before Barney was out in the storm. Since then she had not remembered she had a heart. Well, no doubt, it betokened the nearness of the end. Nature had given up the struggle. There would be no more pain.

'I'm afraid heaven will be very dull after this past year,' thought Valancy. 'But perhaps one will not remember. Would that be – nice? No, no. I don't want to forget Barney. I'd rather be miserable in heaven remembering him than happy forgetting him. And I'll always remember through all eternity – that he really, really liked me.'

THIRTY-FIVE

Thirty seconds can be very long sometimes. Long enough to work a miracle or a revolution. In thirty seconds life changed wholly for Barney and Valancy Snaith.

They had gone around the lake one June evening in their disappearing propeller, fished for an hour in a little creek, left their boat there, and walked up through the woods to Port Lawrence two miles away. Valancy prowled a bit in the shops and got herself a new pair of sensible shoes. Her old pair had suddenly and completely given out, and this evening she had been compelled to put on the little fancy pair of patent-leather with rather high, slender heels, which she had bought in a fit of folly one day in the winter because of their beauty and because she wanted to make one foolish, extravagant purchase in her life. She sometimes put them on of an evening in the Blue Castle, but this was the first time she had worn them outside. She had not found it any too easy walking up through the woods in them, and Barney guyed her unmercifully about them. But in spite of the inconvenience, Valancy secretly rather liked the look of her trim ankles and high instep above those pretty, foolish shoes and did not change them in the shop as she might have done.

The sun was hanging low above the pines when they left Port Lawrence. To the north of it the woods closed around the town quite suddenly. Valancy always had a sense of stepping from one world to another – from reality to fairyland – when she went out of Port Lawrence and in a twinkling found it shut off behind her by the armies of the pines.

A mile and a half from Port Lawrence there was a small railroad station with a little station-house which at this hour of the day was deserted, since no local train was due. Not a soul was in sight when Barney and Valancy emerged from the woods. Off to the left a sudden curve in the track hid it from view, but over the tree-tops beyond, the long plume of smoke betokened the approach of a through train. The rails were vibrating to its thunder as Barney stepped across the switch. Valancy was a few steps behind him, loitering to gather June-bells along the little, winding path. But there was plenty of time to get across before the train came. She stepped unconcernedly over the first rail.

She could never tell how it happened. The ensuing thirty seconds always seemed in her recollection like a chaotic nightmare in which she endured the agony of a thousand lifetimes.

The heel of her pretty, foolish shoe caught in a crevice of the switch. She could not pull it loose. 'Barney – Barney!' she called in alarm. Barney turned – saw her predicament – saw her ashen face – dashed back. He tried to pull her clear – he tried to wrench her foot from the prisoning hold. In vain. In a moment the train would sweep around the curve – would be on them.

'Go – go – quick – you'll be killed, Barney!' shrieked Valancy, trying to push him away.

Barney dropped on his knees, ghost-white, frantically tearing at her shoelace. The knot defied his trembling fingers. He snatched a knife from his pocket and slashed at it. Valancy still strove blindly to push him away. Her mind was full of the hideous thought that Barney was going to be killed. She had no thought for her own danger.

'Barney – go – go – for God's sake – go!'

'Never!' muttered Barney between his set teeth. He gave one mad wrench at the lace. As the train thundered around the curve he sprang up and caught Valancy – dragging her clear, leaving the shoe behind her. The wind from the train as it swept by turned to icy cold the streaming perspiration on his face.

'Thank God!' he breathed.

For a moment they stood stupidly staring at each other, two white, shaken, wild-eyed creatures. Then they stumbled over to the little seat at the end of the station-house and dropped on it. Barney buried his face in his hands and said not a word. Valancy sat, staring straight ahead of her with unseeing eyes at the great pine woods, the stumps of the clearing, the long, gleaming rails.

There was only one thought in her dazed mind – a thought that seemed to burn it as a shaving of fire might burn her body.

Dr Trent had told her over a year ago that she had a serious form of heart disease – that any excitement might to fatal.

If that were so, why was she not dead now? This very minute? She had just experienced as much and as terrible excitement as most people experience in a lifetime, crowded into that endless thirty seconds. Yet she had not died of it. She was not an iota the worse for it. A little wobbly at the knees, as anyone would have been; a quicker heart-beat, as anyone would have; nothing more.

Why!

Was it possible Dr Trent had made a mistake?

Valancy shivered as if a cold wind had suddenly chilled her to the soul. She looked at Barney, hunched up beside her. His silence was very eloquent: Had the same thought occurred to him? Did he suddenly find himself confronted by the appalling suspicion that he was married, not for a few months or a year, but for good and all to a woman he did not love and who had foisted herself upon him by some trick or lie? Valancy turned sick before the horror of it. It could not be. It would be too cruel – too devilish. Dr Trent couldn't have made a mistake. Impossible. He was one of the best heart specialists in Ontario. She was foolish – unnerved by the recent horror. She remembered some of the hideous spasms of pain she had had. There must be something serious the matter with her heart to account for them.

But she had not had any for nearly three months.

Why!

Presently Barney bestirred himself. He stood up, without looking at Valancy, and said casually:

'I suppose we'd better be hiking back. Sun's getting low. Are your good for the rest of the road?'

'I think so,' said Valancy miserably.

Barney went across the clearing and picked up the parcel he had dropped – the parcel containing her new shoes. He brought it to her and let her take out the shoes and put them on without any assistance, while he stood with his back to her and looked out over the pines.

They walked in silence down the shadowy trail to the lake. In silence Barney steered his boat into the sunset miracle that was Mistawis. In silence they went around feathery headlands and across coral bays and silver rivers where canoes were slipping up and down in the afterglow. In silence they went past cottages echoing with music and laughter. In silence drew up at the landing-place below the Blue Castle.

Valancy went up the rock steps and into the house. She dropped miserably on the first chair she came to and sat there staring through the oriel, oblivious of Good Luck's frantic purrs of joy and Banjo's savage glares of protest at her occupancy of his chair.

Barney came in a few minutes later. He did not come near her, but he stood behind her and asked gently if she felt any the worse for her experience. Valancy would have given her year of happiness to have been able honesty to answer 'Yes'.

'No,' she said flatly.

Barney went into Bluebeard's Chamber and shut the door. She heard him pacing up and down – up and down. He had never paced like that before.

And an hour ago – only an hour ago – she had been so happy!

THIRTY-SIX

Finally Valancy went to bed. Before she went she re-read Dr
Trent's letter. It comforted her a little. So positive. So assured. The
writing so black and steady. Not the writing of a man who didn't
know what he was writing about. But she could not sleep. She
pretended to be asleep when Barney came in. Barney pretended
to go to sleep. But Valancy knew perfectly well he wasn't sleeping
any more than she was. She knew he was lying there, staring
through the darkness. Thinking of what? Trying to face – what?

Valancy, who had spent so many happy wakeful hours of night
lying by that window, now paid the price of them all in this one
night of misery. A horrible, portentous fact was slowly looming
out before her from the nebula of surmise and fear. She could not
shut her eyes to it – push it away – ignore it.

There could be nothing seriously wrong with her heart, no
matter what Dr Trent had said. If there had been, those thirty
seconds would have killed her. It was no use to recall Dr Trent's
letter and reputation. The greatest specialists made mistakes
sometimes. Dr Trent had made one.

Towards morning Valancy fell into a fitful doze with ridiculous
dreams. One of them was of Barney taunting her with having
tricked him. In her dream she lost her temper and struck him
violently on the head with her rolling-pin. He proved to be made
of glass and shivered into splinters all over the floor. She woke
with a cry of horror – a gasp of relief – a short laugh over the
absurdity of her dream – a miserable sickening recollection of
what had happened.

Barney was gone. Valancy knew, as people sometimes know
things – inescapably, without being told – that he was not in the
house or in Bluebeard's Chamber either. There was a curious
silence in the living-room. A silence with something uncanny

about it. The old clock had stopped. Barney must have forgotten
to wind it up, something he had never done before. The room
without it was dead, though the sunshine streamed in through
the oriel and dimples of light from the dancing waves beyond
quivered over the walls.

The canoe was gone but Lady Jane was under the mainland
trees. So Barney had betaken himself to the wilds. He would not
return till night – perhaps not even then. He must be angry with
her. That furious silence of his must mean anger – cold, deep,
justifiable resentment. Well, Valancy knew what she must do first.
She was not suffering very keenly now. Yet the curious numbness
that pervaded her being was in a way worse than pain. It was as
if something in her had died. She forced herself to cook and eat
a little breakfast. Mechanically she put the Blue Castle in perfect
order. Then she put on her hat and coat, locked the door and hid
the key in the hollow of the old pine and crossed to the mainland
in the motor boat. She was going into Deerwood to see Dr Trent.
She must know.

THIRTY-SEVEN

Dr Trent looked at her blankly and fumbled among his recollections.

'Er – Miss – Miss –'

'Mrs Snaith,' said Valancy quietly. 'I was Miss Valancy Stirling
when I came to you last May – over a year ago. I wanted to consult
you about my heart.'

Dr Trent's face cleared.

'Oh, of course. I remember now. I'm really not to blame for
not knowing you. You've changed – splendidly. And married.
Well, well, it has agreed with you. You don't look much like an
invalid now, hey? I remember that day. I was badly upset. Hearing
about poor Ned bowled me over. But Ned's as good as new and

you, too, evidently. I told you so, you know – told you there was nothing to worry over.'

Valancy looked at him.

'You told me, in your letter,' she said slowly, with a curious feeling that someone else was talking through her lips, 'that I had angina pectoris – in the last stages – complicated with an aneurism. That I might die any minute – that I couldn't live longer than a year.'

Dr Trent stared at her.

'Impossible!' he said blankly. 'I couldn't have told you that!'

Valancy took his letter from her bag and handed it to him.

'Miss Valancy Stirling,' he read. 'Yes – yes. Of course I wrote you – on the train – that night. But I told you there was nothing serious –'

'Read your letter,' insisted Valancy.

Dr Trent took it out – unfolded it – glanced over it. A dismayed look came into his face. He jumped to his feet and strode agitatedly about the room.

'Good heavens! This is the letter I meant for old Miss Jane Sterling. From Port Lawrence. She was here that day, too. I sent you the wrong letter. What unpardonable carelessness! But I was beside myself that night. My God, and you believed that – you believed – but you didn't – you went to another doctor –'

Valancy stood up, turned round, looked foolishly about her and sat down again.

'I believed it,' she said faintly. 'I didn't go to any other doctor. I – I – it would take too long to explain. But I believed I was going to die soon.'

Dr Trent halted before her.

'I can never forgive myself. What a year you must have had! But you don't look – I can't understand!'

'Never mind,' said Valancy dully. 'And so there's nothing the matter with my heart?'

'Well, nothing serious. You had what is called pseudo-angina. It's never fatal – passes away completely with proper treatment. Or sometimes with a shock of joy. Have you been troubled much with it?'

'Not at all since March,' answered Valancy. She remembered the marvellous feeling of re-creation she had had when she saw Barney coming home safe after the storm. Had that 'shock of joy' cured her?

'Then likely you're all right. I told you what to do in the letter you should have got. And of course I supposed you'd go to another doctor. Child, why didn't you?'

'I didn't want anybody to know.'

'Idiot,' said Dr Trent bluntly. 'I can't understand such folly. And poor old Miss Sterling. She must have got your letter – telling her there was nothing serious the matter. Well, well, it couldn't have made any difference. Her case was hopeless. Nothing that she could have done or left undone could have made any difference. I was surprised she lived as long as she did – two months. She was here that day – not long before you. I hated to tell her the truth. You think I'm a blunt old curmudgeon – and my letters are blunt enough. I can't soften things. But I'm a snivelling coward when it comes to telling a woman face to face that she's got to die soon. I told her I'd look up some features of the case I wasn't quite sure of and let her know next day. But you got her letter – look here, "Dear Miss S-t-e-r-l-i-n-g".'

'Yes. I noticed that. But I thought it a mistake. I didn't know there were any Sterlings in Port Lawrence.'

'She was the only one. A lonely old soul. Lived by herself with only a little home girl. She died two months after she was here – died in her sleep. My mistake couldn't have made any difference to her. But you! I can't forgive myself for inflicting a year's misery on you. It's time I retired, all right, when I do things like that – even if my son was supposed to be fatally injured. Can you ever forgive me?'

A year of misery! Valancy smiled a tortured smile as she thought of all the happiness Dr Trent's mistake had bought her. But she was paying for it now – oh, she was paying. If to feel was to live she was living with a vengeance.

She let Dr Trent examine her and answered all his questions. When he told her she was fit as a fiddle and would probably live to be a hundred, she got up and went away silently. She knew that there were a great many horrible things outside waiting to be thought over. Dr Trent thought she was odd. Anybody would have thought, from her hopeless eyes and woebegone face, that he had given her a sentence of death instead of life. Snaith? Snaith? Who the devil had she married? He had never heard of Snaiths in Deerwood. And she had been such a sallow, faded, little old maid. Gad, but marriage had made a difference in her, anyhow, whoever Snaith was. Snaith? Dr Trent remembered. That rapscallion 'up back!' Had Valancy Stirling married him? And her clan had let her! Well, probably that solved the mystery. She had married in haste and repented at leisure, and that was why she wasn't overjoyed at learning she was a good insurance prospect, after all. Married! To God knew whom! Or what! Jailbird? Defaulter? Fugitive from justice? It must be pretty bad if she had looked to death as a release, poor girl. But why were women such fools? Dr Trent dismissed Valancy from his mind, though to the day of his death he was ashamed of putting those letters into the wrong envelopes.

THIRTY-EIGHT

Valancy walked quickly through the back streets and through Lover's Lane. She did not want to meet anyone she knew. She didn't want to meet even people she didn't know. She hated to be seen. Her mind was so confused, so torn, so messy. She felt that her appearance must be the same. She drew a sobbing breath of relief as she left the village behind and found herself on the 'up back' road. There was little fear of meeting anyone she knew here. The cars that fled by her with raucous shrieks were filled with strangers. One of them was packed with young people who whirled past her singing uproariously:

> *My wife has the fever, O then,*
> *My wife has the fever, O then,*
> *My wife has the fever,*
> *Oh, I hope it won't leave her,*
> *For I want to be single again.*

Valancy flinched as if one of them had leaned from the car and cut her across the face with a whip.

She had made a covenant with death and death had cheated her. Now life stood mocking her. She had trapped Barney. Trapped him into marrying her. And divorce was so hard to get in Ontario. So expensive. And Barney was poor.

With life, fear had come back into her heart. Sickening fear. Fear of what Barney would think. Would say. Fear of the future that must be lived without him. Fear of her insulted, repudiated clan.

She had had one draught from a divine cup and now it was dashed from her lips. With no kind, friendly death to rescue her. She must go on living and longing for it. Everything was spoiled, smirched, defaced. Even that year in the Blue Castle. Even her unashamed love for Barney. It had been beautiful because death waited. Now it was only sordid because death was gone. How could anyone bear an unbearable thing?

She must go back and tell him. Make him believe she had not meant to trick him – she must make him believe that. She must say goodbye to her Blue Castle and return to the brick house on Elm Street. Back to everything she had thought left behind forever. The old bondage – the old fears. But that did not matter. All that mattered now was that Barney must somehow be made to believe she had not consciously tricked him.

When Valancy reached the pines by the lake she was brought out of her daze of pain by a startling sight. There, parked by the side of old, battered ragged Lady Jane, was another car. A wonderful car. A purple car. Not a dark, royal purple but a blatant, screaming purple. It shone like a mirror and its interior plainly indicated the car caste of Vere de Vere. In the driver's seat sat a haughty chauffeur in livery. And in the tonneau sat a man who opened the door and bounced out nimbly as Valancy came down the path to the landing-place. He stood under the pines waiting for her and Valancy took in every detail of him.

A stout, short, pudgy man, with a broad, rubicund, good-humoured face – a clean-shaven face, though an unparalysed little imp at the back of Valancy's paralysed mind suggested the thought, 'Such a face should have a fringe of white whisker around it.' Old-fashioned, steel-rimmed spectacles on prominent blue eyes. A pursey mouth; a little round, knobby nose. Where – where – where, groped Valancy, had she seen that face before? It seemed as familiar to her as her own.

The stranger wore a green hat and a light fawn overcoat over a suit of a loud check pattern. His tie was a brilliant green of lighter shade; on the plump hand he outstretched to intercept Valancy an enormous diamond winked at her. But he had a pleasant, fatherly smile, and in his hearty, unmodulated voice was a ring of something that attracted her.

'Can you tell me, Miss, if that house yonder belongs to a Mr Redfern? And if so, how can I get to it?'

Redfern! A vision of bottles seemed to dance before Valancy's eyes – long bottles of bitters – round bottles of hair tonic – square bottles of liniment – short, corpulent little bottles of purple pills – and all of them bearing that very prosperous, beaming moon-face and steel-rimmed spectacles on the label. Dr Redfern!

'No,' said Valancy faintly. 'No – that house belongs to Mr Snaith.' Dr Redfern nodded.

'Yes, I understand Bernie's been calling himself Snaith. Well, it's his middle name – was his poor mother's. Bernard Snaith Redfern – that's him. And now, Miss, you can tell me how to get over to that island? Nobody seems to be home there. I've done some waving and yelling. Henry, there, wouldn't yell. He's a one-job man. But old Doc Redfern can yell with the best of them yet, and ain't above doing it. Raised nothing but a couple of crows. Guess Bernie's out for the day.'

'He was away when I left this morning,' said Valancy. 'I suppose he hasn't come home yet.'

She spoke flatly and tonelessly. This last shock had temporarily bereft her of whatever little power of reasoning had been left her by Dr Trent's revelation. In the back of her mind the aforesaid little imp was jeeringly repeating a silly old proverb, 'It never rains but it pours.' But she was not trying to think. What was the use?

Dr Redfern was gazing at her in perplexity.

'When you left this morning? Do you live – over there?'

He waved his diamond at the Blue Castle.

'Of course,' said Valancy stupidly. 'I'm his wife.'

Dr Redfern took out a yellow silk handkerchief, removed his hat and mopped his brow. He was very bald, and Valancy's imp whispered, 'Why be bald? Why lose your manly beauty? Try Redfern's Hair Vigor. It keeps you young.'

'Excuse me,' said Dr Redfern. 'This is a bit of a shock.'

'Shocks seem to be in the air this morning.' The imp said this out loud before Valancy could prevent it.

'I didn't know Bernie was – married. I didn't think he would have got married without telling his old dad.'

Were Dr Redfern's eyes misty? Amid her own dull ache of

misery and fear and dread, Valancy felt a pang of pity for him.

'Don't blame him,' she said hurriedly. 'It – it wasn't his fault. It – was all my doing.'

'You didn't ask him to marry you, I suppose,' twinkled Dr Redfern. 'He might have let me know. I'd have got acquainted with my daughter-in-law before this if he had. But I'm glad to meet you now, my dear – very glad. You look like a sensible young woman. I used to sorter fear Barney'd pick out some pretty bit of fluff just because she was good-looking. They were all after him, of course. Wanted his money? Eh? Didn't like the pills and the bitters but liked the dollars. Eh? Wanted to dip their pretty little fingers in old Doc's millions. Eh?'

'Millions!' said Valancy faintly. She wished she could sit down somewhere – she wished she could have a chance to think – she wished she and the Blue Castle could sink to the bottom of Mistawis and vanish from human sight forevermore.

'Millions,' said Dr Redfern complacently. 'And Bernie chucks them for – that.' Again he shook the diamond contemptuously at the Blue Castle, 'Wouldn't you think he'd have more sense? And all on account of a white bit of a girl. He must have got over that feeling, anyhow, since he's married. You must persuade him to come back to civilisation. All nonsense wasting his life like this. Ain't you going to take me over to your house, my dear? I suppose you've some way of getting there.'

'Of course,' said Valancy stupidly. She led the way down to the little cove where the disappearing propeller boat was snuggled.

'Does your – your man want to come, too?'

'Who? Henry. Not he. Look at him sitting there disapproving. Disapproves of the whole expedition. The trail up from the road nearly gave him a conniption. Well, it was a devilish road to put a car on. Whose old bus is that up there?'

'Barney's.'

'Good Lord! Does Bernie Redfern ride in a thing like that? It looks like the great-great-grandmother of all the Fords.'

'It isn't a Ford. It's a Grey Slosson,' said Valancy spiritedly. For some occult reason, Dr Redfern's good-humoured ridicule of dear old Lady Jane stung her to life. A life that was all pain but still life. Better than the horrible half-dead-and-half-aliveness of the past few minutes – or years. She waved Dr Redfern curtly into the boat and took him over to the Blue Castle. The key was still in the old pine – the house still silent and deserted. Valancy took the doctor through the living-room to the western veranda. She must at least be out where there was air. It was still sunny, but in the southwest a great thundercloud, with white crests and gorges of purple shadow, was slowly rising over Mistawis. The doctor dropped with a gasp on a rustic chair and mopped his brow again.

'Warm, eh? Lord, what a view! Wonder if it would soften Henry if he could see it.'

'Have you had dinner?' asked Valancy.

'Yes, my dear – had it before we left Port Lawrence. Didn't know what sort of wild hermit's hollow we were coming to, you see. Hadn't any idea I was going to find a nice little daughter-in-law here all ready to toss me up a meal. Cats, eh? Puss, puss! See that. Cats love me. Bernie was always fond of cats! It's about the only thing he took from me. He's his poor mother's boy.'

Valancy had been thinking idly that Barney must resemble his mother. She had remained standing by the steps, but Dr Redfern waved her to the swing seat.

'Sit down, dear. Never stand when you can sit. I want to get a good look at Barney's wife. Well, well, I like your face. No beauty – you don't mind my saying that – you've sense enough to know it, I reckon. Sit down.'

Valancy sat down. To be obliged to sit still when mental agony urges us to stride up and down is the refinement of torture. Every nerve in her being was crying out to be alone – to be hidden. But she had to sit and listen to Dr Redfern, who didn't mind talking at all.

'When do you think Bernie will be back?'

'I don't know – not before night probably.'

'Where did he go?'

'I don't know that either. Likely to the woods – up back.'

'So he doesn't tell you his comings and goings, either? Bernie was always a secretive young devil. Never understood him. Just like his poor mother. But I thought a lot of him. It hurts me when he disappeared as he did. Eleven years ago. I haven't seen my boy for eleven years.'

'Eleven years.' Valancy was surprised. 'It's only six since he came here.'

'Oh, he was in the Klondike before that – and all over the world. He used to drop me a line now and then – never give any clue to where he was but just a line to say he was all right. I s'pose he's told you all about it.'

'No. I know nothing of his past life,' said Valancy with sudden eagerness. She wanted to know – she must know now. It hadn't mattered before. Now she must know all. And she could never hear it from Barney. She might never even see him again. If she did, it would not be to talk of his past.

'What happened? Why did he leave his home? Tell me. Tell me.'

'Well, it ain't much of a story. Just a young fool gone mad because of a quarrel with his girl. Only Bernie was a stubborn fool. Always stubborn. You never could make that boy do anything he didn't want to do. From the day he was born. Yet he was always a quiet, gentle little chap, too. Good as gold. His poor mother died when he was only two years old. I'd just begun to make money with my Hair Vigor. I'd dreamed the formula for it, you see. Some dream that. The cash rolled in. Bernie had everything he wanted. I sent him to the best schools – private schools. I meant to make a gentleman of him. Never had any chance myself. Meant he should have every chance. He went through McGill. Got honours and all that. I wanted him to go in for law. He hankered after journalism and stuff like that. Wanted me to buy a paper for him – or back him in publishing what he called a "real, worthwhile, honest-to-goodness Canadian Magazine". I s'pose I'd have done it – I always did what he wanted me to do. Wasn't he all I had to live for? I wanted him to be happy. And he never was happy. Can you believe it? Not that he said so. But I'd always a feeling that he wasn't happy. Everything he wanted – all the money he

could spend – his own bank account – travel – seeing the world –
but he wasn't happy. Not till he fell in love with Ethel Traverse.
Then he was happy for a little while.'

The cloud had reached the sun and a great, chill, purple shadow
came swiftly over Mistawis. It touched the Blue Castle – rolled
over it. Valancy shivered.

'Yes,' she said, with painful eagerness, though every word was
cutting her to the heart. 'What – was – she – like?'

'Prettiest girl in Montreal,' said Dr Redfern. 'Oh, she was a
looker, all right. Eh? Gold hair – shiny as silk – great, big, soft,
black eyes – skin like milk and roses. Don't wonder Bernie fell for
her. And brains as well. She wasn't a bit of fluff. B.A. from McGill.
A thoroughbred, too. One of the best families. But a bit lean in the
purse. Eh! Bernie was mad about her. Happiest young fool you
ever saw. Then – the bust-up.'

'What happened?' Valancy had taken off her hat and was absently
thrusting a pin in and out of it. Good Luck was purring beside her.
Banjo was regarding Dr Redfern with suspicion. Nip and Tuck were
lazily cawing in the pines. Mistawis was beckoning. Everything
was the same. Nothing was the same. It was a hundred years since
yesterday. Yesterday, at this time, she and Barney had been eating
a belated dinner here with laughter. Laughter? Valancy felt that she
had done with laughter forever. And with tears, for that matter. She
had no further use for either of them.

'Blest if I know, my dear. Some fool quarrel, I suppose. Bernie
just lit out – disappeared. He wrote me from the Yukon. Said his
engagement was broken and he wasn't coming back. And not to
try to hunt him up because he was never coming back. I didn't.
What was the use? I knew Bernie. I went on piling up money
because there wasn't anything else to do. But I was mighty lonely.
All I lived for was them little notes now and then from Bernie
– Klondike – England – South Africa – China – everywhere. I
thought maybe he'd come back some day to his lonesome old dad.
Then six years ago even the letters stopped. I didn't hear a word of
or from him till last Christmas.'

'Did he write?'

'No. But he drew a check for fifteen thousand dollars on his bank account. The bank manager is a friend of mine – one of my biggest shareholders. He'd always promised me he'd let me know if Bernie drew any checks. Bernie had fifty thousand there. And he'd never touched a cent of it till last Christmas. The check was made out to Aynsley's, Toronto –'

'Anysley's?' Valancy heard herself saying Aynsley's! She had a box on her dressing-table with the Aynsley trademark.

'Yes. The big jewellery house there. After I'd thought it over a while, I got brisk. I wanted to locate Bernie. Had a special reason for it. It was time he gave up his fool hoboing and come to his senses. Drawing that fifteen told me there was something in the wind. The manager communicated with the Aynsleys – his wife was an Aynsley – and found out that Bernard Redfern had bought a pearl necklace there. His address was given as Box 444, Port Lawrence, Muskoka, Ont. First I thought I'd write. Then I thought I'd wait till the open season for cars and come down myself. Ain't no hand at writing. I've motored from Montreal. Got to Port Lawrence yesterday. Enquired at the post-office. Told me they knew nothing of any Bernard Snaith Redfern, but there was a Barney Snaith had a P. O. box there. Lived on an island out here, they said. So here I am. And where's Barney?'

Valancy was fingering her necklace. She was wearing fifteen thousand dollars around her neck. And she had worried lest Barney had paid fifteen dollars for it and couldn't afford it. Suddenly she laughed in Dr Redfern's face.

'Excuse me. It's so – amusing,' said poor Valancy.

'Isn't it?' said Dr Redfern, seeing a joke – but not exactly hers. 'Now, you seem like a sensible young woman, and I dare say you've lots of influence over Bernie. Can't you get him to come back to civilisation and live like other people? I've a house up there. Big as a castle. Furnished like a palace. I want company in it – Bernie's wife – Bernie's children.'

'Did Ethel Traverse ever marry?' queried Valancy irrelevantly.

'Bless you, yes. Two years after Bernie levanted. But she's a widow now. Pretty as ever. To be frank, that was my special reason for wanting to find Bernie. I thought they'd make it up, maybe. But, of course, that's all off now. Doesn't matter. Bernie's choice of a wife is good enough for me. It's my boy I want. Think he'll soon be back?'

'I don't know. But I don't think he'll come before night. Quite late, perhaps. And perhaps not till tomorrow. But I can put you up comfortably. He'll certainly be back tomorrow.'

Dr Redfern shook his head.

'Too damp. I'll take no chances with rheumatism.'

'Why suffer that ceaseless anguish? Why not try Redfern's Liniment?' quoted the imp in the back of Valancy's mind.

'I must get back to Port Lawrence before rain starts. Henry goes quite mad when he gets mud on the car. But I'll come back tomorrow. Meanwhile you talk Bernie into reason.'

He shook her hand and patted her kindly on the shoulder. He looked as if he would have kissed her, with a little encouragement, but Valancy did not give it. Not that she would have minded. He was rather dreadful and loud – and – and – dreadful. But there was something about him she liked. She thought dully that she might have liked being his daughter-in-law if he had not been a millionaire. A score of times over. And Barney was his son – and heir.

She took him over in the motor boat and watched the lordly purple car roll away through the woods with Henry at the wheel looking things not lawful to be uttered. Then she went back to the Blue Castle. What she had to do must be done quickly. Barney might return at any moment. And it was certainly going to rain. She was thankful she no longer felt very bad. When you are bludgeoned on the head repeatedly, you naturally and mercifully become more or less insensible and stupid.

She stood briefly like a faded flower bitten by frost, by the hearth, looking down on the white ashes of the last fire that had blazed in the Blue Castle.

'At any rate,' she thought wearily, 'Barney isn't poor. He will be able to afford a divorce. Quite nicely.'

THIRTY-NINE

She must write a note. The imp in the back of her mind laughed. In every story she had ever read when a runaway wife decamped from home she left a note, generally on the pin-cushion. It was not a very original idea. But one had to leave something intelligible. What was there to do but write a note? She looked vaguely about her for something to write with. Ink? There was none. Valancy had never written anything since she had come to the Blue Castle, save memoranda of household necessaries for Barney. A pencil sufficed for them, but now the pencil was not to be found. Valancy absently crossed to the door of Bluebeard's Chamber and tried it. She vaguely expected to find it locked, but it opened unresistingly. She had never tried it before, and did not know whether Barney habitually kept it locked or not. If he did, he must have been badly upset to leave it unlocked. She did not realise that she was doing something he had told her not to do. She was only looking for something to write with. All her faculties were concentrated on deciding just what she would say and how she would say it. There was not the slightest curiosity in her as she went into the lean-to.

There were no beautiful women hanging by their hair on the walls. It seemed a very harmless apartment, with a commonplace little sheet-iron stove in the middle of it, its pipe sticking out through the roof. At one end was a table or counter crowded with odd-looking utensils. Used no doubt by Barney in his smelly operations. Chemical experiments, probably, she reflected dully. At the other end was a big writing desk and swivel-chair. The side walls were lined with books.

Valancy went blindly to the desk. There she stood motionless for a few minutes, looking down at something that lay on it. A bundle of galleyproofs. The page on top bore the title Wild Honey, and under the title were the words 'by John Foster'.

The opening sentence – 'Pines are the trees of myth and legend. They strike their roots deep into the traditions of an older world, but wind and star love their lofty tops. What music when old Æolus draws his bow across the branches of the pines –' She had heard Barney say that one day when they walked under them.

So Barney was John Foster!

Valancy was not excited. She had absorbed all the shocks and sensations that she could compass for one day. This affected her neither one way nor the other. She only thought:

'So this explains it.'

'It' was a small matter that had, somehow, stuck in her mind more persistently than its importance seemed to justify. Soon after Barney had brought her John Foster's latest book she had been in a Port Lawrence bookshop and heard a customer ask the proprietor for John Foster's new book. The proprietor had said curtly, 'Not out yet. Won't be out till next week.'

Valancy had opened her lips to say, 'Oh, yes, it is out,' but closed them again. After all, it was none of her business. She supposed the proprietor wanted to cover up his negligence in not getting the book in promptly. Now she knew. The book Barney had given her had been one of the author's complimentary copies, sent in advance.

Well! Valancy pushed the proofs indifferently aside and sat down in the swivel-chair. She took up Barney's pen – and a vile one it was – pulled a sheet of paper to her and began to write. She could not think of anything to say except bald facts.

> Dear Barney:
>
> I went to Dr Trent this morning and found out he had sent me the wrong letter by mistake. There never was anything serious the matter with my heart and I am quite well now.
>
> I did not mean to trick you. Please believe that. I could not bear it if you did not believe that. I am very sorry for the mistake. But surely you can get a divorce if I leave you. Is desertion a ground for divorce in Canada? Of course if there is anything I can do to help or hasten it I will do it gladly, if your lawyer will let me know.

I thank you for all your kindness to me. I shall never forget it. Think as kindly of me as you can, because I did not mean to trap you. Goodbye.
Yours gratefully,
Valancy

It was very cold and stiff, she knew. But to try to say anything else would be dangerous – like tearing away a dam. She didn't know what torrent of wild incoherences and passionate anguish might pour out. In a postscript she added:

Your father was here today. He is coming back tomorrow. He told me everything. I think you should go back to him. He is very lonely for you.

She put the letter in an envelope, wrote 'Barney' across it, and left it on the desk. On it she laid the string of pearls. If they had been the beads she believed them she would have kept them in memory of that wonderful year. But she could not keep the 15,000 dollar gift of a man who had married her of pity and whom she was now leaving. It hurt her to give up her pretty bauble. That was an odd thing, she reflected. The fact that she was leaving Barney did not hurt her – yet. It lay at her heart like a cold, insensible thing. If it came to life – Valancy shuddered and went out.

She put on her hat and mechanically fed Good Luck and Banjo. She locked the door and carefully hid the key in the old pine. Then she crossed to the mainland in the disappearing propeller. She stood for a moment on the bank, looking at her Blue Castle. The rain had not yet come, but the sky was dark, and Mistawis grey and sullen. The little house under the pines looked very pathetic – a casket rifled of its jewels – a lamp with its flame blown out.

'I shall never again hear the wind crying over Mistawis at night,' thought Valancy. This hurt her, too. She could have laughed to think that such a trifle could hurt her at such a time.

FORTY

Valancy paused a moment on the porch of the brick house in Elm Street. She felt that she ought to knock like a stranger. Her rosebush, she idly noticed, was loaded with buds. The rubber-plant stood beside the prim door. A momentary horror overcame her – a horror of the existence to which she was returning. Then she opened the door and walked in.

'I wonder if the Prodigal Son ever felt really at home again,' she thought.

Mrs Frederick and Cousin Stickles were in the sitting-room. Uncle Benjamin was there, too. They looked blankly at Valancy, realising at once that something was wrong. This was not the saucy, impudent thing who had laughed at them in this very room last summer. This was a grey-faced woman with the eyes of a creature who had been stricken by a mortal blow.

Valancy looked indifferently around the room. She had changed so much – and it had changed so little. The same pictures hung on the walls. The little orphan who knelt at her never-finished prayer by the bed whereon reposed the black kitten that never grew up into cat. The grey 'steel engraving' of Quatre Bras, where the British regiment forever stood at bay. The crayon enlargement of the boyish father she had never known. There they all hung in the same places. The green cascade of 'Wandering Jew' still tumbled out of the old granite saucepan on the windowstand. The same elaborate, never-used pitcher stood at the same angle on the sideboard shelf. The blue and gilt vases that had been among her mother's wedding-presents still primly adorned the mantelpiece, flanking the china clock of berosed and besprayed ware that never went. The chairs in exactly the same places. Her mother and Cousin Stickles, likewise unchanged, regarding her with stony unwelcome.

Valancy had to speak first.

'I've come home, Mother,' she said tiredly.

'So I see.' Mrs Frederick's voice was very icy. She had resigned herself to Valancy's desertion. She had almost succeeded in forgetting there was a Valancy. She had rearranged and organised her systematic life without any reference to an ungrateful, rebellious child. She had taken her place again in a society which ignored the fact that she had ever had a daughter and pitied her, if it pitied her at all, only in discreet whispers and asides. The plain truth was that, by this time, Mrs Frederick did not want Valancy to come back – did not want ever to see or hear of her again.

And now, of course, Valancy was here. With tragedy and disgrace and scandal trailing after her visibly.

'So I see,' said Mrs Frederick. 'May I ask why?'

'Because – I'm – not – going to die,' said Valancy huskily.

'God bless my soul!' said Uncle Benjamin. 'Who said you were going to die?'

'I suppose,' said Cousin Stickles shrewishly – Cousin Stickles did not want Valancy back either – 'I suppose you've found out he has another wife – as we've been sure all along.'

'No. I only wish he had,' said Valancy. She was not suffering particularly, but she was very tired. If only the explanations were all over and she were upstairs in her old, ugly room – alone. Just alone! The rattle of the beads on her mother's sleeves, as they swung on the arms of the reed chair, almost drove her crazy. Nothing else was worrying her; but all at once it seemed that she simply could not endure that thin, insistent rattle.

'My home, as I told you, is always open to you,' said Mrs Frederick stonily, 'but I can never forgive you.'

Valancy gave a mirthless laugh.

'I'd care very little for that if I could only forgive myself,' she said.

'Come, come,' said Uncle Benjamin testily. But rather enjoying himself. He felt he had Valancy under his thumb again. We've had enough of mystery. What has happened? Why have you left that fellow? No doubt there's reason enough – but what particular reason is it?'

Valancy began to speak mechanically. She told her tale bluntly and barely.

'A year ago Dr Trent told me I had angina pectoris and could not live long. I wanted to have some – life – before I died. That's why I went away. Why I married Barney. And now I've found it is all a mistake. There is nothing wrong with my heart. I've got to live – and Barney only married me out of pity. So I have to leave him – free.'

'God bless me!' said Uncle Benjamin. Cousin Stickles began to cry.

'Valancy, if you'd only had confidence in your own mother –'

'Yes, yes, I know,' said Valancy impatiently, 'What's the use of going into that now? I can't undo this year. God knows I wish I could. I've tricked Barney into marrying me – and he's really Bernard Redfern. Dr Redfern's son, of Montreal. And his father wants him to go back to him.'

Uncle Benjamin made a queer sound. Cousin Stickles took her black-bordered handkerchief away from her eyes and stared at Valancy. A queer gleam suddenly shot into Mrs Frederick's stone-grey orbs.

'Dr Redfern – not the Purple Pill man?' she said.

Valancy nodded. 'He's John Foster, too – the writer of those nature books.'

'But – but –' Mrs Frederick was visibly agitated, though not over the thought that she was the mother-in-law of John Foster – 'Dr Redfern is a millionaire!'

Uncle Benjamin shut his mouth with a snap.

'Ten times over,' he said.

Valancy nodded.

'Yes. Barney left home years ago – because of – of some trouble – some – disappointment. Now he will likely go back. So you see – I had to come home. He doesn't love me. I can't hold him to a bond he was tricked into.'

Uncle Benjamin looked incredibly sly.

'Did he say so? Does he want to get rid of you?'

'No. I haven't seen him since I found out. But I tell you – he only married me out of pity – because I asked him to – because he thought it would only be for a little while.'

Mrs Frederick and Cousin Stickles both tried to speak, but Uncle Benjamin waved a hand at them and frowned portentously.

'Let me handle this,' wave and wave and frown seemed to say. To Valancy:

'Well, well, dear, we'll talk it over later. You see, we don't quite understand everything yet. As Cousin Stickles says, you should have confided in us before. Later on – I dare say we can find a way out of this.'

'You think Barney can easily get a divorce, don't you?' said Valancy eagerly.

Uncle Benjamin silenced with another wave the exclamation of horror he knew was trembling on Mrs Frederick's lips.

'Trust to me, Valancy. Everything will arrange itself. Tell me this, Dossie. Have you been happy up back? Was Sn – Mr Redfern good to you?'

'I have been very happy and Barney was very good to me,' said Valancy, as if reciting a lesson. She remembered when she studied grammar at school she had disliked the past and perfect tenses. They had always seemed so pathetic. 'I have been' – it was all over and done with.

'Then don't worry, little girl.' How amazingly paternal Uncle Benjamin was! 'Your family will stand behind you. We'll see what can be done.'

'Thank you,' said Valancy dully. Really, it was quite decent of Uncle Benjamin. 'Can I go and lie down a little while? I'm – I'm – tired.'

'Of course you're tired.' Uncle Benjamin patted her hand gently – very gently. 'All worn out and nervous. Go and lie down, by all means. You'll see things in quite a different light after you've had a good sleep.'

He held the door open. As she went through he whispered, 'What is the best way to keep a man's love?'

Valancy smiled wanly. But she had come back to the old life – the old shackles. 'What?' she asked as meekly as of yore.

'Not to return it,' said Uncle Benjamin with a chuckle. He shut the door and rubbed his hands. Nodded and smiled mysteriously round the room.

'Poor little Doss!' he said pathetically.

'Do you really suppose that – Snaith – can actually be Dr Redfern's son?' gasped Mrs Frederick.

'I see no reason for doubting it. She says Dr Redfern has been there. Why, the man is rich as wedding-cake. Amelia, I've always believed there was more in Doss than most people thought. You kept her down too much – repressed her. She never had a chance to show what was in her. And now she's landed a millionaire for a husband.'

'But –' hesitated Mrs Frederick, 'he – he – they told terrible tales about him.'

All gossip and invention – all gossip and invention. It's always been a mystery to me why people should be so ready to invent and circulate slanders about other people they know absolutely nothing about. I can't understand why you paid so much attention to gossip and surmise. Just because he didn't choose to mix up with everybody, people resented it. I was surprised to find what a decent fellow he seemed to be that time he came into my store with Valancy. I discounted all the yarns then and there.'

'But he was seen dead drunk in Port Lawrence once,' said Cousin Stickles. Doubtfully, yet as one very willing to be convinced to the contrary.

'Who saw him?' demanded Uncle Benjamin truculently. 'Who saw him? Old Jemmy Strang said he saw him. I wouldn't take old Jemmy Strang's word on oath. He's too drunk himself half the time to see straight. He said he saw him lying drunk on a bench in the Park. Pshaw! Redfern's been asleep there. Don't worry over that.'

'But his clothes – and that awful old car –' said Mrs Frederick uncertainly.

'Eccentricities of genius,' declared Uncle Benjamin. 'You heard Doss say he was John Foster. I'm not up in literature myself, but I heard a lecturer from Toronto say that John Foster's books had put Canada on the literary map of the world.'

'I – suppose – we must forgive her,' yielded Mrs Frederick.

'Forgive her!' Uncle Benjamin snorted. Really, Amelia was an incredibly stupid woman. No wonder poor Doss had gone sick and tired of living with her. 'Well, yes, I think you'd better forgive her! The question is – will Snaith forgive us!'

'What if she persists in leaving him? You've no idea how stubborn she can be,' said Mrs Frederick.

'Leave it all to me, Amelia. Leave it all to me. You women have muddled it enough. This whole affair has been bungled from start to finish. If you had put yourself to a little trouble years ago, Amelia, she would not have bolted over the traces as she did. Just let her alone – don't worry her with advice or questions till she's ready to talk. She's evidently run away in a panic because she's afraid he'd be angry with her for fooling him. Most extraordinary thing of Trent to tell her such a yarn! That's what comes of going to strange doctors. Well, well, we mustn't blame her too harshly, poor child. Redfern will come after her. If he doesn't, I'll hunt him up and talk to him as man to man. He may be a millionaire, but Valancy is a Stirling. He can't repudiate her just because she was mistaken about her heart disease. Not likely he'll want to. Doss is a little overstrung. Bless me, I must get in the habit of calling her Valancy. She isn't a baby any longer. Now, remember, Amelia. Be very kind and sympathetic.'

It was something of a large order to expect Mrs Frederick to be kind and sympathetic. But she did her best. When supper was ready she went up and asked Valancy if she wouldn't like a cup of tea. Valancy, lying on her bed, declined. She just wanted to be left alone for a while. Mrs Frederick left her alone. She did not even remind Valancy that her plight was the outcome of her own lack of daughterly respect and obedience. One could not – exactly – say things like that to the daughter-in-law of a millionaire.

FORTY-ONE
❦

Valancy looked dully about her old room. It, too, was so exactly the same that it seemed almost impossible to believe in the changes that had come to her since she had last slept in it. It seemed – somehow – indecent that it should be so much the same. There was Queen Louise everlastingly coming down the stairway, and nobody had let the forlorn puppy in out of the rain. Here was the purple paper blind and the greenish mirror. Outside, the old carriage-shop with its blatant advertisements. Beyond it, the station with the same derelicts and flirtatious flappers.

Here the old life waited for her, like some grim ogre that bided his time and licked his chops. A monstrous horror of it suddenly possessed her. When night fell and she had undressed and got into bed, the merciful numbness passed away and she lay in anguish and thought of her island under the stars. The campfires – all their little household jokes and phrases and catch words – their furry beautiful cats – the lights agleam on the fairy islands – canoes skimming over Mistawis in the magic of morning – white birches shining among the dark spruces like beautiful women's bodies – winter snows and rose-red sunset fires – lakes drunken with moonshine – all the delights of her lost paradise. She would not let herself think of Barney. Only of these lesser things. She could not endure to think of Barney.

Then she thought of him inescapably. She ached for him. She wanted his arms around her – his face against hers – his whispers in her ear. She recalled all his friendly looks and quips and jests – his little compliments – his caresses. She counted them all over as a woman might count her jewels – not one did she miss from the first day they had met. These memories were all she could have now. She shut her eyes and prayed.

'Let me remember every one, God! Let me never forget one of them!'

Yet it would be better to forget. This agony of longing and loneliness would not be so terrible if one could forget. And Ethel Traverse. That shimmering witch woman with her white skin and black eyes and shining hair. The woman Barney had loved. The woman whom he still loved. Hadn't he told her he never changed his mind? Who was waiting for him in Montreal. Who was the right wife for a rich and famous man. Barney would marry her, of course, when he got his divorce. How Valancy hated her! And envied her! Barney had said, 'I love you' to her. Valancy had wondered what tone Barney would say 'I love you' in – how his dark-blue eyes would look when he said it. Ethel Traverse knew. Valancy hated her for the knowledge – hated and envied her.

'She can never have those hours in the Blue Castle. They are mine,' thought Valancy savagely. Ethel would never make strawberry jam or dance to old Abel's fiddle or fry bacon for Barney over a campfire. She would never come to the little Mistawis shack at all.

What was Barney doing – thinking – feeling now? Had he come home and found her letter? Was he still angry with her? Or a little pitiful. Was he lying on their bed looking out on stormy Mistawis and listening to the rain streaming down on the roof? Or was he still wandering in the wilderness, raging at the predicament in which he found himself? Hating her? Pain took her and wrung her like some great pitiless giant. She got up and walked the floor. Would morning never come to end this hideous night? And yet what could morning bring her? The old life without the old stagnation that was at least bearable. The old life with the new memories, the new longings, the new anguish.

'Oh, why can't I die?' moaned Valancy.

FORTY-TWO

It was not until early afternoon the next day that a dreadful old car clanked up Elm Street and stopped in front of the brick house. A hatless man sprang from it and rushed up the steps. The bell was rung as it had never been rung before – vehemently, intensely. The ringer was demanding entrance, not asking it. Uncle Benjamin chuckled as he hurried to the door. Uncle Benjamin had 'just dropped in' to enquire how dear Doss – Valancy was. Dear Doss – Valancy, he had been informed, was the same. She had come down for breakfast – which she didn't eat – gone back to her room, come down for dinner – which she didn't eat – gone back to her room. That was all. She had not talked. And she had been let, kindly, considerately, alone.

'Very good. Redfern will be here today,' said Uncle Benjamin. And now Uncle Benjamin's reputation as a prophet was made. Redfern was here – unmistakably so.

'Is my wife here?' he demanded of Uncle Benjamin without preface.

Uncle Benjamin smiled expressively.

'Mr Redfern, I believe? Very glad to meet you, sir. Yes, that naughty little girl of yours is here. We have been –'

'I must see her,' Barney cut Uncle Benjamin ruthlessly short.

'Certainly, Mr Redfern. Just step in here. Valancy will be down in a minute.'

He ushered Barney into the parlour and betook himself to the sitting room and Mrs Frederick.

'Go up and tell Valancy to come down. Her husband is here.'

But so dubious was Uncle Benjamin as to whether Valancy could really come down in a minute – or at all – that he followed Mrs Frederick on tiptoe up the stairs and listened in the hall.

'Valancy dear,' said Mrs Frederick tenderly, 'your husband is in the parlour, asking for you.'

'Oh Mother.' Valancy got up from the window and wrung her hands. 'I cannot see him – I cannot! Tell him to go away – ask him to go away. I can't see him!'

'Tell her,' hissed Uncle Benjamin through the keyhole, 'that Redfern says he won't go away until he has seen her.'

Redfern had not said anything of the kind, but Uncle Benjamin thought he was that sort of a fellow. Valancy knew he was. She understood that she might as well go down first as last.

She did not even look at Uncle Benjamin as she passed him on the landing. Uncle Benjamin did not mind. Rubbing his hands and chuckling, he retreated to the kitchen, where he genially demanded of Cousin Stickles:

'Why are good husbands like bread?'

Cousin Stickles asked why.

'Because women need them,' beamed Uncle Benjamin.

Valancy was looking anything but beautiful when she entered the parlour. Her white night had played fearful havoc with her face. She wore an ugly old brown-and-blue gingham, having left all her pretty dresses in the Blue Castle. But Barney dashed across the room and caught her in his arms.

'Valancy, darling – oh, you darling little idiot! Whatever possessed you to run away like that? When I came home last night and found your letter I went quite mad. It was twelve o'clock – I knew it was too late to come here then. I walked the floor all night. Then this morning Dad came – I couldn't get away till now. Valancy, whatever got into you? Divorce, forsooth! Don't you know –'

'I know you only married me out of pity,' said Valancy, brushing him away feebly. 'I know you don't love me – I know –'

'You've been lying awake at three o'clock too long,' said Barney, shaking her. 'That's all that's the matter with you. Love you! Oh, don't I love you! My girl, when I saw that train coming down on you I knew whether I loved you or not!'

'Oh, I was afraid you would try to make me think you cared,' cried Valancy passionately. 'Don't – don't! I know all about Ethel

Traverse – your father told me everything. Oh, Barney, don't torture me! I can never go back to you!'

Barney released her and looked at her for a moment. Something in her pallid, resolute face spoke more convincingly than words of her determination.

'Valancy,' he said quietly, 'Father couldn't have told you everything because he didn't know it. Will you let me tell you – everything?'

'Yes,' said Valancy wearily. Oh, how dear he was! How she longed to throw herself into his arms! As he put her gently down in a chair, she could have kissed the slender, brown hands that touched her arms. She could not look up as he stood before her. She dared not meet his eyes. For his sake, she must be brave. She knew him – kind, unselfish. Of course he would pretend he did not want his freedom – she might have known he would pretend that, once the first shock of realisation was over. He was so sorry for her – he understood her terrible position. When had he ever failed to understand? But she would never accept his sacrifice. Never!

'You've seen Dad and you know I'm Bernard Redfern. And I suppose you've guessed that I'm John Foster – since you went into Bluebeard's Chamber.'

'Yes. But I didn't go in out of curiosity. I forgot you had told me not to go in – I forgot –'

'Never mind. I'm not going to kill you and hang you up on the wall, so there's no need to call for Sister Anne. I'm only going to tell you my story from the beginning. I came back last night intending to do it. Yes, I'm "old Doc. Redfern's son" – of Purple Pills and Bitters fame. Oh, don't I know it? Wasn't it rubbed into me for years?'

Barney laughed bitterly and strode up and down the room a few times. Uncle Benjamin, tiptoeing through the hall, heard the laugh and frowned. Surely Doss wasn't going to be a stubborn little fool. Barney threw himself into a chair before Valancy.

'Yes. As long as I can remember I've been a millionaire's son. But when I was born Dad wasn't a millionaire. He wasn't even a doctor – isn't yet. He was a veterinary and a failure at it. He and

Mother lived in a little village up in Quebec and were abominably poor. I don't remember Mother. Haven't even a picture of her. She died when I was two years old. She was fifteen years younger than Father – a little school teacher. When she died Dad moved into Montreal and formed a company to sell his hair tonic. He'd dreamed the prescription one night, it seems. Well, it caught on. Money began to flow in. Dad invented – or dreamed – the other things, too – Pills, Bitters, Liniment and so on. He was a millionaire by the time I was ten, with a house so big a small chap like myself always felt lost in it. I had every toy a boy could wish for – and I was the loneliest little devil in the world. I remember only one happy day in my childhood, Valancy. Only one. Even you were better off than that. Dad had gone out to see an old friend in the country and took me along. I was turned loose in the barnyard and I spent the whole day hammering nails in a block of wood. I had a glorious day. When I had to go back to my roomful of playthings in the big house in Montreal I cried. But I didn't tell Dad why. I never told him anything. It's always been a hard thing for me to tell things, Valancy – anything that went deep. And most things went deep with me. I was a sensitive child and I was even more sensitive as a boy. No one ever knew what I suffered. Dad never dreamed of it.

'When he sent me to a private school – I was only eleven – the boys ducked me in the swimming-tank until I stood on a table and read aloud all the advertisements of Father's patent abominations. I did it – then' – Barney clinched his fists – 'I was frightened and half drowned and all my world was against me. But when I went to college and the sophs tried the same stunt I didn't do it.' Barney smiled grimly. 'They couldn't make me do it. But they could – and did – make my life miserable. I never heard the last of the Pills and the Bitters and the Hair Tonic. "After using" was my nickname – you see I'd always such a thick thatch. My four college years were a nightmare. You know – or you don't know – what merciless beasts boys can be when they get a victim like me. I had few friends – there was always some barrier between me and the kind of people I cared for. And the other kind – who would have been very willing to be intimate with rich old Doc. Redfern's son – I didn't care for. But I had one friend – or thought I had. A clever, bookish chap – a bit of a writer. That was a bond between us – I had some secret aspirations along that line. He was older than I was – I looked up to him and worshipped him. For a year I was happier than I'd ever been. Then – a burlesque sketch came out in the college magazine – a mordant thing, ridiculing Dad's remedies. The names were changed, of course, but everybody knew what and who was meant. Oh, it was clever – damnably so – and witty. McGill rocked with laughter over it. I found out he had written it.'

'Oh, were you sure?' Valancy's dull eyes flamed with indignation.

'Yes. He admitted it when I asked him. Said a good idea was worth more to him than a friend, any time. And he added a gratuitous thrust. "You know, Redfern, there are some things money won't buy. For instance – it won't buy you a grandfather." Well, it was a nasty slam. I was young enough to feel cut up. And it destroyed a lot of my ideals and illusions, which was the worst thing about it. I was a young misanthrope after that. Didn't want to be friends with anyone. And then – the year after I left college – I met Ethel Traverse.'

Valancy shivered. Barney, his hands stuck in his pockets, was regarding the floor moodily and didn't notice it.

'Dad told you about her, I suppose. She was very beautiful. And I loved her. Oh, yes, I loved her. I won't deny it or belittle it now. It was a lonely, romantic boy's first passionate love, and it was very real. And I thought she loved me. I was fool enough to think that. I was wildly happy when she promised to marry me. For a few months. Then – I found out she didn't. I was an involuntary eavesdropper on a certain occasion for a moment. That moment was enough. The proverbial fate of the eavesdropper overtook me. A girl friend of hers was asking her how she could stomach Doc. Redfern's son and the patent-medicine background.

'"His money will gild the Pills and sweeten the Bitters," said Ethel, with a laugh. "Mother told me to catch him if I could. We're on the rocks. But pah! I smell turpentine whenever he comes near me."

"'Oh, Barney!" cried Valancy, wrung with pity for him. She had forgotten all about herself and was filled with compassion for Barney and rage against Ethel Traverse. How dared she?

'Well,' – Barney got up and began pacing round the room – 'that finished me. Completely. I left civilisation and those accursed dopes behind me and went to the Yukon. For five years I knocked about the world – in all sorts of outlandish places. I earned enough to live on – I wouldn't touch a cent of Dad's money. Then one day I woke up to the fact that I no longer cared a hang about Ethel, one way or another. She was somebody I'd known in another world – that was all. But I had no hankering to go back to the old life. None of that for me. I was free and I meant to keep so. I came to Mistawis – saw Tom MacMurray's island. My first book had been published the year before, and made a hit – I had a bit of money from my royalties. I bought my island. But I kept away from people. I had no faith in anybody. I didn't believe there was such a thing as real friendship or true love in the world – not for me, anyhow – the son of Purple Pills. I used to revel in all the wild yarns they told of me. In fact, I'm afraid I suggested a few of them myself. By mysterious remarks which people interpreted in the light of their own prepossessions.

'Then – you came. I had to believe you loved me – really loved me – not my father's millions. There was no other reason why you should want to marry a penniless devil with my supposed record. And I was sorry for you. Oh, yes, I don't deny I married you because I was sorry for you. And then – I found you the best and jolliest and dearest little pal and chum a fellow ever had. Witty – loyal – sweet. You made me believe again in the reality of friendship and love. The world seemed good again just because you were in it, honey. I'd have been willing to go on forever just as we were. I knew that, the night I came home and saw my homelight shining out from the island for the first time. And knew you were there waiting for me. After being homeless all my life it was beautiful to have a home. To come home hungry at night and know there was a good supper and a cheery fire – and you.

'But I didn't realise what you actually meant to me till that moment at the switch. Then it came like a lightning flash. I knew I couldn't live without you – that if I couldn't pull you loose in time I'd have to die with you. I admit it bowled me over – knocked me silly. I couldn't get my bearings for a while. That's why I acted like a mule. But the thought that drove me to the tall timber was the awful one that you were going to die. I'd always hated the thought of it – but I supposed there wasn't any chance for you, so I put it out of my mind. Now I had to face it – you were under sentence of death and I couldn't live without you. When I came home last night I had made up my mind that I'd take you to all the specialists in the world – that something surely could be done for you. I felt sure you couldn't be as bad as Dr Trent thought, when those moments on the track hadn't even hurt you. And I found your note – and went mad with happiness – and a little terror for fear you didn't care much for me, after all, and had gone away to get rid of me. But now, it's all right, isn't it, darling?'

Was she, Valancy being called 'darling'?

'I can't believe you care for me,' she said helplessly. 'I know you can't. What's the use, Barney? Of course, you're sorry for me – of course you want to do the best you can to straighten out the mess. But it can't be straightened out that way. You couldn't love me – me.' She stood up and pointed tragically to the mirror over the mantel. Certainly, not even Allan Tierney could have seen beauty in the woeful, haggard little face reflected there.

Barney didn't look at the mirror. He looked at Valancy as if he would like to snatch her – or beat her.

'Love you! Girl, you're in the very core of my heart. I hold you there like a jewel. Didn't I promise you I'd never tell you a lie? Love you! I love you with all there is of me to love. Heart, soul, brain. Every fibre of body and spirit thrilling to the sweetness of you. There's nobody in the world for me but you, Valancy.'

'You're – a good actor, Barney,' said Valancy, with a wan little smile. Barney looked at her.

'So you don't believe me – yet?'

'I – can't.'

'Oh – damn!' said Barney violently.

Valancy looked up startled. She had never seen this Barney. Scowling! Eyes black with anger. Sneering lips. Dead-white face.

'You don't want to believe it,' said Barney in the silk-smooth voice of ultimate rage. 'You're tired of me. You want to get out of it – free from me. You're ashamed of the Pills and the Liniment, just as she was. Your Stirling pride can't stomach them. It was all right as long as you thought you hadn't long to live. A good lark – you could put up with me. But a lifetime with old Doc Redfern's son is a different thing. Oh, I understand – perfectly. I've been very dense – but I understand, at last.'

Valancy stood up. She stared into his furious face. Then – she suddenly laughed.

'You darling!' she said. 'You do mean it! You do really love me! You wouldn't be so enraged if you didn't.'

Barney stared at her for a moment. Then he caught her in his arms with the little low laugh of the triumphant lover.

Uncle Benjamin, who had been frozen with horror at the keyhole, suddenly thawed out and tiptoed back to Mrs Frederick and Cousin Stickles.

'Everything is all right,' he announced jubilantly.

Dear little Doss! He would send for his lawyer right away and alter his will again. Doss should be his sole heiress. To her that had should certainly be given.

Mrs Frederick, returning to her comfortable belief in an overruling Providence, got out the family Bible and made an entry under 'Marriages'.

FORTY-THREE

'But, Barney,' protested Valancy after a few minutes, 'your father – somehow – gave me to understand that you still loved her.'

'He would. Dad holds the championship for making blunders. If there's a thing that's better left unsaid you can trust him to say it. But he isn't a bad old soul, Valancy. You'll like him.'

'I do, now.'

'And his money isn't tainted money. He made it honestly. His medicines are quite harmless. Even his Purple Pills do people whole heaps of good when they believe in them.'

'But – I'm not fit for your life,' sighed Valancy. 'I'm not – clever – or well-educated – or –'

'My life is in Mistawis – and all the wild places of the world. I'm not going to ask you to live the life of a society woman. Of course, we must spend a bit of the time with Dad – he's lonely and old –'

'But not in that big house of his,' pleaded Valancy. 'I can't live in a palace.'

'Can't come down to that after your Blue Castle,' grinned Barney. 'Don't worry, sweet. I couldn't live in that house myself. It has a white marble stairway with gilt bannisters and looks like a furniture shop with the labels off. Likewise it's the pride of Dad's heart. We'll get a little house somewhere outside of Montreal – in the real country – near enough to see Dad often. I think we'll build one for ourselves. A house you build for yourself is so much nicer than a hand-me-down. But we'll spend our summers in Mistawis. And our autumns travelling. I want you to see the Alhambra – it's the nearest thing to the Blue Castle of your dreams I can think of. And there's an old-world garden in Italy where I want to show you the moon rising over Rome through the dark cypress-trees.'

'Will that be any lovelier than the moon rising over Mistawis?'

'Not lovelier. But a different kind of loveliness. There are so many kinds of loveliness. Valancy, before this year you've spent all your life in ugliness. You know nothing of the beauty of the world. We'll climb mountains – hunt for treasures in the bazaars of Samarcand – search out the magic of east and west – run hand in hand to the rim of the world. I want to show you it all – see it again through your eyes. Girl, there are a million things I want to show you – do with you – say to you. It will take a lifetime. And we must see about that picture by Tierney, after all.'

'Will you promise me one thing?' asked Valancy solemnly.

'Anything,' said Barney recklessly.

'Only one thing. You are never, under any circumstances or under any provocation, to cast it up to me that I asked you to marry me.'

FORTY-FOUR

Extract from letter written by Miss Olive Stirling to Mr Cecil Bruce:

It's really disgusting that Doss' crazy adventures should have turned out like this. It makes one feel that there is no use in behaving properly.

I'm sure her mind was unbalanced when she left home. What she said about a dust-pile showed that. Of course I don't think there was ever a thing the matter with her heart. Or perhaps Snaith or Redfern or whatever his name really is fed Purple Pills to her, back in that Mistawis hut and cured her. It would make quite a testimonial for the family ads, wouldn't it?

He's such an insignificant-looking creature. I mentioned this to Doss but all she said was, 'I don't like collar ad men.'

Well, he's certainly no collar ad man. Though I must say there is something rather distinguished about him, now that he has cut his hair and put on decent clothes. I really think, Cecil, you should exercise more. It doesn't do to get too fleshy.

He also claims, I believe, to be John Foster. We can believe that or not, as we like, I suppose.

Old Doc Redfern has given them two millions for a wedding-present. Evidently the Purple Pills bring in the bacon. They're going to spend the fall in Italy and the winter in Egypt and motor through Normandy in apple-blossom time. Not in that dreadful old Lizzie, though. Redfern has got a wonderful new car.

Well, I think I'll run away, too, and disgrace myself. It seems to pay.

Uncle Ben is a scream. Likewise Uncle James. The fuss they all make over Doss now is absolutely sickening. To hear Aunt Amelia talking of 'my son-in-law, Bernard Redfern' and 'my daughter, Mrs Bernard Redfern'. Mother and Father are as bad as the rest. And they can't see that Valancy is just laughing at them all in her sleeve.

FORTY-FIVE

Valancy and Barney turned under the mainland pines in the cool dusk of the September night for a farewell look at the Blue Castle. Mistawis was drowned in sunset lilac light, incredibly delicate and elusive. Nip and Tuck were cawing lazily in the old pines. Good Luck and Banjo were mewed and mewing in separate baskets in Barney's new, dark-green car en route to Cousin Georgiana's. Cousin Georgiana was going to take care of them until Barney and Valancy came back. Aunt Wellington and Cousin Sarah and Aunt Alberta had also entreated the privilege of looking after them, but to Cousin Georgiana was it given. Valancy was in tears.

'Don't cry, Moonlight. We'll be back next summer. And now we're off for a real honeymoon.'

Valancy smiled through her tears. She was so happy that her happiness terrified her. But, despite the delights before her – 'the glory that was Greece and the grandeur that was Rome' – lure of the ageless Nile – glamour of the Riviera – mosque and palace and minaret – she knew perfectly well that no spot or place or home in the world could ever possess the sorcery of her Blue Castle.

BIOGRAPHICAL NOTE

Lucy Maud Montgomery was born in 1874 on Prince Edward Island, Canada. Her mother having died a few years later, Maud was brought up by her grandparents in Cavendish, since her father was too grief-stricken to care for her.

Maud began a career as a teacher but soon found that her talents lay in writing. Her tale of orphan, Anne of Green Gables, was an amazing success. Read worldwide, it was followed by a number of sequels. Her writing depicted Canadian landscape and shared it with a worldwide public. Her career produced twenty novels, over five hundred short stories as well as poetry and an autobiography.

Her love life was rather tumultuous and she found herself engaged a number of times. She eventually married Ewen Macdonald in 1911. Together they moved to Leaskdale and had three sons.

Attempting to balance the sometimes stultifying life of a minister's wife with her career as a successful writer was difficult. Montgomery was also prone to bouts of depression. She died in April 1942, apparently as a result of coronary thrombosis however rumours have since surfaced that she might have committed suicide.

SELECTED TITLES FROM HESPERUS PRESS

Author	Title	Foreword writer
Pietro Aretino	*The School of Whoredom*	Paul Bailey
Pietro Aretino	*The Secret Life of Nuns*	
Jane Austen	*Lesley Castle*	Zoë Heller
Jane Austen	*Love and Friendship*	Fay Weldon
Honoré de Balzac	*Colonel Chabert*	A.N.Wilson
Charles Baudelaire	*On Wine and Hashish*	Margaret Drabble
Giovanni Boccaccio	*Life of Dante*	A.N.Wilson
Charlotte Brontë	*The Spell*	
Emily Brontë	*Poems of Solitude*	Helen Dunmore
Mikhail Bulgakov	*Fatal Eggs*	Doris Lessing
Mikhail Bulgakov	*The Heart of a Dog*	A.S. Byatt
Giacomo Casanova	*The Duel*	Tim Parks
Miguel de Cervantes	*The Dialogue of the Dogs*	Ben Okri
Geoffrey Chaucer	*The Parliament of Birds*	
Anton Chekhov	*The Story of a Nobody*	Louis de Bernières
Anton Chekhov	*Three Years*	William Fiennes
Wilkie Collins	*The Frozen Deep*	
Joseph Conrad	*Heart of Darkness*	A.N.Wilson
Joseph Conrad	*The Return*	Colm Tóibín
Gabriele D'Annunzio	*The Book of the Virgins*	Tim Parks
Dante Alighieri	*The Divine Comedy: Inferno*	
Dante Alighieri	*New Life*	Louis de Bernières
Daniel Defoe	*The King of Pirates*	Peter Ackroyd
Marquis de Sade	*Incest*	Janet Street-Porter
Charles Dickens	*The Haunted House*	PeterA ckroyd
Charles Dickens	*A House to Let*	
Fyodor Dostoevsky	*The Double*	Jeremy Dyson
Fyodor Dostoevsky	*Poor People*	Charlotte Hobson
Alexandre Dumas	*One Thousand and One Ghosts*	
George Eliot	*Amos Barton*	Matthew Sweet
Henry Fielding	*Jonathan Wild the Great*	Pete Ackroyd

F. Scott Fitzgerald	*The Popular Girl*	Helen Dunmore
Gustave Flaubert	*Memoirs of a Madman*	Germaine Greer
Ugo Foscolo	*Last Letters of Jacopo Ortis*	Valerio Massimo Manfredi
Elizabeth Gaskell	*Lois the Witch*	Jenny Uglow
Théophile Gautier	*The Jinx*	Gilbert Adair
André Gide	*Theseus*	
Johann Wolfgang von Goethe	*The Man of Fifty*	A.S. Byatt
NikolaiGogol	*The Squabble*	Patrick McCabe
E.T.A. Hoffmann	Mademoiselle de Scudéri	Gilbert Adair
Victor Hugo	*The Last Day of a Condemned Man*	Libby Purves
Joris-Karl Huysmans	*With the Flow*	Simon Callow
Henry James	*In the Cage*	Libby Purves
Franz Kafka	*Metamorphosis*	Martin Jarvis
Franz Kafka	*The Trial*	Zadie Smith
John Keats	*Fugitive Poems*	Andrew Motion
Heinrich von Kleist	*TheMarquise of O–*	Andrew Miller
Mikhail Lermontov	*A Hero of OurTime*	Doris Lessing
Nikolai Leskov	*Lady Macbeth of Mtsensk*	Gilbert Adair
Carlo Levi	*Words are Stones*	Anita Desai
Xavier deMaistre	*A Journey Around my Room*	Alain de Botton
André Malraux	*The Way of the Kings*	Rachel Seiffert
Katherine Mansfield	*Prelude*	William Boyd
Edgar Lee Masters	*Spoon River Anthology*	Shena Mackay
Guy de Maupassant	*Butterball*	Germaine Greer
Prosper Mérimée	*Carmen*	Philip Pullman
Sir Thomas More	*The History of King Richard III*	Sister Wendy Beckett
Sándor Petöfi	*John the Valiant*	George Szirtes
Francis Petrarch	*My Secret Book*	Germaine Greer
Luigi Pirandello	*Loveless Love*	
Edgar Allan Poe	*Eureka*	Sir Patrick Moore
Alexander Pope	*The Rape of the Lock and A Key to the Lock*	Peter Ackroyd

Antoine-François Prévost	*Manon Lescaut*	Germaine Greer
Marcel Proust	*Pleasures and Days*	A.N.Wilson
Alexander Pushkin	*Dubrovsky*	Patrick Neate
Alexander Pushkin	*Ruslan and Lyudmila*	Colm Tóibín
François Rabelais	*Pantagruel*	Paul Bailey
François Rabelais	*Gargantua*	Paul Bailey
Christina Rossetti	*Commonplace*	Andrew Motion
George Sand	*The Devil's Pool*	Victoria Glendinning
Jean-Paul Sartre	*The Wall*	Justin Cartwright
Friedrich von Schiller	*The Ghost-seer*	Martin Jarvis
Mary Shelley	*Transformation*	
Percy Bysshe Shelley	*Zastrozzi*	Germaine Greer
Stendhal	*Memoirs of an Egotist*	Doris Lessing
Robert Louis Stevenson	*Dr Jekyll and Mr Hyde*	Helen Dunmore
Theodor Storm	*The Lake of the Bees*	Alan Sillitoe
Leo Tolstoy	The Death of Ivan Ilych	
Leo Tolstoy	Hadji Murat	Colm Tóibín
IvanTurgenev	*Faust*	Simon Callow
Mark Twain	*The Diary of Adam and Eve*	John Updike
Mark Twain	*Tom Sawyer, Detective*	
Oscar Wilde	*The Portrait of Mr W.H.*	Peter Ackroyd
Virginia Woolf	*Carlyle's House and Other Sketches*	Doris Lessing
Virginia Woolf	*Monday or Tuesday*	Scarlett Thomas
Emile Zola	*For a Night of Love*	A.N.Wilson